Last to Know

About the author

Liz Allen was born in Dublin in 1969. She wrote her first newspaper article at the age of 15, whilst still at school. She worked on several national newspapers in Dublin for 13 years, a career which took her into the depths of the Irish underworld and the judicial system, where she was called by the State to give evidence against several high-profile gangland figures.

She lives in Dublin with her husband, Andrew and their daughter, Elise.

LIZ ALLEN

Last to Know

Hodder & Stoughton

First published in Great Britain in 2004 by Hodder and Stoughton
A division of Hodder Headline

A CIP catalogue record for this title
is available from the British Library

ISBN 0 340 82925 7

Typeset in Plantin by Hewer Text Ltd, Edinburgh
Printed in Great Britain by
Clays Ltd, St Ives plc

Hodder and Stoughton
A division of Hodder Headline
338 Euston Road
London NW1 3BH

For Andrew and Elise

PROLOGUE

Dublin City, 2002

Deborah Parker was in way over her head. She was officially a target. A marked woman.

Criminals, the most ruthless and vicious, wanted revenge.

The police, including the best investigator in the land, wanted her head on a silver platter.

Time was nearly up. She had no place left to run.

I

Knocktopher Village, County Kilkenny, November 1972

They walked purposefully. It was a long, cold half-mile to the 'big house'. The man was engulfed in bitterness for his daughter. He was about to throw her to the lions.

The rain cut bitterly into Sheila Dunne's face and the razor-sharp gusts of wind tore through her like a blade. But the torture of the elements was nothing in comparison with the torrent of abuse heaped on her by her father over the previous six days since he had heard the news. To him, now she was a slut, a harlot, a cheap trollop, who had brought the ultimate shame on the family. Her dirty secret threatened their good name and their home.

Her explanations had fallen on deaf ears. Love? She didn't know the meaning of the word. Love, her father had said, was reserved for the privileged classes. Everyone else just found a respectable partner with whom they could build a family. This was rural Ireland and that was the way things were, said Jimmy Dunne. Working-class Catholics didn't get involved with landed Protestant gentry – and now she was bearing the fruit of her sordid liaison.

The grey granite structure loomed in the distance. Soon she would be inside, surrounded by blazing fires her mother had lit with logs Jimmy Dunne had chopped. But there was little comfort to be gained from that. If they were lucky, Sheila's parents would

3

be permitted to stay on in the lodge at the entrance to the two-hundred-acre estate. It was a matter of compliance, her father had warned, and she would accept whatever was decided. There would be no pleadings of love tonight, he had told her. This would be the last time she would cross the threshold of the big house, and unless she wanted him and her mother to suffer the same fate, she had better stay silent while her future was decided.

A little later, Sheila was listening to her parents' employers from the church bench in the hallway outside the drawing room. She heard no raised voices, just her father agreeing to the stipulations of his employers. For the first time in her eighteen years, Sheila realised that her father lacked backbone. As did the father of her unborn child, who had just broken his promise to stand by her.

When the doctor offered to drive them back to the lodge, Jimmy told him not to fuss on account of the girl's condition. The walk in the storm would do her no harm.

2

Dublin, July 2002

Mugsy Mooney sat in his leather swivel chair with his feet propped up on his magnificent yew-wood desk. As he listened to his speaker-phone, he massaged his temple. A headache was coming on.

'Listen, Johnny, tell the stupid prick to get out here quick sharp. Like now! Where the fuck did you say the girl is? The Rotunda? The fucking Sexual Assault Unit, was it? You get in there and make her sweet, OK? Promise her the sun, moon and stars, whatever the fuck you think will make her keep her trap shut. She'll be too afraid to refuse. And tell him to be here within the hour. I don't want him going anywhere near his own pad before he talks to me.'

He swung his feet to the floor and stood up, pressing his palms into the wood. He was afraid that if he moved them he would grab some heavy object and smash it into the mahogany-panelled walls that had set him back twelve grand not six months ago. He'd kill the bastard if he brought the cops to his door. Those kind of visits had been all well and good when he lived in Finglas where the locals knew what he was made of, but out here on Killiney Hill, where he was known as Michael Mooney Senior, property speculator *extraordinaire*, they were inconceivable. While it was clear to those born and bred on

5

this stretch of South Dublin coastline that he was not of the old school, they assumed that he was one of the thousands of new-money men, all products of the Celtic Tiger economy that had placed Ireland at last on the world economic stage. As far as Michael Mooney was concerned, his six-bedroom Georgian house, set in almost an acre of grounds, gave him the veneer of respectability that could only be associated with class. But to the locals, the gold-painted falcons beside his electronically controlled gates and the floodlit garden gave the game away. Definitely new, and probably tainted, money.

He was in his study, listening now to the eleven a.m. RTE Radio One news bulletin. When he heard that a woman discovered in a lane off Baggot Street in the early hours of the morning was unconscious at the Sexual Assault Unit of the Rotunda Hospital, his heart lifted. With a bit of luck, she wouldn't regain consciousness and Michael Junior would be out of the woods. But the reporter went on, 'Experienced detectives were shocked by the vicious nature of the assault. Officers have revealed that in addition to having her face and upper body slashed with blades, the woman suffered con-siderable internal injuries, which they believe were inflicted with heavy instruments. Detectives say they will leave no stone unturned until the culprits are apprehended.'

Just then, a bright red BMW convertible screeched up the driveway, stereo blaring, its occupant apparently oblivious to the trouble he was in. His son's *laissez-faire* attitude stuck in Mugsy's craw. Hadn't the kid learned anything from him in his twenty-five years?

A few moments later, the young man strode into the room, flopped on to the red velvet *chaise-longue* and announced that he'd a bit of bother with one of the new recruits last night. 'I had to sort her out, Da. Two of me regulars were standin' by for a threesome with her and at the last minute she decided she wasn't coming up with the goods. Prissy fuckin' bitch. Three hundred smackers each they paid me for two hours with her, and it was her only job of the night. Fuck sake, Da, I had to teach her a lesson, didn't I? I mean, there was four other girls in the penthouse and I had to set an example so they wouldn't be takin' advantage, like. It cost us an' all. I had to provide a replacement and throw in another for free.'

Michael Junior saw his father clench his fists. The knuckles turned white, foreshadowing an imminent outburst of rage. He decided against telling him how he had taught the girl a lesson – before he had beaten her to within an inch of her life. He'd save that for his cronies.

Mugsy knew that if he lost his rag the inquisition would be futile so he kept a veneer of calm. 'What about the punters, son? Do they know what went on?'

'Jasus, Da, they were well cut by eleven and the slag didn't start acting up until close to midnight. They were ten fuckin' sheets to the wind 'cos me girls had filled them full of that fancy champagne those briefs think is the only thing good enough for them to drink. They were even more pissed by the time I got back from sortin' out the silly cow.'

Mugsy's eyes narrowed at the information his son had saved until last that their customers had been briefs. That was why he was so cocky. The lad was a chip off the old block yet, he mused proudly. 'What class of brief are we talking about here, son? Anyone who might be useful to us?'

Michael Junior stood up, his toned body outlined by the tight white T-shirt and black jeans that comprised his daily uniform. 'Let's just say, Da, I reckon these punters are going to be in a position to pay us through the nose if we need to call on their services. And, I can say with me hand on me heart that they'll be in a position to provide us with sterling services. Even if they'd only had a glass of Seven-Up last night, I can guarantee that they'll forget their whereabouts or anything they witnessed in the penthouse.'

Mugsy was still furious that his son had placed his operation in jeopardy by causing strife with one of the girls in the presence of customers, but he consoled himself with the knowledge that the key civilian witnesses would want to distance themselves, for professional reasons, it seemed, from the scene of the crime. And, anyway, hadn't the news said that the girl was unconscious? With a bit of luck, she wouldn't last the week.

He took out his mobile and dialled Johnny Collins. 'Have you reached your destination yet?'

'I'm heading through the main doors, boss. Sorry it's taking so long. I had to queue in the flower shop to get a nice big bunch of posies for me missus, like. A man couldn't be goin' into the Rotunda Maternity Hospital without a bouquet for his wife now, could he?'

Five minutes later, Collins was *en route* back to Killiney.

Mugsy was pleased with the way things were working out. He hadn't wanted Collins to set foot near the girl and he would only send him back if the media reported that she was improving, which seemed unlikely.

The older man looked at the woman briefing him. She had been a wise choice for the job, he thought. Although she had little experience of this kind of work, his instincts told him that she would prove effective with his 'clients', as he referred to the people he and his colleagues dealt with.

'She's a bit sketchy on the details,' the woman continued, 'but I think by this afternoon I should be able to get more information about what happened from her. What she has said so far gives us something to work with. I'm hoping that if she's as co-operative this afternoon as she was early this morning, a more experienced person like yourself might be able to pin-point the individual she's talking about. I mean, this has to be someone from within the established circles we're familiar with. Right?'

Hanley took in her curvaceous frame, all five foot nine of it. She was wearing a smart trouser suit and her long wavy blonde hair cascaded down the black fabric. Yes, Maria Lynch was different from the other women he had taken on over the years. For a start she didn't dress to give away her occupation at a glance, which considerably enhanced her value to him. The twenty-seven-year-old had an unassuming way about her, which invited people to open up and had made her a success with his clients.

'OK, Lynch,' he said. 'Off you go and talk to the poor girl. She'll probably be a bit more reticent this afternoon, now that the drugs they gave her will have worn off, and she might be a bit more cautious about protecting her own back. Just remind her gently that it's better, for her own safety, that she work with us rather than against us.'

Rita Brady looked a right mess. Her long red hair was still matted with blood and the left side of her face was bandaged to cover the six stitches she had received from the blade wound. The right side was swollen and badly bruised from hitting the ground after she was thrown out of the car.

Lynch was still as shocked by the woman's appearance as she had been six hours earlier. Even in her line of work, this had been an exceptionally vicious attack. And Lynch feared that she and the rest of the team would be indirect casualties if they let it go unpunished. The media would have a field day, stirring up a scare about attacks on working girls if they didn't solve this one.

She stood at the foot of the bed, not wanting to invade the woman's space for fear of frightening her off. 'Would you like something to drink? I brought you a bottle of Lucozade because I figured you wouldn't be telling too many people that you're in here.'

It was one of Maria's usual tricks. The recipients of her interrogations didn't usually anticipate such acts of kindness, no matter how small, and let down their guard.

It worked with Rita Brady.

3

The offices of Jennings and Associates, Dublin

Deborah Parker could hardly believe the turn of events. Wait until her boss, Paul Jennings, heard about this! A second major criminal client, and she had only started with him six weeks ago. Her excitement was enhanced by the knowledge that the Mooney family was one of the biggest crime families in the country. Outsiders might take a dim view of her elation at landing such a notorious clan, but professionally it was a scoop. Yet even though she had worked hard to get where she was, Deborah was still amazed that major criminals could approach her for help. It was surreal: her own life was so far removed from this world.

Jenings had recruited her because of her growing reputation within the criminal-law community. His firm was one of the top three criminal-law practices in the country and he was constantly on the look-out for new talent. The majority of the firm's clients would have been described as the scum of the earth by the city's other leading law practices, and the firm's reputation for taking on big-time criminals at times caused Jennings difficulty with finding good staff. Ireland had become so litigious that commercial and personal-injury law practices seemed to attract the *crème de la crème*, which meant that he often had to train many of his associates from scratch. To many of the young apprentices emerging from college, criminal law lacked the cachet of the commercial field.

In Deborah Parker, Jennings had discovered a gem: she possessed a rare ability to connect with her criminal clients, and could break down the barriers erected by the preconceived notions criminals frequently held about solicitors. It was strange: criminals in deep trouble often chose the firm because of its great reputation, yet they invariably arrived at its doors with such suspicion of anyone associated with the law that they risked damaging their cases. Deborah saw straight through the lies her clients told her and secured quick results. This told them that she meant business.

She knew why Jennings had recruited her. He had witnessed her in action in the drab environs of the Bridewell courts in Dublin city centre where she had been representing a recidivist burglar. Jennings had observed the verbal exchange between her and the notoriously cranky Judge Brendan Smithers, and decided on the spot that she was going to work at his firm. The crims loved her.

She had been unaware of the effect her courtroom manner had on the gathered criminal fraternity while she questioned the judge on every decision he took. Judge Smithers had known that she was challenging him to gain favour with the criminals – it was an old trick, which many new solicitors were not shrewd or mature enough to take on board. But Deborah was not just about clever tactics: she went the extra mile for every client, believing that if she did not do her utmost to plead their case, then there was no point in having a justice system. On almost every occasion she appeared in open court, word spread to other criminals in need of a brief that Parker was one of them. Even when she lost a case, her clients recommended her to their associates. Deborah had no idea why – as far as she was concerned, she was just doing her job. But as far as her clients were concerned, she fought hard for them and they respected her for it. In the criminal community, respect was an important word.

One of her first big court appearances had involved a twenty-three-year-old drug addict who had tortured a two-year-old child in front of its mother to force her to give him money she didn't have. Strung out on heroin, the addict had systematically ripped out the child's fingernails while the mother looked on from the chair she was tied to. Only after the ninth did the addict relent – and slashed the mother's face with a Stanley knife.

There had been no defence in the case, except to plead addiction to drugs and a deprived background for her client, whose life had been devoid of any moral guidance – he had been beaten to a pulp by his alcoholic mother and deserted by his unemployed father, who had inflicted even more vicious beatings on both mother and child. But Deborah's client had insisted on pleading not guilty.

She had entered the usual pleas for mitigating circumstances and had presented her client to the court as what he was: a victim of an impoverished, violent home whose welfare had been, as she told the jury, 'relegated to the lost-property compartment of public conscience'. But even as she uttered the words, which were true, the look on the jurors' faces had told her that her client was going down.

She spent the two weeks after the trial in despair, recalling the photographs of the mother and child's injuries, and wondering why she had opted to plead mercy for the dregs of society.

The simple answer was that she was good at what she did. During their mock trials her law lecturers had told her that she would make a brilliant defence solicitor, and later, during her apprenticeship at a small criminal practice, the clients had begun asking for her, rather than the firm's fifty-three-year-old senior partner.

When she walked into their regular nine o'clock Monday meeting to discuss the firm's cases for the week, Deborah's demeanour did not indicate that she had just hooked one of the biggest fish in the criminal sea. Instead, she listened to Patrick Mangan tell Jennings, 'I have a fucking great week lined up, lots of faces who'll get the firm's name in the papers and two pretty definite strike-outs because the State has exceeded the acceptable time-frame in preparing books of evidence. I'm applying for dismissal in both cases.'

Deborah didn't know Mangan very well. He achieved decent results, but he measured his success by the number of his cases that made it into the headlines. She couldn't care less if her cases featured in the newspapers. She was happier sifting through case studies and trying to find loopholes in the State's evidence against her clients. But she knew that the defection of the Mooneys from their long-time firm, W.H. Benson, would make headline news in legal circles and in the media. There was also no doubt in her mind that Mangan, an employee of Jennings and Associates for five years and Deborah's equal in court experience and salary, would have loved to have such high-profile clients. But she didn't want to undermine him so she delivered her news calmly. 'I'm afraid, boys, I'm going to have to hand over my load for today and possibly tomorrow to somebody else. I got a live one this morning on two counts of statutory rape and one assault occasioning actual bodily harm. I have a client in Donnybrook Garda station. He's taking a nap now and the boys from the NBCI say they're waking him at ten thirty to begin questioning after he's been examined by a doctor. He was deemed intoxicated when they took him in in the early hours of the morning.' She didn't volunteer the name of her new client because she wanted to let the significance sink in of what she had told them. First, assault causing serious harm, buggery and rape, were serious charges, which brought with them maximum sentences of life imprisonment. But, more importantly, the fact that her client had been arrested by the National Bureau of Criminal Investigation, the Garda's élite investigation unit, had told her colleagues that her client was a big fish.

'So, who's the lucky man who gets to spend several hours in a cosy little room with you, then?' Mangan asked.

Deborah thought she could see resentment in his face. With Paul Jennings, he was all sweetness, light and support, but elsewhere he was another man. She had hoped that he and she would make a good team; but so far Mangan had been reluctant to form any professional bond with her. 'Believe it or not, it's the one and only Mugsy Mooney,' she said.

Paul Jennings looked flabbergasted, as well he might. This was a real catch. He was savvy enough not to belittle Mangan's own contribution by telling Deborah how she had just justified her appointment to his firm, but no observer could have missed his expression of delight. 'Goodness, Debs,' he said, 'nobody has managed to lift Mugsy in a long time. They must have some good stuff on him to haul him in.'

'Well, my first impression is that they're on a fishing expedition. I mean, everything I've heard about Mooney suggests to me that he's not stupid enough to leave himself open to being nabbed for such a crime. Rape and battery leave too many fingerprints and he's been in this business too long not to know the significance of DNA. I would suggest that the real perp is among his cronies and they're just trying to get his back up by bringing him in,' she said.

'You'll find out soon enough. Needless to say, I don't have to emphasise the importance of providing the best possible service to our new client. You get to it, and Patrick will handle your caseload. Well done. I don't know how you reeled him in, but keep at it.'

Patrick Mangan folded his arms. 'Yeah, good for you, Debs, and don't worry about your other little bits and pieces – I'll take care of them.'

Deborah did not miss the insult, but she had more important things to consider now that she was on her way to meet Mugsy Mooney.

When the two squad cars and the unmarked Opel Vectra screeched to a halt outside Mount Argento at five a.m. on Monday, the occupants of the house were fast asleep beneath their duvet. The previous evening had turned into an impromptu celebration between Mugsy and Johnny Collins: Michael Junior appeared to be out of the woods.

The news had come to them courtesy of the TV3 evening news bulletin. They had opened the first bottle of whiskey after the newsreader reported that the woman attacked in the city centre during the early hours of Saturday morning had died from her injuries.

It wasn't that Mugsy was pleased that the girl was dead, just relieved that there was now no link between her and his son, as far as he was concerned. Business was business and had the girl been able to describe young Michael to the cops, it wouldn't have taken them long to establish the perp's identity.

When Lelia Mooney thumped her husband's shoulder and yelled, 'Wake the fuck up and look who's at the gate,' Mugsy thought he was having a bad dream. Then he saw the moving images on the CCTV screen, which was set into his built-in wardrobe.

He shot upright in bed. 'Jesus, Mary and holy Saint Joseph! What the bleedin' hell is goin' on here? What the fuck do they want? What's the stupid fucker done now?' The intercom buzzed.

Lelia pushed her tousled peroxide-blonde hair off her face. 'Why do you think my Michael has anything to do with it? You're always blamin' him for everything.'

'Cos your Michael, who happens, unfortunately, to be my son too, is a stupid little prick who has lost the run of himself, thanks to you spoilin' him all his life, that's why. Now, say nothin' when they come in. He was here with us all Friday night until ten o'clock on Saturday morning. We got a video out. I don't need to tell you which one we watched, love.'

He leapt out of bed and pressed the intercom. 'What's the problem, officers? Is there something I can help you with?'

Detective Inspector Brendan Hanley sniggered quietly. He'd been after Mooney for years and each time their paths crossed the man had managed to sound like the local Neighbourhood Watch co-ordinator, as if butter wouldn't melt in his mouth.

'Michael Mooney Senior?' Detective Garda Maria Lynch spoke into the intercom.

'That's me,' came the response.

'Mr Mooney, can you open the gates, please, and come to your front door. I'm arresting you for questioning under Section Four of the Criminal Justice Act. You do not have to say anything, but anything you do say will be taken down and used against you in a court of law . . .'

★   ★   ★

Mooney knew that, under that section of the law, they could hold him initially for a period of six hours, then approach a superintendent for an extension of a further six hours. He also knew that, under the same law, the police must reasonably suspect an arrested person of having committed a serious offence and that, if a charge was brought, it would carry a sentence of at least five years. They're on a trawl, he thought, because they've got nothing on me. He decided to play along – he might discover what they had, if anything, on his son.

He pressed the buzzer. 'OK, love. You don't have to continue. I know the drill and there's obviously been a mistake. That said, being the good citizen I am, I'm more than happy to help you with your inquiries. Now, come on in and I'll have my wife put the kettle on. But before you do, tell those fuckers to turn off their sirens. They'll wake me neighbours.'

'The audacity of it,' Lynch said to Hanley. 'I'll give him a cup of tea!'

'Don't let him get to you,' Hanley told her. 'That's just what he's trying to achieve. He's pissed off that the neighbours will have seen and heard the sirens – I knew *that* would get to him. And I wouldn't worry about having to stay for tea either. He'll want us out of here so fast he'll be waiting for us when we get to the front door.'

Immediately, Maria felt calmer. Her mentor always had that effect on her. It came from years of dealing with hard-core criminals who enjoyed nothing better than seeing their inter-rogators' faces redden with anger. He never rose to the bait. Not publicly.

It was eleven a.m. on Monday by the time Deborah was sitting alongside her new client. Under the arrest regulations, a suspect is entitled to a consultation with a solicitor out of earshot of police before being interviewed. Deborah was painfully aware that she was flying by the seat of her pants: she would have to exercise extreme caution over questions she allowed Mooney to answer. She prayed he wouldn't fly off the handle, which he was likely to do, given his well-known hatred of the police.

She had her own way of dealing with them, which didn't involve antagonism. Her approach was one of reasonable co-operation. It didn't mean that her clients were forced to hold up their hands and plead guilty – they always told her they were innocent, anyway – just that they should answer all reasonable questions and seem to co-operate. The police usually thought of defence solicitors as obstructionist, but Deborah's philosophy was two-fold: she had to defend her clients, and at the same time, she was mindful that she would have to deal with the police for the rest of her career.

In the case of Michael Mooney, she would play it all by the book. Anyway, he probably knew the law better than she did.

'As you know, Michael, you have the right to say nothing, but they may ask your whereabouts on last Friday night or in the early hours of Saturday morning. You will have to account for yourself. You probably know that you're not obliged to sign any statement. OK? We can take it from there,' she told him.

As far as Mugsy was concerned, he didn't need Parker, but he knew that bringing in a big-shot criminal firm would force the cops to play it straight. He was not surprised when Hanley allowed Maria Lynch to take the lead in the interview. It was commonplace when a big fish was in for questioning that senior officers allowed their subordinates to open the questioning. It left them free to observe, then intervene when flaws in the story began to emerge. That tactic often knocked a suspect off-guard.

'Mr Mooney, can you tell us of your whereabouts last Friday night and into the early hours of Saturday morning, please?' Lynch said.

'Sure thing. I was at home in my house in Killiney with my wife, Lelia, and my son, Michael Junior. The three of us watched a video and we had a Chinese takeaway.'

'Can you tell us the title of the video you watched?'

'Certainly. It was a family favourite – *Babe*. It's about pigs.' He paused. 'Animal pigs, that is.'

Such swipes were part and parcel of the everyday exchanges between the criminal fraternity and their interrogators and a seasoned officer like Hanley wouldn't lose any sleep over them, or Lynch, whose pinched lips showed she was furious, but she didn't react. All she said was, 'I would have thought a man of your age might have advanced beyond cartoons.' Then, 'Are you the proprietor of a business called Executive Escorts, Mr Mooney?'

Mugsy replied with a nod that he was.

'And can you tell us the nature of that business, please?'

It was an escort agency, Mugsy said, providing dates for men requiring female companionship.

'And do those companionship services also include sexual services?'

'They definitely do not, although what the girls get up to in their time off with men they meet through my service is none of my business,' Mooney shot back.

'So, are you telling us that you believe some of the girls working for you might provide sexual services to the men they meet through your agency?'

'Detective, I have already told you that my agency provides dating services for men requiring companionship. I object to your innuendo that anything untoward might take place on the premises.'

Lynch jumped at the opportunity Mooney had handed her: 'To the contrary, Mr Mooney, I was not suggesting that the sexual activity I am inquiring about occurred on the premises in Sandymount.'

'Exactly what sexual activity *are* you inquiring about?' Mooney asked.

It was another golden opportunity. 'I am inquiring about the repeated rape and battering of a young woman who commenced work at your premises in Sandymount last Friday night. She was systematically violated and beaten and then dumped in the city centre in the early hours of Saturday morning. Ring any bells, Mr Mooney?'

Deborah intervened: 'Detective, my client has already told you of his whereabouts.'

'I am responding to his question for clarification, Miss Parker. I am asking him about his knowledge of an incident involving a member of staff at one of his premises,' Lynch said.

Mugsy looked solemn. 'That incident certainly does not ring any bells with me, and if any of our customers committed such an act against one of my girls, I guarantee you, I'd be in here reporting it myself.'

Lynch sat back in her chair, tucked her blonde hair behind her ears and gazed at him. 'Oh. Perhaps you misunderstood me, Mr Mooney. I wasn't suggesting that a customer might have perpetrated such a crime. I was referring to your son, Michael. Is he not the person who runs the agency on your behalf?'

Mooney was unfazed by this salvo. 'As I've already told you,

Michael Junior was at home with me and Lelia watching our favourite video on Friday night. You've got the wrong person if you think you're fingering him for what happened to that poor girl. Ask any of the others who were working that night and they'll tell you he wasn't there. Do you think I reared a fuckin' animal?'

'Well, Mr Mooney, the victim of the attack certainly seemed to think so, and we'll see how you fare for aiding and abetting a suspect when this case gets to court. We'll let the jury decide whether or not your precious son is an animal, shall we?'

Mugsy's, face was turning red. 'This isn't going anywhere near the fucking courts! What are you going to do? Call a chief witness who just happens to be six bleedin' feet under?'

Hanley stood up abruptly and announced that the interview was terminated. Then he said, 'That is where you're wrong. I wouldn't be ordering my wreath for her funeral just yet – these journalists are always getting their facts wrong. Imagine them saying the poor girl was dead when she is, in fact, recovering steadily.'

The colour drained from Mugsy's face.

'There's no need to feel stupid, Mugsy,' Hanley went on. 'You're not the only one who got it wrong. You see, when you were getting sloshed last night, we took the liberty of bringing your son in for a chat. And you know what? He was so convinced she was dead, too, that he didn't even take us up on our offer to call his brief. A lovely girl, he said she was. He told us she was in fine form leaving your premises on Friday night, in his company. That, of course, was before we gave him the good news that she isn't dead after all.'

Hanley rubbed his hands in satisfaction as he left the interview room with Maria Lynch. It had been his idea to feed the line to the reporter that the girl had died, but the hack would forgive him when he fed him the exclusive about the son of one of the country's top crime bosses being charged with such a heinous crime . . .

Deborah left the interview room with Mooney. Her client had handled himself reasonably well. There had been no need for her to object to the line of questioning because it had only been a preliminary trawl by the police and they hadn't overstepped the boundaries. Still, she would put money on it that Mooney knew more than he was letting on.

But she didn't have time to ask him. At the main door of the police station, he uttered a stream of expletives about his son, shouted at her that he would be in touch, then jumped into a passing taxi.

4

Knocktopher, December 1972

The weather reflected the atmosphere. There had been no let-up from the vicious November winds and the rain pelted down from a cold grey sky. Nor had there been any let-up in Jimmy Dunne's relentless cruel remarks about his harlot daughter and the shame she had visited upon his family.

Sheila sat silent, gazing into the kitchen fire. Since her father had told her of her fate, she had felt sick. Tomorrow she would move out of the lodge to Gardener's Lane to live with the man who by then would be her husband. Two weeks earlier, when Jimmy had announced his solution to her predicament, Sheila had pleaded with him: 'But I don't want to marry him, Dad. He repulses me. I don't love him. Send me to Dublin or Cork – England, even – but don't make me marry him.'

'You really don't get it, Sheila, do you? You're in my house and you'll do as I say. You should be glad enough that his family has agreed to let him marry you. You'll have a father for your child and a roof over your head for the rest of your life. You should be thankful that someone has agreed to take you on, considering the disgrace you've brought upon yourself and this family,' he told her. 'The only saving grace is that no one else around here seems to know. You'd better hope it stays that way, lassie, or he'll throw you out on your ear, married or not.'

When the wind bellowed through the house, signalling her father's return, Sheila knew that he would be more resolved than ever. He had come from a final meeting with her future in-laws at Gardener's Lane.

'So, now. You'd better be getting yourself off to bed. It's bad enough you being sick from being knocked up without you falling down altogether from exhaustion on your wedding day. Eamon's family will want you looking your best to avoid any suspicions.'

But Sheila was dying inside from the pain of what she suspected lay ahead. Sure, she would have some degree of security, being married to the gardener on the only other estate left in the village. Eamon's parents had even fixed up the little six-room cottage that stood alongside theirs and which their employers had promised to their only son when he married. Sheila suspected that the only reason the cottage had been promised to him was because no one had ever believed he would find a wife.

In rural Ireland in the 1970s most men over the age of thirty were married and settled, so it had come as a shock even to Eamon to find himself entering into a union at the age of thirty-six. He knew he was no oil painting, so he was willing to overlook Sheila Dunne's dirty little secret in return for a wife. And what a wife he had caught, a beautiful, fresh-faced, dark-haired teenager who, he had decided, would bear many more children than the one she was already carrying. He would see to it that she was punished every day for her sins. As he told his father excitedly, 'At least we know that she's up to being a proper wife, Dad. I'll ride the living daylights out of her and teach her to show how grateful she should be to me.'

Sheila knew that her marriage to Eamon would indeed be a penance. As she lay in bed, contemplating her future with him, she remembered the first time she had encountered him. It was only eight years ago when she was ten and he was a twenty-eight-year-old bachelor, drinking his way to an early grave. Her father had taken her to Gardener's Lane to borrow a wheelbarrow and Eamon had made no secret of his interest in the child. His mouth curved into a leering grin. When he realised that Jimmy Dunne had noticed his ruddy face had reddened even more.

Sheila wondered if she should remind her father of how he had cursed Eamon for the way he had looked at her that day. But as the tears trickled down her face, she realised her father would only tell her it was no more than she deserved.

The wedding went off without incident. Sheila returned from the church to her new cottage and served out the salads prepared by her mother-in-law. There was no question of any help from either family when she went outside to fetch more logs for the fire. As the men drank the two bottles of whiskey sent by the doctor for the celebrations, she prayed that they would slow down and thereby put off the encounter she knew was looming between herself and a man she had never even kissed.

By seven o'clock, the bottles were empty and it was pitch black outside. Nobody uttered any objection when Eamon announced that he was tired and suggested that everyone should get going before the weather worsened.

When the door had closed behind both sets of parents, Sheila hurried to clear the table. 'There's no need to do that now, my love. You can do it after,' he told her.

Sheila shivered as she sat opposite him before the fire. 'Well, you'd better let me get a look at your belly, then. It is my baby you're supposed to be carrying,' he said.

'But, Eamon, hadn't we better go to the bedroom and turn off the light?' she said, her voice quivering.

'You're my wife now, Sheila, and I'm entitled to what any married man is due. Open your dress from the bosom down and let me see your belly.'

Her fingers fumbled, and she could sense that he was losing patience.

'Hurry up,' he bellowed. 'You'd no problems getting your clothes off for the doctor's son, so the least you can do is accommodate your husband.'

Tears streamed down her face as the fifth button opened at her waist. 'Now lean forward and take your arms out of the dress. I want to see my wife's body.'

She tried to cover her breasts with her long dark hair, but he instructed her to push it back on her shoulders. 'Undo it all the way down now and open your legs wide for me, love,' he said.

'Oh, Eamon. This just isn't normal. It's not the way it's supposed to be the first time. Please, let's go to the bedroom,' she implored.

But he was playing with his zip. 'All in good time, my love. After all, it's not your first time, is it? Now, open your legs before I take my hand to you.'

It went on for at least an hour, him staring at her as he ordered her to remove her undergarments and touch herself. And then, with a violence that Sheila had never imagined, he pulled her from her chair, swept the dishes off the kitchen table, ordered her to bend over and ploughed into her. The stench of whiskey on his breath made her retch as he whispered obscenities in her ear. Then he turned her on to her back and entered her again, staring at her in a frenzy of desire.

When he was finished, he got up and told her, 'Don't worry, my love. It will get easier with practice. And, believe me, there'll be plenty of that. Now, clean up and come to my bed. I'll be waiting for you.'

5

'Where on earth is Deborah? She knows this is the one meeting of the week I need her here for,' Paul Jennings said to Patrick Mangan.

'It's a bit strange all right,' Mangan responded. 'It's probably just the Monday-morning blues. It can't be easy for her, having started here only a few months ago and being thrown in at the deep end with Mooney and his crew. That lot are a tough bunch, Paul, and she's not cut from the same cloth as they are. It's bound to be hard on her. Maybe she had one too many last night in anticipation of the week ahead.'

Jennings looked alarmed. 'Are you trying to tell me you reckon the pressure of this job's too much for her, Patrick?'

'Look, boss, I don't want to speak out of turn about our star player or anything. I'm just saying that maybe you should go a bit easier on her. She was saying in the pub on Friday after you left that she feels an awful lot is expected of her.' Mangan did not add that she had said that was why she loved the job. The pressure gave her a buzz.

Jennings hunched forward and stabbed his pen at his blotter. 'Jesus, Patrick, of *course* an awful lot is expected of her. I'm not paying her over forty grand a year to take a holiday. She's on a case that's been all over the papers and I

29

don't have to tell you that the way this is handled will determine a lot about the volume of business we get from the likes of Mooney in the future. Those pressures are an inherent part of the job.'

Mangan pushed his greasy blond fringe out of his eyes and sat back in his chair. Cupping his chin in his right hand, he sat pensively, tugging at a loose piece of skin on his lip.

'Come on, Patrick. What's on your mind?' Jennings asked.

Mangan frowned, as if trying to find the words for something he didn't feel comfortable saying.

'Look, if there's a problem with her, I want to know. Spill the beans here between the two of us. It will go no further,' Jennings pressed.

'Look, Paul, I could be wrong here, but since this Mooney rape and assault case has been in the papers, she seems to have lost her focus. It's as if the case is the only thing the firm is handling and everything else, including the rest of us, just pales into insignificance alongside it. You and I both know that you're only as good as your last court appearance and you can't trade on one case for ever.'

Jennings was about to speak, when Mangan continued, 'I suppose I'm a bit fed up carrying the can for her. She's a grand girl and everything, but I've got my own workload and I've been handling about eighty per cent of her minor stuff for the past two months. It becomes a bit of pain when she doesn't recognise that – you know, by not even turning up for the one important meeting of the week.'

'OK, Patrick. I hear what you're saying. I'll bring another junior on board to take some of Deborah's pressure off you. How does that sound?'

Patrick Mangan was ecstatic, but not because he was going to offload some of Deborah's cases: he had twisted a knife into

Deborah Parker with the subtlety of a seasoned backstabber.
And he had made himself look more conscientious and hard-
working in the process. It had been a valuable meeting, he
mused as he left the office.

When Mangan was gone, Jennings pressed the speed-dial
button on his speakerphone and waited for Deborah to
answer her mobile. He was annoyed when he was diverted
to the voicemail service. He left a message reminding her
that it was now half past ten on Monday morning, would
she ring him and let him know her whereabouts. He needed
her in the office immediately. He was not to know that his
own direct-line voicemail was out of service and that Deborah had left a message on Mangan's phone at eight
o'clock that morning saying that she was in Killiney with
Mugsy Mooney, who had telephoned her at eleven o'clock
on Sunday night, demanding to see her about his son's
impending court appearance.

Lelia Mooney opened her front door to find Deborah outside.
Although she was the wife of a wealthy businessman and spent
a fortune on clothes, she never felt secure with other women.
Self-consciously, she ran her right hand, which bore four huge
gold rings, down her white-leather clad thigh. She appraised
Deborah, in silence, for at least twenty seconds.

'Mrs Mooney, I'm Deborah Parker,' Deborah said. 'I'm
representing your son in court and I have an appointment with
your husband.'

'I know who ye are. You're the one who's going to get my
Michael off those charges being made by that scheming little
slut. My Michael would never do those things she's accusing
him of. Now, come with me and I'll show ye where his father

is. Then you'll have to excuse me. I'm having a coffee morning in the lounge.'

Deborah followed her through the house and Lelia stopped to show her the drawing room. The white leather couch was occupied by three similarly jewelled women. The gold eagles that had been embossed on to each of the seating panels replicated those outside the house. Two foxes' masks hung on the wall at either side of the fireplace and a bear's head stood on a pedestal at the other end of the room. Deborah had never seen anything like. She wondered if an interior designer had been at work, or if this was Lelia's doing. She supposed that Lelia might employ the services of a designer for the kudos of being able to say so. But she also reckoned that a woman like Lelia would have a strong sense of the 'style' she wanted and would probably disregard any designer's advice.

A huge arrangement of satin roses occupied the hearth and Deborah noticed two bottles of white wine on the white coffee-table in the centre of the room.

Evidently Lelia had noticed the look of awe on her face. 'I see you're admirin' me settee, love. Even if I do say so meself, it's lovely, isn't it? It was very expensive to have it done, but it just goes to show ye, doesn't it? Money buys taste after all!'

'It's obvious you've spent a lot of money on the house, Mrs Mooney. It's beautiful.' Architecturally, it *was* a beautiful building.

By the time she reached the more subdued environs of Mugsy's library, Lelia was rejoining her friends.

Mugsy Mooney recognised the look of relief on her face. He'd moved out here to the south side so that people with money and class couldn't look down on him any more. But even he conceded that his wife's taste in furnishings was an affront to good taste. And even if people were too polite to comment, he knew what they thought of Lelia's interiors. 'Go ahead, love,' he said. 'You may as well have a good laugh at Lelia's decorating skills. Everybody else does.' He beckoned her to take a seat in the velvet-upholstered wing chair facing his desk. 'But, Miss Parker, I see in my Lelia what she sees in our Michael. She might be a bit rough around the edges but she has a heart of gold.'

The analogy sickened Deborah. She couldn't forget the findings of the forensic medical report, which disclosed the details of the attack the Mooneys' son was accused of perpetrating on the twenty-year-old university student, Rita Brady, a month earlier. She made no reference to the furnishings – it was of no concern to her how her clients decorated themselves or their homes. What she found interesting was that they cared what she thought. Insecurity, despite the trappings of wealth.

Mugsy Mooney had sought an urgent meeting with Deborah because he had spent the weekend worrying that his chain of escort agencies was going to go down the tubes if his son was convicted. Since the attack on Rita, Johnny Collins had been running Exclusive Escorts in place of Michael Junior, and Collins had informed Mugsy on Friday night that business was down almost sixty per cent because of the publicity surrounding the case. The only part of the Sandymount business that remained was a string of working girls who were too frightened to leave so that they could work for the opposition.

'If you can get him off this charge,' Mugsy said now, 'I am prepared to pay full fees, plus an annual retainer of twenty grand to your company. In addition, I will transfer all of my business dealings to your firm. If Michael is found guilty and we have to appeal I'll just have to go to another firm,' he told her.

Deborah didn't know what the man expected her to do, but she was not going to be threatened. Her main priority was to give the best kind of representation. And that included telling her client the facts. 'Look, Michael, it's not as simple as you offering us a further financial incentive to get your son off. It's our job to provide the best possible defence for him but no amount of money is going to alter the outcome of the case.'

But he was not to be dissuaded. 'Look, I have the back-up to stop this case going ahead if I want to take that route, but I'm not suggesting it. All I'm saying is it's worth my while to give you every incentive to get him off. I'm sure your boss won't turn his nose up at a retainer of twenty grand a year, before costs.'

Deborah was taken aback by Mooney's candour. The man was tacitly admitting that he was prepared to blackmail and or injure potential witnesses or jurors – or even his own son, for all she knew – to prevent a guilty verdict. She was well aware that the more powerful criminal gangs had the means to intimidate witnesses, but it discomfited her to know that a client could admit it to her. In her line of work, she divorced herself from the gruesome reality of her clients' capabilities and dealt with them on a need-to-know basis. None the less, she was shocked to realise, for the first time, that they saw her as one of them.

She stood her ground: 'Michael, I have to tell you that the weight of evidence lies heavily in favour of the State. There's the DNA for starters. The strands of hair found on the girl's clothing match Michael's. His hair was found on her body, and hers in his BMW. As I have said before, it would be prudent to consider a guilty plea. If we were to get lucky, we could stand a chance of bargaining it down to assault causing serious harm. The State wants a trial no more than you do, what with the huge backlog in the courts, and they might be amenable to talking on that basis to save us all a lot of time and money. We could possibly end up with a sentence as short as five years. I have to ask you again to consider it.'

Mooney rose from his leather swivel chair and walked round the side of the desk. He stopped inches from where Deborah sat. He stabbed the index finger of his right hand into the desk to reinforce his point: 'I've heard what you've been saying about copping a guilty plea but we're not going for it, and that's that. The fact of the matter is, I could have stayed with the tossers in that other firm if I wanted to get him to plead guilty. Now, there's going to be no pleading guilty and I'm giving you the twenty grand as a retainer, starting now. His mother will kill me if he goes down – so, you see, you have to help me out here, love.'

He was writing the cheque before she could respond. She had fulfilled her ethical duty in advising him of the best approach to take in the case, but he was the client and she was obliged to take instruction from him. If they lost the case, which was a very real possibility, at least Jennings and Associates would pull in considerable fees, plus the one-off twenty thousand pounds' retainer he had just signed.

'So, where are we at in our defence, Miss Parker?' he asked, as he folded the cheque in two and handed it to her.

It wasn't normal procedure for a solicitor to receive a cheque from a client before a bill had been issued, but Deborah did not want to antagonise him. It represented a minor departure from the norm but many of her clients thought money could buy everything. In some instances, she knew, they were right. 'Well, Michael, on the downside, there is the question of your son's hair on the victim's body and hers in his BMW. We also have the matter of the jack being missing, the same type of car jack with which the victim says she was assaulted. And then there is the question of Michael admitting while in custody that he had hired the girl and that she had been on his premises earlier that night. He even gave a hair sample, although he says he was not advised of his rights not to do so.'

Mooney tried to intervene, but Deborah held up her right hand to signal that she should not be interrupted. They were now on her territory. '*However,* there are some plus factors on our side. For starters, the prosecution have a strong case to answer in terms of the manner in which they conducted their initial interview with your son. He had no legal representative present and, as you know – despite the protestations of Hanley and Lynch to the contrary – Michael insists that he was not afforded an opportunity to contact his solicitor. We will be making a strong point about this in court and senior counsel says that this in itself could break the case. As you know, Michael says that he was not notified immediately orally and in writing, as is a suspect's right, of his entitlement to access to a solicitor. We are bringing in a handwriting specialist to analyse the custody records to ascertain exactly when he was afforded this right.

'Additionally, the fact that Michael has admitted to having been in the girl's company on the night in question could go in his favour. It demonstrates that he had nothing to hide as is his contention.

'Third, Michael is adamant that he gave the girl a lift into the city centre and he says further that they had a kiss and more than a cuddle. This will go some way to accounting for the hair samples.

'Lastly, the missing jack. Forensics are saying that the nature of the injuries inflicted on her chest and arms are consistent with the standard jack for a 320 BMW convertible. Aside from the testimony of the girl herself, this is the State's strongest piece of evidence and, as you also know, the jack was not found at the scene and Michael has a witness, yourself, who will say that he mistakenly left his jack at the side of the road after changing a spare tyre about three weeks prior to the incident. The fact is that, unless the State are in a position to produce the jack used in the attack, the absence of the tool from Michael Junior's car is merely circumstantial.

'Those are the technical weaknesses in the State's case, which may help us. On the witness side of things, senior counsel is not advising that we put Michael in the witness box because we don't want to give the other side an opportunity to cross-examine him. As you also know, his previous convictions may not be referred to in court and hopefully the jury-selection process will enable us to eliminate any potential jurors who might have read about his previous activities in the Sunday tabloids.

'We need the three women from the escort agency to verify that Michael took twenty minutes to drop the girl into town, before returning to Sandymount for the night, and we will more than likely put them on the stand. You and Lelia will both say in your evidence that you were mistaken about the night you watched the video at home with him and that will just come down to whom the jury believes. Anyway, that's a long way off yet. Let's just get through the preliminary hearings.

'Now that the case has been sent forward for trial by the District Court to the Circuit Criminal Court, we'll see if the Circuit Criminal judge will grant us our motion to return to the District Court to depose some of the State's witnesses.

Your son seems to believe that he will get a fairer hearing from Judge Deering in the District Court. I think your family knows enough about the law to understand that this is an indictable offence, which cannot be tried at District Court level, but if we can get the Circuit Court to refer it back to the District Court to take depositions from some of the Garda witnesses, the District Court might agree that there is some loophole that might prevent the State's case going on. We can try this. It is what your son wants.'

Then Deborah reminded him that a year earlier the traditional preliminary examination of a case by the District Court had been abandoned. 'You see, Michael, under the new procedure, either side wishing to take pre-trial evidence from a witness, for the purposes of relevance and admissibility in court, must make an application to the trial judge in the Circuit Criminal Court. It is up to that judge to decide if it would be in the interests of justice to return the case – before the trial hearing – to the District Court to rule on the admissibility of certain evidence.'

Privately, Deborah was uneasy about Michael Junior's insistence that his legal team apply for preliminary examination of certain witnesses in the District Court. He had even used the relevant legal terms when telling her that he wanted her to make the application for a return to district level. His knowledge of the new legislation had been so thorough that she had wondered if he had taken separate legal advice on the issue.

Still, it was her job to take instruction from her client and there was nothing she cherished more than her oath to represent them to the best of her ability. She would interpret his wishes and go through the evidence with a fine-tooth comb in an effort to discover flaws in the State's case.

★   ★   ★

When she had finished, Mugsy was impressed. He'd watched enough court cases to know that a case could fall on the smallest technicality and it seemed to him that the bulk of the State's case rested on circumstantial evidence. He couldn't get over the way she had taken control of the situation. She had even prevented him interrupting! Did she know who she was dealing with? She looked so innocent, but her knowledge and confidence with her business was awe-inspiring.

He was happy with what he had heard so far. But there was one thing he couldn't understand, and after Deborah Parker had left his house, he wondered about it again. Why was Michael Junior being so cocky about this case? And why had he failed to display any anxiety about his fate? They were serious charges, carrying a potential sentence of at least five years, yet his son could barely be bothered to turn up for meetings with his legal team. Mugsy suspected that something his son had said the morning after the attack lay behind his flippant attitude, but he couldn't remember what it was.

It was close on eight o'clock when Deborah drove up to the gates of the Dalkey apartment complex where she had lived for the past six years, right beside a picturesque little harbour. The Sea View apartments, offering stunning views of the South Dublin coastline, comprised two rows of three-storey build-ings on either side of a small avenue, which ran directly down to the sea below. If she walked to the edge of the perimeter wall at the sea end of the complex and looked right, she could see over to Killiney Bay, where Mugsy Mooney's pile sat perched high in the hills. He was welcome to it.

Deborah pressed the remote-control keypad on her dash-board and the electronic gates swept open, leading her on to the little avenue and down to where her apartment perched in the corner site. It was a beautiful September evening, unusually warm, and the sky a palette of red and blue above a sea that was so still it looked like a sheet of glass.

As she hopped out of her two-year-old Volkswagen GTI convertible, Deborah thanked her lucky stars for evenings like these. The car had been an extravagance, which she still felt guilty about because the Irish weather did not frequently lend itself to driving open-top. But on good weekend days, or on evenings such as this, there was nothing more exhilarating than to drive along the coast from Dalkey to Killiney with the wind blowing through her hair. She was about to go into her apartment when she glanced into the back seat and saw the two boxes of files for the Mooney case. She had gone straight to the Law Library to examine case studies after her meeting with Mugsy and hadn't returned to the office.

She walked to the wrought-iron rail that separated the complex from the boulders that led down to the sea and strolled down the steps. She sat on one of the big flat rocks that formed the sea wall, kicked off her black slingbacks and threw back her head. She closed her eyes and felt the breeze waft over her face.

Fifteen minutes later, she was disturbed by the sound of her telephone ringing through the open window of her apartment, two storeys above. Abruptly, she sat up and put her shoes on. She hadn't got where she was today by sitting around being lulled by sea breezes. As she collected her briefcase and the files from the car, Deborah recalled the motto her mother had instilled in her from an early age; 'If you want to succeed, work hard. If you want others to help you succeed, work harder than them.' She had followed it and it had certainly paid off. She had had a good education, which had led to a great job, a nice home and a car. She had fantastic friends, although she rarely saw them these days, and life was good for Deborah Parker. She had come a long way.

Now it was time to get back to work. No doubt the flickering light on the answering-machine heralded a message from a friend, inviting her out for a drink in one of the cosy little pubs in Dalkey. No doubt, too, that whoever it was hadn't expected her to accept – she'd become a virtual recluse since she'd begun working for Jennings and Associates.

She dumped the files in the middle of the living room and grabbed her diary. If it was the only personal thing she achieved, she would take care of her telephone banking business before getting back to work. She dialled the number and took out a pile of bills: two for electricity, two for the phone and two for Visa, total amount owing twelve hundred pounds. She swore. Having to pay off a sum like this would throw her finances into disarray. She made the payments, and was about to replace the receiver when she decided she needed a confidence boost. She transferred to the account-balance inquiry system and checked the details on her dual account. The automated voice informed her: 'Account balance thirty-four thousand and five hundred pounds. Last transaction September 01 account credit five hundred pounds.'

The money was there yet again, just as the solicitor had informed her it would be shortly after her mother died six years ago. To this day, Deborah could not understand why they had lived in almost abject poverty when her mother had clearly been a woman of considerable means. It was strange, too, that the solicitor had refused to confirm that the money had been left to her by her mother. No will had been made, yet she had begun receiving the lump sums just after her mother's death. It *must* have come from her. Deborah had no other living family . . .

By the time she had finished poring over documents in the Mooney case, it was half past eleven. She sat back and stretched her arms up to the ceiling. Another good day's work done.

As she passed the flickering answering-machine *en route* to the double bed she feared she would never share with any man if she continued working such long hours, she pressed play. She learned that the missed phone call hadn't been from a friend inviting her out for a drink. Instead, she was greeted by a clearly irate Paul Jennings, wondering 'where the bloody hell you've been all day.'

She curled up in bed, exhausted, but sleep wouldn't come. She couldn't stop wondering how he hadn't known where she had been. She had left two messages with Patrick Mangan about her movements. Perhaps her colleague was blacking her because she had refused him the kiss he had asked for after five pints in the pub last Friday night. Surely not, she thought. He couldn't be that petty, surely?

6

Offices of the Garda National Bureau of Criminal
Investigation, Dublin, September 2002

Maria Lynch sat with her boss and the rest of the team at a circular conference table in their offices at Harcourt Square. It was from these Dublin headquarters that all major national investigations were spearheaded. The building housed a cross-section of intelligence gatherers who, despite the usual inter-departmental rivalry, pooled resources and information to provide the teams with the bigger picture on those under investigation.

In the case of the Mooney inquiry, the NBCI officers, under Detective Inspector Brendan Hanley, had accessed the databases of the Organised Crime Unit and the Criminal Assets Bureau to build a full profile of the Mooney clan and its activities. Their colleagues had parted grudgingly with the information. None wanted to see Hanley's team get the credit for solving a crime with intelligence that had been painstakingly gathered by officers with no links to him. It was nothing personal, just the politics of the job.

Hanley's team were hoping to use the ancillary information to put pressure on the Mooneys and build a stronger case against Michael Mooney Junior in court next month. The problem was, Michael Junior had few previous convictions of any note and, in any case, under the rules of evidence, previous convictions were inadmissible at trial in Ireland. But they could be entered in the court record in the case of a judge passing sentence on a guilty verdict. Hanley, known among his colleagues as the 'Attorney General' because of his vast knowledge of the legal system, pointed this out.

He perused the printout obtained from the intelligence-records section. Mooney Junior had a lengthy record for petty misdemeanours. There were several car thefts, burglaries, driving without a licence or insurance, assault on a traffic warden . . .

'There's no point in us even attempting to go the route of slipping his previous into evidence,' Hanley said. 'It will result in a dismissal of the jury at least and a striking-out of the case at worst. The only instance where previous are admissible is when there is a striking similarity between a previous offence and the current offence for which the person is being tried. For instance, if Mooney had been found guilty of an earlier offence perpetrated in the same fashion as the offence on Rita Brady, then we could introduce it. But that's not the case here, so we can forget it. We have to go on the hard evidence and, God knows, we have enough of that.'

It was one of Hanley's trademarks that he imparted as much as possible of his thirty-odd years' policing knowledge to his juniors when investigating a case. An avuncular figure of the old school, he was known as one of the toughest taskmasters in the force, but also as one of the best when it came to interrogating suspects and teaching his subordinates the tricks of the trade.

His team listened attentively. His take on the case would tell them how to play it in court. Piled high on the circular table were all of the documents the prosecution would present to the court. Bulkiest of all was the Book of Evidence, which contained everything they had against Mooney Junior, including medical reports and witness statements. Without the Book, as it was known to the police, a trial could not go ahead. As Hanley leafed through its 390 pages, he recalled the hours he had often spent with victims' relatives, explaining to them that the police were obliged to hand it over to suspects before their trials began.

'But why should suspects get access to the document containing all of the State's evidence against them?' he was often asked by distraught families who wanted their loved ones' attackers brought to justice.

He would try to explain that criminals, or suspects, as he was obliged to call them, were entitled to due process: 'It's the law. We are obliged to let them know what we have on them so that a defence can be mounted. They have rights too.' Then he would pause, and add, 'Unfortunately.'

The Book had been served on Mooney Junior in the District Court. Its completion was indication that Hanley's team was ready to proceed with the trial. Once it had been served, the Dublin District Court had returned the case for trial to the Central Criminal Court.

'You've checked the index here and everything is in order?' he asked Lynch.

Lynch had spent the night ensuring that all of the witness statements matched the evidence. She nodded in a way that told Hanley exactly how thorough she had been. None the less, he went through his usual checklist: nothing should be overlooked or taken for granted. Despite the high hopes he held for Lynch in the force, he had no intention of taking her word that everything was up to speed. Over the years he had seen too many eager officers burn the midnight oil to the detriment of an important case. There was no room for exhaustion-related cock-ups on this one.

'Our barristers have already seen this anyway, lads, but are we positive that the medical reports tally with what the doctors and nurses from the Sexual Assault Unit will say in court?' he asked.

Lynch let out a sigh, and Hanley glanced at her. He smirked at the look of impatience on her face. He was only too aware that his meticulous approach irked his juniors. But they would all have to live with it. The minute some of them got into the NBCI they thought they were the top dogs. Not that Lynch was like that, he mused – but they all had to learn that patience and attention to detail were vital to this line of work. His protégés had to grasp that they should never rush to judgement because all seemed well on the surface. In Hanley's world, there was no room for shoddy policing.

'Everything's in order, boss. The medical reports are almost verbatim identical to what the medical staff have said in their statements. There are no grey areas open to exploitation by the defence.' Lynch eyed him with a level gaze that said, 'Here we go again.'

Enjoying her frustration now, Hanley had a knowing twinkle in his eye.

Lynch closed the files before her and folded her arms in a statement of boredom. 'As I said, boss, all is in order. I have thoroughly checked everything.'

But Hanley continued, as though she had not spoken: 'The forensics reports tally with our placing Mooney with the girl? Your statements regarding what she told you in the first and subsequent interviews are in here? Mooney's statement to us on the morning he was lifted is in here? Have you checked and double-checked everything, Lynch?'

This time she glared at him. She was one of the few officers who could do it and know that he would laugh it off. 'For God's sake, boss, you should have come home with me last

46

night and stood over me. It would have been quicker than this. Every scintilla of evidence has been corroborated. Sure don't I know what a finicky, belligerent taskmaster you are?'

Suddenly, the mood changed and Hanley looked at her sternly. She had crossed the line. 'Lynch. I have no idea why you think you can refer to your superior as finicky and belligerent. I am now formally reminding you to think before you open your mouth again.' He paused, then added, 'Especially if you expect me to take you up on that invitation to come home with you. Now, what way is that to talk to a prospective suitor?'

The whole room, including Lynch, fell about laughing. It wasn't often that they heard Hanley flirt. In fact, it had never occurred before. He obviously liked Lynch. A lot.

Hanley closed the Book of Evidence and picked up another weighty volume, containing the scenes-of-crime evaluation evidence. In other policing jurisdictions, it was known as the Exhibits Book. It contained photographs of the scene where the victim had been located and of her injuries after admission to the Rotunda Hospital. Hanley relaxed as he fingered the plastic covering on the document. A picture told a thousand stories, and in this instance, the jury would be repulsed when they saw the extent of the harm done to Rita Brady. But for all the pleasure it gave Hanley to know that the pictures before him would convince any jury of Mooney Junior's deviant behaviour, he hated Exhibits Books. Invariably they depicted an increasingly valueless society where human lives were debased to the point of worthlessness. Hanley couldn't countenance the fact that one human being could inflict such torture on another.

He closed the book, his face flushed now with rage, then asked Lynch, 'How is she doing? Will she hold up for us? It's a lot to ask of anyone, especially given that she is admitting to having agreed to work at the agency.' From his own experience, Hanley knew she would be concerned about the girl's performance in court. She had brought the witness on board so she was responsible for her. Hanley noted Lynch's defensive body language, but paid it little regard. He had been there himself on many occasions. When a defendant was put on trial, he or she was not the only person being judged. The officers who put the cases together were under constant scrutiny, by their superiors, the public, the media and, most importantly, by the victims of crime. Furthermore, there was a unique responsibility on whichever officer brought in the key witness for a case. Even though everybody knew that a police officer couldn't be responsible for a witness's performance, the burden nonetheless always fell to the officer in charge of the key witness. If the witness did well, the officer was a hero – and vice versa. If the witness performed badly, the officer felt like hell. And the worst thing about the huge responsibility was that there was nothing at all anybody could do about a 'bad witness', as Hanley and his colleagues referred to weak courtroom performers.

'She's bearing up well, under the circumstances, but I have to say she's distraught at the prospect of cross-examination and the fact that it is going to be suggested to her that she consented to sex with him,' Maria said.

'I wouldn't be too worried about her coming across as a bit volatile under cross. With the medical evidence we're presenting, the jury is bound to see why she would take offence at such a suggestion,' Hanley told her. 'The woman had a car jack pressed on her back to hold her down while he committed anal penetration. The photographs show she has the scars to prove it and, to be honest, the more emotional scars she shows in the witness box, the better.'

Maria squirmed visibly in her chair, and she was not alone. Every officer was uncomfortable with the idea that any victim of such a hideous crime should have to relive the ordeal to bring its perpetrator to justice.

Hanley could offer her no comfort. It was his opinion that policing was a nasty business and you either coped with the harsh realities or you shouldn't be in the job.

He continued to outline the possibilities for Mooney Junior: 'Let's look at what our client, the not-so-lovely Mr Mooney, is looking at here. Under section four of the Criminal Law (Rape) Act, 1990, penetration, however slight, of the anus or mouth by the penis where the victim does not consent and the accused knows or is reckless as to whether they consent or not, could attract a maximum penalty of a life sentence. Now, we all know that our suspect won't get life, but with charges of assault causing serious harm, and rape, he should receive a sentence of at least 15 years.'

Lynch intervened, sounding depressed: 'Yes, boss, and we all also know that if he goes down, he'll only serve six or seven years at best. And a big thanks to the overcrowding problem in our prisons. No doubt Mooney will be cheering the revolving-door system as he goes in at the front and out at the back – and hoping that the media doesn't find out that the State won't keep a rapist for the full term of his sentence. It's bloody sickening.'

He gave her a reprimanding glare, but he supposed she was entitled to her views. It was his view, however, that they should remain personal and private. He hoped he hadn't been wrong about her. 'Tell me this, Lynch. You've got to know the girl pretty well by now. Why would a final-year student at one of the best universities in the country sign up to work at an escort agency? What motivates someone with so much going for her, and a bit of a stunner too, to demean herself in that way?'

As the father of a twenty-two-year-old, Hanley couldn't countenance the idea of his daughter either suffering a similar ordeal or working for an escort agency.

'According to her, it's not as uncommon as you might think. She says she knows a medical student and an architect who are at the same thing. The Celtic Tiger economy produced a lot of new money and a lot of broken marriages. Rita Brady says she saw it as easy money – a few hours with a professional man once or twice a week and she could walk away with four hundred quid in her pocket. That's what she was promised, you see, an introduction, as the advert for Exclusive Escorts said, to "refined, professional gentlemen requiring companionship". She swears blind that although she never came out of the bedroom she was in, or set eyes on the two clients Mooney had waiting for her, they were professional types. It's a booming business in Dublin and it seems to give hardened thugs like the Mooneys the image of respectability they crave.'

'So why risk her future career by waiving the right to anonymity afforded to rape victims?' Hanley queried.

'Well, she will be insisting in the box that she took the word "escort" literally, and that she was under the firm impression that she was selling her services as a companion, nothing more. At the end of the day, her impressions of what the job was about are of no material relevance to the case.

'With regard to why she is going public, I think it will be cathartic for her. She is so repulsed by Mooney's vicious assault on her that she has decided the only way she will ever get over it is to confront him face-on, so to speak, although she will be giving evidence by video link. Mind you, she only knew she had *that* right when I told her about it. She was prepared to stand up in court,' Lynch said.

Hanley made a mental note to talk to Lynch later about the

advice she had volunteered to Brady regarding the video link. In terms of the impact their victim would have on the jury, it would have been better if she had been prepared to appear in person. Brady's figure in the courtroom would have really affected the jury. Lynch had to learn to think strategically.

'So, the only conceivable problem we are going to encounter is Mooney's contention that we contravened the Treatment of Prisoners in Custody regulations,' Hanley said. 'Read that section in the book to us, Lynch, and we'll figure out where this gobshite is coming from on this.'

Lynch wished he had asked one of the others to do it. She knew they referred to her as Hanley's Golden Girl and she didn't want to be ostracised by the rest of the team because of his attentions, which she didn't court. If only he knew the truth about her . . . She didn't need to read the law to her boss: she knew it verbatim. 'Under the 1987 Act, a detainee in a police station is entitled to be notified of his or her right to consult a solicitor. Once an arrested person has asked for a solicitor, they may not be asked to make a written statement until a reasonable time for the attendance of a solicitor has elapsed. Indeed, if the nominated solicitor fails to show, the detainee is entitled to name another. The arrested person may then consult with the solicitor out of earshot of investigator.

'As we are all too aware, it's a strong element of Mooney Junior's case that he was afforded no such opportunity when in custody.'

Hanley raised his eyebrows, a bemused look on his lined face. 'How quickly he forgot all he said to us about not needing a brief because, as far as he was concerned, the girl was dead and we would never have a case against anyone anyway. It will be a simple case of our word against his and, given the strength of the girl's evidence and everything else we have that's tangible, I don't foresee it being a major problem.'

His telephone rang. It was the Chief State Solicitor's Office, to inform him that Mooney Junior's team intended to make an application to the trial judge in the Central Criminal Court the following Tuesday morning.

The others listened as he repeated the words into the mouth-piece: 'They want to send the case back to the District Court for depositions from some of the Garda witnesses? Why? What do they think they're going to achieve by doing that?'

'We think it's just a trawl for loopholes. Look at the calibre of his legal team. They'll try every trick in the book before this goes to trial,' the solicitor replied.

Hanley put down the receiver. He had decided that this was just a trawl by the defence, one of the many delaying tactics that seasoned criminals like the Mooneys employed to try to frustrate the course of justice. He instructed his team to meet him on Tuesday.

The following Tuesday morning, the Mooneys received a telephone call from Deborah Parker. The Central Criminal Court had agreed to their application to take preliminary evidence in the district court from four police witnesses: Brendan Hanley and Maria Lynch – who had formally ar-rested Michael Junior – Sergeant Brian Williamson, who had cautioned him before bringing in a doctor to take hair samples for analysis, and Dr Claire Byrnes, the forensic scientist who had conducted the tests.

When she hung up, Deborah Parker tried to work out her client's motive in insisting that the team get the case back into the District Court.

7

It was a crisp October morning, with the sun shining brilliantly on the Bridewell garda station at the back of the Four Courts. The assembled media was in full feeding frenzy. Television cameras from TV3, RTE and even Sky had gathered to capture pictures of the notorious Mooney clan turning up to do battle with the police over the charges levelled against Michael Junior and his alleged attack on the prostitute. The journalists could barely believe that the Mooneys had been successful in their application four weeks earlier to have depositions taken.

The media posse also included photographers from all of the national print publications, anxious to get a clear picture of the man the police had labelled 'the most ruthless sex fiend in Ireland'. That tag had been applied before the charges were brought against Mooney in court, and although reporting of the case was now confined to what transpired in court, the description of the crime issued by the police before they had made an arrest had ensured that every development received a high-level airing in the media.

The attention was just what Hanley and his team wanted to keep up the pressure on the Mooneys.

The deposition hearings were due to get under way in one of

the courtrooms at the back of the Bridewell, but under the rules of the Courts Service, television cameras and photographers were not allowed to film inside the building. This meant that the wrought-iron gates at the car-park entrance were closed to the cameramen and photographers who were gathered outside. The Mooneys would have to battle through the scrum to get in. 'All the better to embarrass the living daylights out of the scumbags,' Hanley had gloated, as he and Lynch were photographed through the windows of his Opel Vectra while they waited for the garda in charge of the court to open the gates and let them through.

The Mooneys had had to suffer the indignity of walking from Church Street, round the corner, to the court building, giving the media ample opportunity to film them. When they reached the gates, they had been forced to wait while the garda fumbled with his keys until he found the correct one. Such delaying tactics formed part of the unspoken agreement between the police and the media. The police were anxious to embarrass criminals they particularly disliked: getting them into a fury before they entered the courts often meant that they exploded before the presiding judge.

Hanley, Lynch and the rest of the investigation team stood laughing at the spectacle from an upstairs window in the court building.

From the corner of her eye, Deborah Parker was observing them. Standing back from the gates to allow the Mooneys to go through ahead of her, she warned them not to let the police see they had noticed them laughing. But Lelia Mooney, in her leopard-print knee-length skirt and black patent leather stilettos, couldn't conceal her anger. The next morning an image of the peroxide blonde giving the two fingers towards a hazy figure in the window made a sensational picture in two of the daily newspapers.

To add insult to injury, Deborah, her client and his parents were forced to stand in the courtroom while the court garda ushered the assembled media from the front seats normally reserved for legal representatives and their clients. Because of the overcrowding in most Dublin courtrooms, it wasn't uncommon for members of the press to end up squashed into a tiny space on a bench beside the solicitors, but Deborah knew that in this case the court authorities would be aware that, because depositions were being taken, she and her barrister needed the bench to themselves so that they could spread out their case notes, legal textbooks and pads.

Lelia was furious at having to wait while the press moved to other seats. 'I thought you said this case was being held in secret, Miss Parker. What in hell is all these reporters doin' here?' she demanded.

Deborah explained that this part of the hearing was indeed being held *in camera*, 'But they have a right to be here for deposition hearings,' she muttered. 'They just can't report anything that's said until there is a verdict after the trial has concluded.'

Michael Junior appeared calm, regardless of what might be ahead. 'We're here today to see that this goes no further,' he told his mother, 'so don't be thinkin' that because Ms Parker says stuff about "after the trial" that she's right. We're here today to see that this case doesn't go that far. Isn't that right, Miss Parker?'

Deborah stared at her client, icy cool in his black Hugo Boss suit, crisp white shirt and crimson silk tie. She could not fathom any legitimate reason for her client's unfailing optimism. He seemed to possess an unfounded degree of confidence . . . or was it knowledge, even, that the case would go no further than today's hearing. It was one of the most troubling aspects of the case.

Judge Thomas Deering was a notoriously meticulous judge. When they had drawn him for the initial hearings, Deborah had been disappointed because he had a reputation for playing things strictly by the book. He was known to dislike lengthy legal argument in his courtroom.

One of the golden rules of courtroom politics, no matter which side a solicitor is representing, is not to upset the judge. If that means not embarking on areas of argument a judge is known to want to avoid, then so be it. In the case of Judge Deering, the presentation of lengthy legal arguments were pretty much off-limits from the outset, as far as Michael Junior's defence team was concerned. Legally, of course, they had the right to present any argument they chose, but they did not want to irritate the judge with their strategy. However, Deborah and her barrister, Marcus Daly, perceived themselves as having drawn a 'bad judge' for the hearing because of the tactics they would employ.

One thing that both sides could be sure of, however, was precision, and it was bang on half past ten when the judge ordered his clerk to call the first witness whose evidence the defence wanted to examine.

Dr Claire Byrnes, from the Garda Forensics Unit at Garda Headquarters in the Phoenix Park, took the stand. She answered a series of mundane questions about her qualifications and estimated that she had worked on approximately sixty cases over the past four years in which DNA had been extracted from hair for forensic testing. The media scribbled as she told the court that she had been given two samples of

Mooney's hair for testing, one an intimate sample, the second non-intimate.

Hanley and his team fought to conceal their mirth as they heard her tell the court about the method of testing the samples. 'The intimate sample comprised several strands of Michael Mooney's pubic hair and this sample, in accordance with the stipulations of the Forensic Evidence Act of 1990, was taken by a medical doctor who was called to Donnybrook garda station on the morning of Mr Mooney's arrest.'

Hanley could almost see the headlines at the end of the case. 'Crime Boss Pubic Hair Leads To Conviction.' Michael Mooney Junior would be the laughing-stock of the gangland scene.

Claire Byrnes continued: 'The non-intimate sample comprised strands of the defendant's scalp hair. These were taken by the duty sergeant, Brian Williamson.'

Judge Deering stroked his own silver grey hair as he listened to her explain how she had tested the scalp hair and come up with the first set of results, which Hanley's team insisted linked Mooney to the Brady attack. 'Every Garda team has a hair-sample kit, which they get from us at the forensics lab. We suggest that when the kit is being used, the head is combed through thoroughly. If this doesn't yield much hair, we suggest that a sample is either cut or pulled from the root. That hair is then presented to us for the initial stages of analysis.'

'And can you tell us how exactly that hair was tested, Doctor?' Marcus Daly asked.

Hanley could imagine the press pack comparing Claire Byrnes to Dr Kay Scarpetta, the forensic pathologist in Patricia Cornwell's novels. It would make for great colour in background pieces about the case. He chuckled to himself.

Byrnes continued: 'I took the hair from the suspect and I mounted it on a microscopic slide. There were several strands. I then took a comparison microscope, and I mounted the hairs found on the victim beside those of the suspect and I examined the strands millimetre by millimetre. This type of microscopic examination is essentially a physical examination of hair, which demonstrated that the hairs found on the victim's clothing were consistent with the hair samples of the defendant.'

Marcus Daly stood up. 'Are you telling this court that you based your findings on a mere physical examination of the evidence? Can you tell us how scientifically accurate this might be?' he quizzed her.

Byrnes played to the barrister, allowing him to think that he was about to score a point. 'That's correct, Judge. I took the non-intimate sample for microscopic examination,' she said. 'It was hair that was combed from the defendant's head by the investigating gardai. The match was high, but it would not be correct to say that it is absolutely scientific.'

Daly looked at Judge Deering, with incredulity written on his face. He told the judge that, on the basis of this non-scientific evidence, he would be applying for the charges against his client to be dropped.

Byrnes allowed the buzz in the courtroom to subside, then said, 'Judge, if I might add, this microscopic examination was merely the first part of my analysis.'

Daly sat down, looking defeated, and the judge told Byrnes to proceed.

'I then extracted DNA through an alternative and altogether more advanced scientific method. DNA comes from the root, not from the hair shaft, and from it, a scientist can extract the same profile as from blood or semen. The hairs I worked on were not the same ones as I used in the microscopic examination. The second set were left at the crime scene. They were not shed hairs – that is, hair without roots – they had been pulled out by the victim in the struggle. These hairs were discovered on her clothing and in the scrapings under her fingernails.'

Judge Deering was engrossed in what she was saying, and noting down every detail.

'I used a system known as PCR, or Polymerase Chain Reaction, in which the hairs are placed in a tube and incubated in such a way as to liberate the DNA from the root. This kind of profiling is known as Short Tandem Repeat and it is the system that is used by policing agencies throughout Europe.

'I separated the DNA on a gel, in a process known as electrophoresis. Here, the molecules are separated in an electrical field and as the hairs move about, a laser moves back and forth and the DNA pattern gets repeated, leaving us with a DNA profile. The chance of two people having the same DNA profile is less than one in one hundred million. I secured a match between the hair found on the victim and the suspect's hair, which was presented to me by the gardai,' she finished.

In an almost off-hand manner, Daly asked, 'And can you tell us when exactly this evidence was presented to you for examination?' Given that Byrnes had volunteered that the hairs she used had been obtained at the crime scene, the question was of crucial importance to the case.

'The evidence was presented to me for analysis on the morning of the victim's admission to hospital on the ninth of July,' she answered.

'And when, Dr Byrnes, did you return your results to the investigating team?' Daly asked.

'I returned my findings on the tenth,' she answered.

The assembled media and legal teams were huddled together in groups, waiting for Judge Deering to emerge from his chambers with his ruling on the admissibility of evidence.

All of Hanley's previous concerns about the Treatment of Persons in Custody Regulations, and Mooney's contention that he had been denied access to a solicitor, had gone out of the window as he had heard the legal argument presented by both sides.

The court clerk announced the judge's imminent return and there was hushed silence as Judge Deering took his seat and began to speak. 'Clearly, from the evidence of Dr Byrnes, the State was in possession of near-incontrovertible proof of the defendant's guilt from the tenth of July. This means that when the defendant was arrested on the eleventh, he should not have been questioned, as the investigating team clearly had ample evidence with which to charge him. As both sides are aware, the law states that a suspect may not be questioned further when the State already has sufficient evidence to charge them.'

The journalists were already out of their seats and running to file the sensational collapse of the case to their news desks.

Judge Deering told them not to leave his courtroom until he had finished.

'I am ruling that Mr Mooney was held in unlawful custody when being questioned at the garda station and, therefore, his alleged admissions that he had been with the victim at the time of her attack are inadmissible, as are the hair samples taken by the sergeant. I thank Dr Byrnes for her succinct evidence. The case is dismissed. You are free to go, Mr Mooney.'

As he sat in his chambers, Judge Thomas Deering reflected on his ruling. It was legally sound and unlikely to be overturned by any other judge. In any case, he had given it prolonged consideration since Michael Mooney Junior had first appeared before him almost four months ago . . .

8

Sandymount, Dublin, Four Weeks Later

The penthouse that housed one of Exclusive Escorts' five Dublin bases was buzzing for the first time in months. In the reception room, where clients mingled with the girls before choosing one – or more – for the evening, several well-heeled professional men were drinking cocktails or champagne, dispensed by attractive young women in black-and-white maids' uniforms.

The agency had been closed to non-regulars for the night, in accordance with the instruction of Michael Mooney Senior. He didn't want to give Hanley and his crew a chance to raid it. His son hadn't agreed with Mugsy's order that no new girls were to be signed up for the foreseeable future and was hosting his own party in the master bedroom, with three cronies to help him vet the prospective new talent. Whacker Browne was his coke supplier, and Niallo Dunne the bagman, who deposited at the bank the cash collected from the Exclusive Escorts' premises. Johnny Foley helped out with security. The four had grown up together in Finglas on the north side of the city. They had been born into the working class and, unlike most of the children from the many decent families in the area, had been allowed to run wild from an early age. None had completed any formal education and they had shared many a police cell. These days, they sported Gucci shades and Rolex watches, and drove souped-up cars with tinted windows.

Michael Junior was on his fourth can of Heineken. He was sprawling on the vast heart-shaped bed, boasting about his antics with Rita Brady months earlier. 'She knew what she was gettin' into, lads, didn't she? Fuckin' posh bitches like her don't frighten the likes of us. Think they can come to a place like this with their fancy degrees and not work, they do. Jesus, lads, I taught her some lesson, I did. I showed her what real work is all about and what a workin' girl has to do to earn it. Bleedin' south-side snob she was.'

The irony of what he was saying was lost on him and his companions. They had no problem taking money from middle-class women and men or living alongside them, but they all had a chip on the shoulder about the divisions that existed between the middle classes and 'our lot' as they referred to themselves. The irony was that it was actually the likes of Mooney and co who created the barriers. It was their absolute rejection of the law and of what most people deemed socially acceptable behaviour, which served to erect the class barriers they so resented.

He continued, 'Last year, I made over a quarter of a mill on this place alone for me da. He'd kill me if he knew I was tellin' yous this, but that's the fact of it. Ye don't make that kind of loot providin' convent girls to go to fuckin' tea in the Westbury Hotel, now, do ye? No, siree. Ye make it by providin' convent girls to get their kit off.

'Jesus, they don't call me "Mick the Prick" for nothing,' he said, unzipping his trousers and waving his hard penis about, sending his friends into a frenzy of laughter. They could never understand how he seemed able to maintain an erection when drinking copious amounts of alcohol. But when they discussed it privately, Whacker had volunteered the theory that their friend got a huge thrill out of inflicting all manner of degradation on the women who worked for him and that he only needed to think about violating a woman to get a hard-on. They envied him his asset, as they referred to it.

The nickname had actually been attributed to Michael Mooney by the girls who worked for him because he was regarded as an unmitigated thug and a pervert. He, however, had taken it as a compliment when he heard it first, deciding that it was his sexual prowess and infinite reserves of energy for 'testing' his girls which won him the name. His friends hadn't dared tell him differently, lest they lose their livelihoods.

'Jesus lads. Look at me. I've gone all hard even thinkin' about the money we make from these girls. Get them out here now and we'll do a bit of servicing,' he enthused.

Whacker, Johnny and Niallo were dying for a bit of action themselves, but Niallo Dunne wanted to know how his friend had been so right in predicting that his legal team would win their motion for dismissal of the charges against him in the District Court.

'So how did ye know you'd get off, Mick? Jasus, you were pretty cocksure about that one,' Niallo Dunne asked.

But Michael Junior wasn't about to let his guard down, even for his trusted lieutenants. Especially when even his father didn't know the real reason why he had insisted that his legal team return to the District Court. 'Let's just say I have faith in the legal system and some of those who make the decisions in it. You'd be amazed what they do in their spare time.' He winked.

His three friends were stunned into silence by the significance of what he had told them, but they knew not to press him any further. If the Mooneys wanted to keep things secret they would and, anyway, the less they knew the better. All

63

three had been happy to stay out of it before the charges had been dropped.

At a sign from Michael Junior Dunne stood up and went to get the four women from the adjoining bathroom. They were just finishing the coke they had been given to loosen them up before their trial session for Exclusive Escorts. None of the girls was in any doubt about what would be required of them if they joined the agency. They all scored coke regularly from Whacker Browne and knew the hard work required to keep them in supplies.

The vetting process took the usual format: Michael Junior sampled each 'package', then passed them on to his friends. When they had finished, they sent the girls to clean up while they gave them marks out of ten. Any girl who refused anal sex was automatically dismissed. Tonight all four passed with flying colours and Michael Junior told them to put on maids' uniforms and join the guests. A little later, in the reception area, he took the receptionist aside and pointed to a distinguished-looking man wearing a bespoke suit. 'Anything he wants,' he said, 'is on the house.'

9

Knocktopher Village, May 1976

The child ducked down behind the armchair, her special hiding-place. She always retreated to it when her mother told her to run to her bedroom because he had come home drunk. But young though she was, the little girl's instincts told her to stay and make sure that her mother survived.

It was 7 April and the room was decorated with balloons and streamers. The aroma of freshly baked apple pie wafted through the house and a fire blazed in the kitchen hearth. Until ten minutes earlier, the child had been playing with the doll her mother had given her for her third birthday.

Sheila Dunne, over three years married now, had been determined to give her daughter a happy birthday. That morning her husband had told her that he wouldn't be home until late and Sheila had had the opportunity to do something special.

Ten minutes ago, at half past five, they had been enjoying the celebratory tea. As far as Sheila knew her husband had been at the pub for half an hour, and the evening's drinking stretched ahead of him – if his usual routine was anything to go by. She should have known better than to believe what he had told her.

'Didn't I fucking tell you not to be spoiling that little bastard?'

'Yes, Eamon. I'm sorry, Eamon. I just wanted to give the child a birthday. She's only a baby, for God's sake.'

He threw the pot of tea at her, scalding her arm. 'Take that, you stupid bitch, and don't talk to me about her being a baby. She's no baby of mine. You and that fucking snob of a doctor's son saw to that. I won't have my money spent on her. How many times do I have to tell you?' His face was turning purple with the rage that any mention of the child stirred in him.

'Eamon, I didn't spend any of your money on her. My mother gave her the doll and I did the usual baking. I even made your favourite apple pie for you. We had everything in the house. I beg of you, don't hurt the child.'

Before the last words were out of her mouth, he was scanning the room for the doll he had not yet seen. 'A present, no less? She even gets a present and you try to pass it off as coming from your mother. I'll kill you and then I'll kill the little bitch. She causes nothing but trouble in this house!' he screamed. He pulled the little girl from behind the chair by her hair. 'Give your daddy the doll,' he ordered.

But the child clasped it tightly to her. He picked her up by the collar of her dress and held her before the fire. 'Give me the doll now, or she might fall into the fire,' he bellowed.

Still the child wouldn't relinquish it, although her legs were reddening so close to the flames. Sheila snatched it from her daughter and handed it to her husband. 'There. Take the doll. Now put her down, I beg of you.'

A familiar routine followed. 'You'll beg me all right. You'll beg me for forgiveness for your sins. You'll beg me not to harm your precious child,' he told her, and placed the child in the armchair, where she would have a full view of what was about to happen.

Sheila knew better than to ask him to let her put the child in her room. To do that, she knew, was to risk him injuring the little girl.

He told her, 'Before you beg, you'll take my two children and you'll put them to bed. They don't deserve to see what I have to do to make their mother love them.'

66

Sheila sat in the room with the two younger children and wondered if another might be conceived tonight. She looked at their frightened faces, which always asked the same question: why did their sister always have to stay in the room when Daddy was with Mummy?

She made the sign of the cross and prayed that he would not make her pregnant again. The first time she had conceived by Eamon, she had prayed that the absence of her period was due to stress, or one of the beatings he had given her. Eventually, she went to a doctor in Kilkenny and had a test. She had wept uncontrollably, to the amazement of the doctor, when it had proved positive. When she begged for help in getting rid of the baby, she was told in no uncertain terms that there were no back-street abortionists in Ireland and that she was to go to her local priest and beg forgiveness for her thoughts.

When a little boy arrived after a nine-hour labour, Eamon had come in drunk from the pub and taken her again, delirious with joy at the birth of a son and promising to get another one from her as soon as he could. Three months later, when she was late again, she didn't bother going to a doctor. Her fate was sealed. Now she had a two-year-old son and a year-old daughter and, despite the circumstances of conception, they were as beautiful as her first child.

She clung to the two little ones before leaving their bedroom. Eamon had insisted that neither slept in the same room as her first child. She fought to hold back the tears as she kissed them. She cherished them every bit as much as her first, although they had been conceived in violence and hatred. Every time she thought of the events that had brought them into the world, she felt ill with revulsion.

Sheila returned to her husband. She knelt before him on the linoleum floor, looked into his eyes and begged his forgiveness, in the way he had instructed her during the first week of their marriage. 'Forgive me, Eamon, I beg you. Forgive me, Eamon, I beg you.' On and on she repeated it, until he sent the birthday girl to bed. Then he bent his wife over the kitchen table and violated her. As usual, when he had finished, he instructed her to clear the table and the floor, then 'Hurry up and come to my bed,' where she would lie, quivering with fear, and ask herself, Why don't I have the strength to leave him? Why don't I get away?

But the answer was obvious: Sheila Dunne had little education and no money to her name. She swore to herself she would ensure that her girls were never at the mercy of any man. And she prayed that her little boy would not grow up to be like his father.

IO

Deborah Parker was ensconced in Dobbins restaurant in Dublin's south side. It was the first big party her firm had given that she had attended in the seven months since she had joined. She had missed the summer party because she was on holiday, but she had heard enough stories about staff antics at a Jennings and Associates bash to know that she had had a lucky escape.

She was in need of a good knees-up. She had been working so hard that her social life had virtually died. The flagstone-floored restaurant, nestling in a little lane off Dublin's Mount Street, was a favourite with the city's legal, business and professional circles. At busier times of the year, like the Christmas period, it could have been described as the power-house of Irish business.

If one wanted to be seen, Dobbins was one of the key places to dine. And what better way for Paul Jennings to inform his professional rivals that business was booming, than to take his staff of fourteen there?

Six bottles of Châteauneuf du Pape stood on the table and most were already nearly empty, although the group had only been in the restaurant for fifty minutes. It was lining up to be a good afternoon. The festivities would undoubtedly transfer to the Shelbourne Hotel on St Stephen's Green, where the famous Horseshoe Bar would be lined with the city's best-known faces.

Sandwiched between Jennings and Patrick Mangan, Deborah was aware of the glances her cleavage was attracting, particularly from Mangan, after she had removed her formal black jacket. She was also aware of their colleague Geena Williams's interest in Mangan. Williams, it seemed, had taken an intense dislike to her lately. She had been less than co-operative when Deborah had asked for help in unearthing case files stored in the filing cabinets in Williams's office. The woman's behaviour was odd, given that she was a junior solicitor in the firm, but Deborah put it to the back of her mind – perhaps the twenty-six-year-old was finding it hard to cope with the pressures of work.

It had been after the first in a series of interviews with Deborah had appeared in one of the weekend newspapers, that Williams's attitude towards her had changed. She had told Deborah acidly the following Monday morning that she was honoured to be working alongside a 'celebrity solicitor', as the newspaper had called her.

To Deborah, the initial approaches from the media had seemed bizarre. She had laughed when she received a telephone call from a journalist asking for biographical information because she was writing a piece about her. She had told the journalist she didn't want any publicity: self-promotion just wasn't her thing. But when she told Jennings about it, he had insisted she call the reporter back; the article would be good for the firm.

After the first article had appeared, she was inundated with calls from tabloids seeking her views on new legislation aimed at clamping down on the city's crime bosses. One of the broadsheets had carried a full-page article on women lawyers, citing Deborah as 'the pioneering 29-year-old who has been responsible for the breakdown in the barriers erected (by their male colleagues) against women in the legal profession'.

She had been particularly embarrassed by that and had told Jennings she didn't want to give any more interviews. He had retorted that she was being precious: putting forward a positive image of the profession was as much part of her job as representing her clients in court. Lately he had been brusque with her on several occasions. It seemed to Deborah that the closer he became to Mangan, the further her relationship with him deteriorated.

When Jennings rose to make his end-of-year speech to the group, Deborah was at first flattered, then astonished, to hear him single her out. Slurring his words, like the rest of the group now, he said, 'And I would like to take this first opportunity to publicly welcome Deborah on board. I think we would all agree that she has been a fantastic acquisition for the company and the publicity she has had in the papers has been fantastic too, for us as well as for her own personal image.'

Deborah cringed.

Jennings continued: 'And I want to remind all of you that Deborah has had a difficult time since she started with us. She has had to cope with the likes of a certain family, who are now among our top clients, and with the media attention, plus a heavier workload than she had probably anticipated. But it's too late to quit now, Debs! We're all one big family here at Jennings and Associates, and I want all of you to give her as much support as she needs in the coming year. A toast. To Deborah.'

As the glasses clinked, Deborah's face was as red as the wine slopping from Geena Williams's glass – she didn't fail to notice Williams wink at Mangan. It was the most embarrassing moment of Deborah's life. Even more so than the broadsheet article heralding her as the saviour of female solicitors.

For the life of her, Deborah could not understand why Jennings might think she was having a difficult time, as he had implied in his speech. He had sounded as though he felt she wasn't as capable as he had thought her to be. She didn't let her embarrassment show. Instead, she raised her glass and thanked him, then excused herself and went to the ladies' at the other end of the restaurant. Never in her life had she felt so threatened. And she had no idea why . . .

'The most powerful man is the one with most friends,' her mother had always told her. And as she returned to her colleagues at the table, Deborah felt like the most powerless person in the room – and very alone. Someone else had once said that it was wise to 'keep your friends close and your enemies even closer'. Right now, she felt as though she was surrounded by enemies.

Much later, in the Horseshoe Bar, she sat beside Patrick Mangan. Fuelled by the wine, she decided to try to patch up whatever difficulties were causing the atmosphere between them. But before she could begin Mangan had flung a series of questions at her. 'Jasus, Debs, you're some piece of work. Do you know that? You do. Don't you?' Mangan's eyes sloped in the direction of her chest.

Deborah played along with him. He was only engaging in some flirtatious workplace fun. 'That's me, Patrick. I'm such a piece of work that I need the support of the whole firm to keep me standing. I need everybody's co-operation, Patrick. So co-operate with me and tell me what Jennings was actually saying there today.' She said it in a light-hearted way, but even in his inebriated state, Mangan wasn't giving anything away.

★   ★   ★

Over the past few months, Mangan had forged a bond with his boss. The pair frequently went out for a Friday-night pint and Jennings had been to his house twice. It seemed to Mangan that his advice to Jennings about Deborah's difficulties with the job had brought them closer together. He was confident now that his boss had taken him into his confidence, and regarded himself as Jennings's right-hand-man.

Now Patrick sat up straight, but leaned in so close to her that Deborah could feel his shirt brushing against her breasts. 'I'll tell you what, Debs. You let me fuck your brains out and I'll co-operate with you all you like. How does that sound?'

In her seven years in the legal profession, since graduating at twenty-two, Deborah had been subjected to plenty of sexist remarks. It was part and parcel of the business, and any woman who didn't play along was labelled a spoilsport or too weak to compete with her male colleagues. But she had never been propositioned so blatantly. And in such a sinister way. She couldn't let him get away with it. 'You know what, Patrick? I may be drunk, but I'm not that drunk,' she said, and cast a contemptuous look over his body.

She noted that astonishingly, he was taken aback, and took advantage of that to plough on: 'Anyway, is there anyone you want me to call and let them know that I'm putting you in a taxi?'

He ignored her veiled threat. 'Jesus, Debs, I find you irresistible, I really do . . . want to fuck your brains out. But that's not all. I want to be with you. If I could have you, I'd do anything for you. Do you know that, Debs? Anything. No one else would get a look in if I could have you.'

Now he'd gone too far. 'Don't provoke me any more, Patrick. You might regret it in the morning. You never know who might hear of this conversation.'

But Mangan grabbed her arm. 'You, Deborah Parker, are the one who will have the regrets. Think on that, why don't you.'

Deborah realised that Patrick Mangan would either get his own way or destroy her.

It was an hour before she left with three of the secretaries and their accountant to go to a nightclub. Williams and Mangan declined the invite. They said they were sharing a taxi home together.

As Patrick Mangan made his way home in the taxi, having declined Williams' invite to go back to her flat, he was seething with hatred of Deborah Parker. She had been so wrong not to play along with him. And boy, did he intend to make her pay for it. 'By the time I'm finished with her, she will be wishing her life was over,' he said out loud.

The taxi-driver eyed him suspiciously in the rear-view mirror and when he dropped him home, he made a note of his address. The man had a murderous look about him and the driver intended to go to the police if there were any reports of assaults against women in the media later in the day.

At three o'clock in the morning, Deborah stood in a hazy state in a long queue outside of Renard's nightclub, the notoriously trendy hang-out of the celebrity and model set. But Deborah didn't feel in the slightest bit merry. She felt a frightened, but none-the-wiser woman, as she wondered how to solve the problem of the man who was hell-bent on destroying her career – unless she slept with him.

Looking up towards the dark sky, she silently asked her mother what she should do when she couldn't keep an enemy close. All that she could feel was numbness as she waited for an answer, an answer which she would have to find herself . . .

11

The meeting was taking place at Garda Headquarters in the Phoenix Park. As Hanley drove through the wrought-iron gates, he cursed at the sight of the crowded front yard, packed with the cars of the two thousand staff who worked there, the hundreds of visitors and other officers like himself who, no doubt, had been called in to receive reprimands similar to the one he knew he was about to receive.

The duty sergeant on the gate signalled him to turn left and make his way to the officers' club at the other end of the complex. This building, with its beautiful plasterwork, plush carpeting and antique furnishings, was normally reserved for the bigwigs brainstorming sessions. Most of the 10,800 officers in the force had never been inside its double mahogany doors. There was general resentment among rank-and-file officers towards anyone invited there – the honour was only bestowed by the top brass, whose uniforms were decorated with medals.

As he drove up the avenue, Hanley recalled the day he had decided to join the force. He had been a seventeen-year-old schoolboy on his summer holidays, and he could still feel the sweat that had trickled down his back as he ushered the family's fifty pigs along the lane and into a shed. As he walked back along the lane, he had noticed two policemen sitting in a car, the windows down, chuckling as they read their newspapers and drank tea from a flask. That's the job for me, he had thought, and he had never looked back.

In those days, policing had been easy. The odd car accident, a few thefts and complaints about damage to farm property. Then he was moved to Donnybrook, the upper-crust suburb of Dublin. He chortled as he remembered his then sergeant following him on the beat as he strolled through the village – he hadn't forgotten the sting that had raced up his spine when the sergeant had kicked his right buttock because he was 'failing to walk in an upright manner'. In those days, appearances were everything and members of the force expected to command respect. Now, a respectful kid was one who only stuck up two fingers at an officer instead of telling him to fuck off. Drugs were destroying lives and entire communities, while gun-toting thugs killed each other without pause for thought.

When Hanley and his colleagues managed to arrest a suspect – which was becoming increasingly hard because of all the regulations that now had to be observed – they were claiming legal aid and challenging every law in the land before you'd asked a single question. Crims were always looking for loopholes in the law. It was frustrating for the likes of Hanley. Along with most of his colleagues, he held the view that if they were genuinely certain of a suspect's guilt, they should do whatever was necessary to secure a conviction. But there was no question of fit-ups.

Since Hanley had entered the National Bureau of Criminal Investigation in 1998, he had found himself dealing with the godfathers of the Irish organised-crime scene, most of whom employed expensive solicitors and top barristers who were adept at extricating their clients from any awkward situation.

He and his colleagues believed that the new regime of affording suspects any number of civil liberties and rights was a load of crap. As far as Hanley was concerned, these bastards would only be deterred if they were subjected to the beatings and brutality they meted out to others in their own turf wars. But that would have the civil-liberties groups up in arms.

Michael Mooney Junior was a perfect example of this type of criminal and unlike his father, who had grown up in the days when the law commanded respect, he was an unmitigated villain. Hanley was furious that it was because of Mooney Junior that he, an officer with over thirty years' service in the force, had been called here for a rap on the knuckles.

It wasn't so much that he had failed to prepare for the case. It was more that he had prepared to fail by trying to pull a fast one on Mooney's legal team. He knew, in his heart of hearts, that he should not have allowed the weight of the case to rest on the scientist's evidence, but at the same time he had known that Mooney was guilty and that Dr Claire Byrnes had the evidence to support this. He cursed the loopholes and the law, and wondered if it was worth carrying on with all the administrative hassle. But he had his pride, and his pension, to consider. Another few years, and he would gladly leave the younger, degree-laden officers to deal with the underbelly of society. Until then, he would continue to battle against the system, which seemed increasingly to militate against the police and the victims on whose behalf he worked.

When Hanley walked into the long dining room and saw the lone figure of Assistant Commissioner Tom Daly sitting at one end of the rectangular table he stopped in his tracks. Surrounded by a sea of blue manila folders, Daly wore a mischievous expression. Hanley had seen it many times in the early eighties, when he had worked alongside the other man on 'covert operations' in Special Branch.

Daly, round-faced and plump, had a congenial nature that had allowed him to cajole 'intelligence' from the most unlikely informants during his ten years of trying to infiltrate the workings of the Provisional IRA. He hadn't quite succeeded in cracking their operations, but his depth of knowledge regarding their inner workings was encyclopaedic. He was credited with providing the Irish government with a substantial body of the intelligence that had enabled them to work on the 1998 Good Friday Agreement, which had resulted in a form of political harmony in the northern peace process. Now commissioner for the Dublin area, Daly was regarded as shrewd and effective. Hanley loosened the tie he had worn for the occasion and stuffed his hands into his trouser pockets.

His old friend sat back in his chair and smiled. 'You took a bad hit on Mooney, Brendan. The powers-that-be—'

'You are the powers-that-be, Tom,' Hanley interrupted.

'No. Not in this case. I'm talking about the real powers-that-be. This is coming from the top, old pal – the top here and in St Stephen's Green.'

St Stephen's Green was the headquarters of the Department of Justice, known as such because of its location in Dublin city centre. If the instructions on the Mooney case were now coming directly from the Green, that meant the minister wanted the situation addressed. The Garda Commissioner would have had a dressing-down from the minister about organised crime and, consequently, was none too pleased with the way in which the high-profile case had been handled.

'Jesus, Tom, since when did the civil servants begin meddling in the affairs of the police? Are we taking our instructions from the secretary to the Department of Justice now?' he asked, irritated.

Tom Daly crossed his arms and raised his eyebrows. 'For cryin' out loud, Brendan, you're either dying of naïveté, or you don't need me to answer that question for you.'

'Listen, Tom, it comes as no shock to either of us that the department meddles in the affairs on An Garda Siochana, but their interference is generally confined to matters of admin- istration and budgeting. Where's the political gain in this for them? For the life of me, I can't see it.'

The Assistant Garda Commissioner, with responsibility for policing in the Dublin metropolitan area, couldn't see it either, but friend or no friend, he was too powerful to admit this to Hanley. 'The minister wants tabs kept on the Mooneys and their operations monitored closely. The whole issue of whether or not to legalise prostitution is too much of a hot potato for him to take on. But at the same time he's coming under pressure from his female cabinet colleagues and women's pressure groups to protect women who are forced to turn a trick for a living. This was a high-profile case. He wants to be seen to be doing something about millionaire pimps living in luxury houses that his salary could never hope to buy him.'

Daly tapped his index finger on one of the piles of manila folders. 'You've got all you need to start with here. This has been going on since the case collapsed against the Mooneys last October – there's several months of intelligence for you.'

Hanley strolled up to the other end of the table. His own team had already collected everything from the Criminal Assets Bureau and from the Garda National Bureau of Fraud files. What else could there be to which he didn't have access?

This calibre of intelligence didn't come cheaply, and Hanley was delighted, astonished and perplexed by the information contained in the files. The fact that he had been given it meant that senior police officers, the Commissioner himself, senior civil servants, the Minister for Justice and even a High Court judge were involved in the case.

Hanley found it hard to comprehend why the Mooneys had warranted such high-level interest. Despite their wealth and propensity for barbarity, they were still regarded as a two-bit crime family by comparison to some of the other thugs in the city and they confined the violent side of their operations to prostitution, as far as he was aware. The whole picture didn't make sense.

He cursed Tom Daly for having landed him with whatever hornets' nest these files represented. Someone had taken a lot of trouble to get this information. Under the Telecommunications and Interception of Telephones Act, a suspect for whose telephone the police needed a tap had to be under investigation. Then they had to apply for the tap to Garda Headquarters Crime and Security Section. From this top-secret division of the force, issues of State security were decided and controlled.

A senior officer within C&S, as the section was called internally, would then have assessed the application to ensure that it merited consent, before forwarding it to the most senior police officer in the land for subsequent approval.

Even the sanction of the Commissioner was not sufficient itself for the authorisation of such a tap. If the Commissioner had been in agreement that the telephone tap was warranted, he would have forwarded the signed application to the serving Justice Minister who had to agree to its installation.

Who had been responsible for initiating the tap – and, more importantly, why? The files, which contained transcripts of hundreds of telephone conversations from Mooney lines, raised a number of questions in Hanley's mind.

Designed to protect the right to privacy of the ordinary, law-abiding citizen, if, as Hanley mused to himself, there was such a thing anymore, the business of phone-tapping was expensive and time-consuming for all involved.

He conceded it wasn't like his old Special Branch days. Back then, a tap was initiated at a local exchange, recorded by the telephone company at its headquarters in the General Post Office in Dublin's O'Connell Street and the tapes typed out by officers at Garda Headquarters.

These days, they had all sorts of sophisticated technology to cut out the middle men. But still, it was a very costly business. The hub of the operation was still at the GPO and the same administrative procedures which were in place in Hanley's day were still followed. But after that, it was all technology.

Hanley recalled reading in the 'Garda Advances' magazine about the computer whizz-kid new recruits who were being trained in the use of the latest tapping technology. These days, the tapped line was recorded in the GPO alright, but there was no more transcribing the details of conversations from tapes to paper. Instead, a signal from the GPO bounced automatically to a big computer in the Phoenix Park and within a fraction of a second of the conversation taking place, a verbatim account would appear on a screen operated by some young computer genius.

First, the Mooney family had not been under investigation at the time the application for the tap was signed, which flouted the requirements of the legislation. Second, Crime and Security section had clearly ordered the tap internally, because Hanley's National Bureau of Criminal Investigation team knew nothing of it. Or perhaps, he wondered, C and S had known nothing of the tap and the orders had come from higher up. Third, all taps had to be investigated by a High

Court judge, appointed specially by government to inquire into the legitimacy of such taps. This was disturbing. Whoever had made the order had risked exposing themselves to investigation by the highest levels of the force and even the judiciary. He was so troubled by all of this that he didn't even try to dissect the information contained within the transcripts.

12

Marbella, Spain

The sun shone and there was not a cloud in the sky. The water in the oval pool glistened as the rays reflected on its surface, and on the bronze body that lay face down on the lilo. Michael Mooney Senior, at six foot two, with a well-toned frame and gleaming black hair, looked younger than his forty-six years. As he lay sprawled in his naked glory, he was unaware of the video camera recording his every move.

Two women and two other men sat chatting on the luxuriously padded and elegantly crafted wrought-iron sun-loungers. The older woman admired her husband's lean physique. They had what might be called an ambivalent relationship but there was no doubting that Lelia and Michael Mooney were still as attracted to each other as the day they had first had sex in a Finglas confession box thirty-two years ago.

In her Burberry swimsuit, which she'd purchased from Dublin's most exclusive department store, Brown Thomas, Lelia knew that she was lucky to have such a handsome husband. The years had not been as kind to her as they had to him: her skin was leathery and wrinkled from the twice-weekly sun-bed sessions, which she had hoped would give her a fresh healthy glow.

Lying next to Lelia was Michael Junior's latest squeeze,

twenty-seven-year-old Stephanie Dixon. To Lelia's shock, the girl had clearly been brought up far from the world she occupied now. With her olive skin, heart-shaped face and big brown eyes, the tall brunette stirred a resentment in Lelia that she would have displayed openly, were it not for her son, whom she would never upset. Stef, as Michael Junior called her, had been on the scene since just after his big court case and although he had never clarified how he had got to know her, Lelia suspected that she was working for him.

Johnny Collins completed the gathering. His hatred of Michael Junior had intensified since Stephanie had arrived on the scene. Collins, with his tightly cut brown hair and tiny piercing blue eyes, was at first glance the most unlikely of hard men. But he was not known as Michael Senior's equaliser for nothing.

When he had to be, Collins was the most vicious, threatening individual on the Dublin crime scene. Ironically, his lack of physical muscle was one of his chief assets in his work. His adversaries tended to underestimate his capabilities, then had to live with missing limbs or scarred faces that bore testimony to his powers. If you double-crossed a Mooney, or inadvertently got in the way, Collins was dispatched to equalise the score.

Collins had heard on the grapevine that Michael Junior had done a deal with Stephanie: she would provide services to his most select customers for nothing, and in return she lived at the Sandymount penthouse, was taken to nice restaurants and provided with a wardrobe befitting her status as Michael's girlfriend. As far as Collins had ascertained, the problem was that she had answered an advert to work as an escort two or three nights per week. The word from the girls in the apartments was that she was none too happy at becoming Michael's twenty-four-hour prostitute and a vehicle for wealthy men to vent their sexual frustration.

Stephanie, it seemed, despised Michael Junior but was either too terrified, too broke or both to extricate herself from the situation in which she was now trapped. Johnny Collins thought it was disgusting: young Michael had so much money he could get almost any girl of a certain calibre, he wanted. In fact, this had been Michael's reasoning: instead of just acquiring a girlfriend, he was displaying good business sense in utilising her for the benefit of his businesses. Michael knew that soon Stephanie would be knackered from all the shagging and he would dispose of her to one of his less-classy operations.

Mugsy flipped off the lilo, swam a length of the pool and climbed out. He picked up a Ralph Lauren towel and secured it round his waist. He told the maid, Maria, to bring piña coladas for the ladies and several bottles of San Miguel for the men. Then he stretched himself to his full height and threw back his head. 'This, me lovelies, is the life! This is why we all work so hard. This,' he swept his right hand in a grand gesture towards his landscaped grounds, 'is why crime fucking well pays!'

Collins noted that Stephanie's smile was forced.

Michael Mooney Senior was known as 'Mugsy' to his close associates because, as he frequently told his coterie, he had been arrested more times than he could count, had had his mug-shot taken in at least a dozen garda stations in Dublin, yet never once been charged. He prided himself on always coming out smiling in the photos, which was why he called himself Mugsy.

The purchase of the private villa, in 2001, had been his second major extravagance – the first was Mount Argento in

Killiney. Playa del Dunas was a stunning development of villas and condominiums in the heart of Puerto Banus, the social hub of the resort, which stretched to Marbella. It was known, to all of those who returned year after year, as the Golden Mile.

The first time Lelia had set eyes on Puerto Banus and the glitzy tourists who frequented it, she had been totally in awe of the place. She had immediately rushed into the shopping mall at the end of the port and bought a pair of Guess jeans, some painful Prada mules and the biggest gold-plated Moschino belt she could find. Strolling back through the port in her new outfit, Lelia decided that anyone looking at her clothes would know that she belonged here, that she had money. Now she felt at home. It had taken her only a month to persuade Michael to buy them 'a little holiday cottage'.

It was located in one of the flashiest developments in the port. It had been fully interior designed, had five bedrooms and a price tag of three-quarters of a million pounds. Michael had been reluctant to buy it, but Lelia reminded him that the other Irish criminals were further down the coast towards Málaga. 'They are in the real Costa del Crime, Michael, love. Here, it's real class. It shows you're a world apart from those scumbags.'

That had been it. Michael snapped up the villa at Playa del Dunas, where the residents, many of them Irish, comprised leading sports and business figures and were all pillars of the community.

Alex King, investigative journalist, could not believe his luck. This would lead to a sizeable salary increase at his next pay review, maybe even a job offer from the rival television station RTE. His boss had been over the moon when Alex had telephoned him that afternoon to tell him of the footage he had on his video-recorder of the man dubbed 'the most notorious sex fiend in Ireland'. The pictures of Michael Mooney Junior, lazing by the pool in his skin-tight black Speedos, alongside his parents and his father's well-known henchman would cause a stir in Ireland. After last year's court case there was hardly a home in the country that didn't know who the Mooneys were. When this footage was aired on TV3, there would be uproar about criminals living the high life and the police not doing anything about it.

The swimming-pool footage was the tip of the iceberg; Alex had used the sensitive microphone on his Sony DV-Cam to record their conversations from behind the villa's boundary fence.

Now pretending to admire one of the fabulous yachts at the edge of the port, Alex panned his camera across the yacht and over the steady stream of diners entering the restaurant. The Mooney party strolled to the door and were instantly ushered to a window table. In the open, Alex knew that he stood no chance of recording the activity at the party's table, but he decided to stay on, if only to learn more about the brunette with Michael Junior.

Just as the group had finished ordering their food, Mugsy leapt from his chair and ran outside to the queue at the door. A brief conversation with the maître d' and he was back at the table with three young women in tow. They looked uncomfortable and appeared, to Alex, to be refusing his offer of seats at the table. Mugsy was clearly having none of it, gesturing broadly that they should sit down. Eventually they did so.

Alex had been observing the group for about a quarter of an hour before it clicked that someone was missing.

Where was the brunette? Could she have been a hired hand? No. Whatever about Michael Junior, his father was too shrewd to let some stranger in on his business. So what had happened to her? He had been right, he thought, that she wasn't of the same ilk as the Mooneys. And her absence might explain the vicious look on Michael Junior's face.

Back at the villa, Stef was staring at the Louis Vuitton bag Michael Junior had given her the day before they left Dublin. It was now packed. She was ready to leave for Málaga airport. But no matter where she looked she couldn't find the cash he had left lying around the room earlier that day. Nor could she find her passport or airline ticket. And when she keyed in the combination to the safe in their room, it would not open.

She put her hand to the small of her back, which hurt. He had been clever enough not to injure her where his father would see it. After the Rita Brady business, he was conscious of not showing his violent side to Mugsy. The bastard, she thought, reliving the events of four hours earlier when he had shoved her face down on the bed after she had refused him anal sex. She had thought that the presence of his parents would prevent him hurting her, but he had pressed her face so hard into the bed that her screams were muffled. When he had finished, he slapped her face and told her to think over what she had to lose by not fulfilling his desires.

She thought back to the circumstances of her first meeting with Michael Junior. She had had enough of working in fast-food restaurants and bars in Cork, always scrimping and saving to pay for her dingy bed-sit, with the black fungus of damp crawling up the walls and the constant loud music blaring from the rooms of the students who lived above her. She had been sick of listening to them coming in with their friends, reminding her of things she wanted but would never experience.

And she thought back to last October, when she had listened, fascinated, to the television news coverage of the Mooney case, when Michael Junior had walked free from court. That was when she had learned of the huge amounts of money to be made in the escort business. The journalist from RTE had reported, 'These high-class call-girls can make up to a thousand pounds a day,' and Stephanie wanted a security blanket.

A week later, she had left the room that had been her home for the previous two years and took the train to Dublin to begin her new life.

Scanning the adverts in *Dublin Speaks* magazine, she found the one she wanted. It read just as she had imagined it would: 'High-class dating agency requires escorts to entertain professional gentlemen. High-calibre candidates only need apply. Excellent remuneration. For further details, telephone Michael . . .'

It had been as easy as that. There was little the authorities could do to prevent the likes of the Mooneys advertising escort services. The police could infiltrate the agencies, but then they would be in court accused of entrapment. There was no question of getting the girls to speak out: they were all too afraid. Everyone on the scene knew what had happened to Rita Brady.

Michael Mooney had asked Stephanie on the phone if she had ever 'worked' before. When she had answered, 'No,' a shiver of excitement ran through him. Contrary to the assumption that pimps only wanted experienced girls, Mooney loved taking fresh young girls and introducing them to the business. He enjoyed putting them through their trial runs, which were unknown to his father but which Johnny Collins despised. He loved lying on a bed, or sitting on a chair, fully clothed, as he watched the first-timers shiver with nerves as they undressed before him, then followed a list of orders that left them fully aware of what would be required of them if they secured a place in his business.

'I want you to wear something revealing, but sophisticated. You should look like a businesswoman. And don't forget the underwear. It's the most important part of the package,' he had told Stephanie, when arranging her interview. 'If I give you a job, I'm going to have to see that you're fit to accompany my customers on dates, so I will personally look you over,' he had added. He told her to meet him at the Willows hotel in Ballsbridge.

When she alighted from the taxi Stephanie was stunned by the splendour of her surroundings. The head porter opened the cab door for her, and the staff were courteous when she said she was there to meet Martin Maguire, the name under which Mooney had registered.

Mr Maguire had been staying in one of the fabulous suites at the top of the hotel. When he met her at the door of his luxurious suite, she was taken aback by his sharp appearance – she had expected him to look a bit dodgy. She was relieved to find that he was a smooth-talking, expensively dressed man of about her own age.

Mooney had decided on the spot that she had an innocent look about her that would drive the punters wild. But first he had to conduct an 'interview'. He observed the cream co-loured short skirt and jacket she wore. (She had spent her last hundred pounds on the outfit at the end-of-summer sale in Debenhams and had finished it off with a pair of high black strapless mules which she picked up in Marks & Spencer.) He decided he liked the way she had chosen to wear only a lace bra beneath her jacket, which displayed a hint of what were clearly generous breasts. He also liked the way she had chosen to leave her long legs bare, although he would order her to wear stockings and suspenders in the future: middle-aged customers liked them.

He looked at his Rolex and told Stephanie he was running short on time and could only spend two hours with her: he had several more interviews to conduct.

Stephanie was shocked to learn that an interview could take two hours, but she settled into a chair, assuming that she was in for a long chat. Nothing could have been further from the truth.

'Before we start, are you prepared to remove all of your clothes? I have to make sure you're not wired before we begin our session,' he told her, his cool gaze fixed on her.

She was appalled. Eventually, she stammered: 'Do you . . . do you want me to do that now?'

He nodded.

She had begun with the single button on her jacket, then the zip at the back of her skirt.

'Turn round with your buttocks facing me and then pick up your skirt. But stay bent down. I want to observe how supple you are. Flexibility is important in this business,' he told her.

Stephanie was shocked by his lewd behaviour. She had assumed that it would be cold, calculated sex with a string of nameless men, but this was degrading in the extreme. It must have been after three minutes, although it felt like three hours, that she felt his hand on her left buttock. It rested there for some time until his other hand joined it on the right. 'We have a select number of customers who require anal penetration. It's up to the girls if they do it, but it pays an extra hundred and fifty quid. Are you game, love?'

Stephanie had been lucky if she was left with that amount of money to spend on food each month after paying her rent. Now she faced the prospect of earning it for just a few hours' work. Earlier she had decided that she would throw her morals out the window if she got the job, but now she shivered with disgust. Nevertheless, she said, 'That's fine by me, Michael.'

'If I give you a position, you call me Mr Mooney. Do you understand that, girl?'

'Yes, Mr Mooney.' She was close to tears and terrified at the prospect of what she was letting herself in for.

'Kneel down, then, and let's get on with it. I want to see how you are in the backside department, Stef. That's what I'll call you.'

She knelt down. 'You're not going to have sex with me, are you? You said that this was just an interview, Mr Mooney. Isn't this sort of stuff just for the customers?'

'Listen, darlin', if you go for a job in a computer firm, they want you to know how to work a computer. Get my drift? Now, am I in or are you out?'

'You're in, Mr Mooney.'

She tried to concentrate on the plush carpet and the legs of the antique chair opposite her, and told herself that, some day, she would have nice possessions if she worked hard enough.

As he worked hard at entering her, he issued a list of instructions: 'You never talk to the customers unless they talk to you. Do you get that? My customers like it because my girls are obedient. They do as they're told. My customers are important business people who do not like to be questioned and they thrive on the fact that my girls accept their authority. I just want you to know that this isn't some fucking two-bit operation, Stef.'

Five minutes later, he ordered her to turn round and lick

him clean. Then he had knelt down on the floor and stuck three fingers crudely between her legs. Stephanie had stood there, not moving, afraid of what was to come – whatever it was, it could not have been as bad as what he had just done to her on the floor – but the worst was over, as far as she was concerned. And if she wanted to get security, she would just have to get used to doing things she didn't like.

'OK, you'll do fine. But I have to warn you, you need plenty of lubrication in a certain area and I will have to see to that myself to get you ready for my customers.' Then he had put his tongue into her mouth. She had thought she would vomit.

'The rate is a hundred pounds an hour. That's sixty to you and forty to me. If they ask you to dress up, that's an extra fifty pounds an hour and if they want some of what I've just had, that will be an extra hundred and fifty. Here's my card. Ring this number and ask for Tiff. She's me secretary. She'll take you shopping and get you what you need. You can go now. Hurry up. The next one will be here any minute.'

As she had turned the door handle to leave the suite, he called, 'Oh, yeah, and another thing. I'll be testing you regularly meself to make sure you're not losin' it. I won't be payin' for it. OK? It's called in-house training and it's one of the perks of the job.'

When she reached the foyer, the girl on the reception desk had informed her that Mr Maguire would like her to return to his suite for what the receptionist described to Stephanie as 'some unfinished business'. For a split second, she contemplated running out of the hotel and finding some other way to make a decent life for herself, but in the end she had acknowledged the message and returned to the penthouse lift.

She remembered knocking on the door and being called inside. She could still feel the shock she had experienced when she saw the naked woman leaning over the desk. 'You're a quick learner, Stef,' he had said. 'We may as well get on with the second phase of your in-house training. This here is Lucy,' he'd said, slapping the voluptuous redhead's buttocks. 'She's very experienced. She'll show you what to do.'

Now, as she sat forlorn and penniless in Marbella, Stephanie realised that he had her over a barrel. She would just have to bide her time until she had got what she had come to him for.

It had taken Alex King two hours to realise he had a scoop that would make him the envy of the other journalists who had been chasing the Mooney story since the court case. 'Christ, I must be losing my touch,' he said, to nobody in particular. Then again, she was wearing a short skirt and he was not used to seeing her dressed so scantily. What had really thrown him was her hair: tousled and falling over her face, it lent her a sultry aura he had never noticed before. She certainly keeps this side of her hidden at home, he thought, more's the pity . . . God, the woman is so sexy.

It wasn't so much that he could prove she was in business with the Mooneys, but that a picture told a thousand stories. And when the folks back home got to see the footage of a highly respected solicitor dining with one of the most notorious underworld pimps in the most upmarket resort in Spain, questions would certainly be asked – by Deborah Parker's bosses, not to mention the police . . .

13

For Paul Jennings, the media deluge had begun at eleven the previous night, just after the programme had been broadcast on TV3.

'Can you explain the personal links between your firm's top criminal solicitor and the Mooney family, Mr Jennings? Do you believe it is ethical for a representative of your firm to holiday with a notorious criminal family, Mr Jennings? Did Ms Parker pay for the holiday herself, or was the bill paid by the Mooney family, Mr Jennings? You are aware, are you not, that the Mooney family is under investigation by the Criminal Assets Bureau for failure to pay taxes on income, Mr Jennings, income that the CAB says is the proceeds of crime?'

The principal of Jennings and Associates had been preparing to watch RTE's flagship current-affairs programme, *Prime Time*, and had been channel-hopping beforehand when he heard the trailer for TV3's investigative programme *Undercover*. 'Tonight, on *Undercover*, we bring you the real story about the family Irish police say are making three million pounds a year from prostitution. We reveal the jet-set lifestyle of the family police say are top-earning criminals, but whose members remain free to operate their lucrative illegal business.' He paused dramatically. Then: 'And in the most sensational development in the story of the Mooney family to date, we take you behind the scenes and show how the other side really lives and how it rewards those who work for them, including their legal advisers. Don't miss the real story of the relationship between top criminals and the legal profession. Tonight, on *Undercover*, TV3, at ten.'

Jennings had been apoplectic with rage. He had no idea what the reporter had been talking about but he knew two things: first, that there was no way *Undercover* would be running this programme unless they had the material to back-up their allegations; second, the reporter must have had cast-iron proof of whatever links he was alleging, other-wise he would have had to contact Jennings and Associates for an explanation of whatever he had uncovered.

Jennings knew that Alex King had not contacted his firm because he himself would have gone straight to court to secure an injunction to prevent the programme being aired. What-ever the man had, it must be good.

As he waited for the programme to start, Jennings tried to contact Deborah. Three calls to her apartment in Dalkey had yielded no response. He left a message that she should be contactable at all times, and a similar one on her mobile. His only other possible source of information was Patrick Mangan.

Mangan was his usual reticent self when asked about Deborah, until Jennings said, 'Come on, Patrick. I know you don't want to be opening any cans of worms here, but this is no time for misguided loyalties. Your primary respon-sibility is to me. If you know what this programme might contain, you'd better spill the beans.'

'Ah, Jasus, Paul, I don't even know if I'm right here, but she was reluctant to give any info when I asked her about her holiday. I don't know if that's what this is about, though. The only thing I know is that she was in Spain with a group of people and she wouldn't tell me who they were. She went all coy and private when I asked her.' He lapsed into silence for a moment. Then, in a low, conspiratorial voice, he asked Jennings, 'You don't think she was with the Mooneys, do you? I mean, she's more copped on than that, isn't she? Jesus, Paul, surely she knows that if she went with the Mooneys it would be a sackable offence? Wherever she was, though, she was living the high life. Since she came back, she's had a whole new wardrobe of expensive clothes that our salaries couldn't pay for. That's for sure, boss. Geena was remarking on her new look too. According to her, you'd want to be earning a hundred grand to wear the kind of gear she's got. And I wouldn't mind living in that fabulous apartment she has in Dalkey, or driving a fancy convertible car like hers. You can pay me some of what she's on, if you like.'

That left Jennings with a whole new scenario on his hands: was Deborah Parker taking back-handers from the Mooneys? Was she closer to them than she was letting on? How else could she afford such an expensive lifestyle? He tried to rationalise what Patrick had said, then switched to analysing Deborah as he would the facts of any case.

It was true: she lived in a very nice place and dressed smartly. At Dalkey you couldn't pick up a box for less than half a million. And he knew that Deborah owned her apartment. Even though she was on a good salary, it wouldn't meet the repayments on that kind of a mortgage.

Then there was the hotel she had stayed in. He had overheard Geena asking her and had been slightly surprised by the response. You wouldn't have much change out of two hundred pounds a night for a room at the Don Pepe. And, now that he thought about it, she certainly did appear to be even more expensively dressed since her holiday. The Gucci handbag for a start: it was identical to the one he had bought for his wife, Kathleen, last Christmas and which had set him back over five hundred pounds. It was a ridiculous amount of money to pay for a bag, he had told her, but she had got it anyway. Along with a solitaire diamond ring.

He had also noticed the label on Deborah's coat: Prada. And while he hadn't paid much attention to it at the time, a coat like that would have cost well over a grand – he knew that from the fashion magazines Kathleen read in the bathroom while she bathed the children. And on one of her few lunch breaks, he had overheard her talking to an art gallery about the price of a Graham Knuttle painting. From his own collection, he knew that even a small one was worth at least five thousand.

As the evidence mounted up, he tried to suppress it. His gut instincts were normally right and she had certainly done the business since joining his firm. But, still, with this TV3 broad-cast and everything Patrick was hinting at a wall of suspicion was suddenly being built round Deborah Parker's private, and possibly professional, life . . .

When the first of the calls to her mobile had come from Alex King, Deborah had been furious. She wondered how he had got hold of her private number and decided she would have to change it. That had been three weeks ago, at the beginning of June and just after her return from Marbella. Eventually, but only after the sixth unanswered call, the investigative journalist stopped phoning her. She had been curious about what he wanted, given that he was famous for his undercover stories, but had put it out of her mind when the calls had stopped. She had not told Jennings about them because she had feared that he would force her to do another interview. But now, as she sat facing him across his semi-circular glass conference table, she wished she had.

'Are you seriously trying to tell me that the first you heard of this business was when you came in here this morning, Deborah?'

'Paul, I honestly didn't have a clue. Even when I came to the door this morning, I thought the journalists were here for some other reason. I didn't know they were here to talk to me. I was out last night and, as you know, I don't read the papers until I get to my desk.'

Jennings drew back in his seat and removed his glasses. 'Look, Deborah, I want to give you the benefit of the doubt here, as much for my sake as for yours, but something's going on. I don't know what it is yet, but I bloody well intend to get to the bottom of it.'

Deborah could not believe what he was suggesting. She was so caught up in the shock of it that she was unable to answer him back.

She opened her mouth to speak and Jennings pounced on her. 'I have to tell you, Deborah, that you are being less than honest with me. I know that you deliberately ignored King's repeated attempts to get in touch with you. I had an interesting conversation with him this morning and he says he telephoned you half a dozen times and that you never returned his calls. Were you hoping he would just fade away?'

Deborah couldn't understand her boss's insinuations. Was he suggesting that she was trying to conceal some kind of relationship with the Mooneys? That appeared to be so, and she couldn't blame him for not thinking otherwise. She cursed herself for not having told him of her encounter with the Mooneys in Spain, but these days he rarely communicated with her. 'Paul, I bumped into the Mooneys in a restaurant. I was with two friends on a trip we take annually. I felt uncomfortable when he asked us to join him, but he is one of our top-paying clients and we have just taken a twenty-grand annual retainer from him, not to mention twenty-eight thousand in fees for the court case. What did you expect me to do? Rebuff him in front of his family and friends and have him take his business away? What would you have said if I'd come back and told you he was jumping ship?'

Jennings rested his elbows on the edge of the table and joined his hands to point them in her direction. 'I would have said, "What the hell are we talking about? I know nothing of any twenty-grand retainer." That's what I bloody well would have said. I would have said that this plot thickens by the minute.'

'I'm very sorry, but you must have forgotten,' she told him, indignantly. 'It was during all of the drama surrounding Michael Junior's arrest last year. You were in court when I got back from my meeting with his father and I gave the cheque to Patrick for safe-keeping. It was during lunchtime and there was nobody in Accounts. You *must* remember.'

Even as Deborah uttered the words, she felt the ground slipping from beneath her feet. If Jennings had received the cheque, he would have told her so. She even remembered thinking it a bit odd at the time that he had not congratulated her on bringing in such a handsome retainer.

'OK. We can clear the air on at least part of this thing now,' Jennings said, and buzzed Mangan to come in.

They sat in silence as they waited for him. He sauntered in and looked at Deborah as if embarrassed for her.

Jennings asked him evenly, 'Deborah says she gave you a cheque for twenty thousand pounds last year as a retainer from the Mooneys. Any idea why I haven't received it, Patrick?'

Mangan looked at Deborah, then at Jennings, then back at Deborah, an incredulous look on his face. 'Come on, Debs, you must be joking. I think I'd remember if I was given a cheque for that amount of money. You must have done something else with it, because I certainly never had it.'

Deborah stared at Jennings, open-mouthed. Quickly, she recovered herself. She looked Mangan straight in the eyes and told him, 'No. You are very much mistaken. I gave *you* that cheque.'

Then to Jennings, 'Paul, I passed a cheque for twenty thousand pounds to Patrick, and I have no idea what is going on here.'

Now it was Mangan's turn to be indignant. 'Just what are you suggesting by that?' he growled, leaning forward in his seat.

'Now, calm down, Patrick,' Jennings said. 'If Deborah says she gave you the cheque, I think you should consider that as a possibility. She has proven herself to be a very thorough and reliable member of this staff. Perhaps you're mistaken?'

But there was no mistaking the look of resolute denial on Mangan's face. 'I am not taking the fall for missing or, dare I say it . . .' he cast a cutting look at Deborah '. . . stolen monies, which are the property of this firm. I don't care what she thinks she did with the money. It didn't come to me.'

Deborah wanted to lash out at Mangan, but she knew now that he was playing a dangerous game. She intended to steer clear of him and exonerate herself at the same time. She looked at Jennings. 'Just so that you are very clear on this, Paul, my firm position on this is that I gave the cheque to Patrick. Now, if he lost it, it will be redeemable from Mugsy Mooney.'

Mangan pounced on her. 'Deborah, the man is a criminal, for Christ's sake. He doesn't have a decent bone in his body.'

Deborah glared at him. The knives were drawn now. 'He may be a criminal, Patrick, but believe it or not, he considers himself an honest one. I am certain that when I explain the situation regarding your misplacing the cheque that he will write us another on the spot.'

Mangan was about to issue another denial, but Jennings gestured to both of them to stop. Deborah would contact Mooney and, once the cheque was recovered, they would put aside their differences.

Jennings leaned forward and looked at Deborah quizzically. 'There's an awful lot here that doesn't add up. Including our accounts in the Mooney case, it would seem. I want this cleared up, Deborah. Fast. Until then, my position is that something underhand is afoot.'

Deborah was about to say that she agreed, but thought better of it. What accusations could she level against Mangan? None. That he had not been polite to her? That he had tried to get her to sleep with him? She had no witnesses – and, anyway, he would probably plead intoxication. She left the room, shocked to the core, intent on getting a new cheque from her client and resolved to keep a close eye on Mangan.

14

Knocktopher Village, May 1979

Sheila walked up the lane towards the cottage. It was a sunny evening and she had gone out after tea for a walk, just to the end of the lane and back. She rarely left her elder daughter with her husband for fear that he might harm her. But he had fallen asleep in his chair and the children had been playing hide-and-seek.

She had been gone all of twenty minutes. The first thing she noticed when she turned the bend towards their home was the absence of children's voices. Panic swelled inside her when she saw that the floral-print curtains were drawn – it was only ten past seven. Quietly, she crept to the back of the cottage and peered in through the back window. Seconds later, she was pulling herself up from a pool of her own vomit.

Eamon was standing with his back to the wall. His trousers were open, hanging loose on his thighs. Sheila's younger daughter stood before him, his right hand behind her head, pulling her close to him.

Sheila barged in through the back door, all fear of her violent husband forgotten. For years, she had endured the brutality, the violence, to protect her children. It was because of them that she did not fight back. If he killed her, and she knew he was capable of it, they would be left with their savage of a father. And Sheila knew that however bad it was for them to witness violent assaults on their mother it would be ten times worse if they were left alone with him.

She had become used to pain, but not of this type and physical pain paled into insignificance by comparison with what she had just endured. For the first time in her marriage, she saw her husband in shock. He jumped back as she pulled the little girl away from him and screamed at her to go to her room.

It didn't take Eamon long to recover. 'You'll not tell my children to disobey me! You'll not fucking do it. I control this house,' he yelled, and punched her, sending her flying through the open back door. She lay on her back, half in and half out of the house and screamed, praying that the neighbours might hear, 'You filthy, filthy pervert! You're not a man – you're a filthy, disgusting piece of nothing. To do that to my child! You're sick.'

He came to her, dragged her to her feet by the hair and hurled her into the cottage. He swept aside the stewpot on the table, flung her on to it on her back, and began to unbutton his trousers.

Sheila seized the moment. She grabbed the stewpot's handle, never taking her eyes off her husband. He dropped his trousers, then he leaned over her: 'I'll show you filthy and disgusting! Now you're going to know what sick really *is.'*

Three hours later, she sat huddled in a corner of the kitchen. Yet again, she was covered in blood. But this time so was Eamon. She had beaten him relentlessly with the empty stewpot. She had broken several of his teeth and his nose. She thought she might have broken his arm too. She prayed that she had.

She also begged God to give her the strength to send away her younger daughter, now aged four. The daughter he had told her he would 'play' with as often as he liked. 'After all,' he had told her, 'she is my property. Just like you.'

15

'Fuck me! She'll be too terrified to say she saw anything. She's losing her bottle now. It's only a matter of time before she breaks altogether, trust me. And there's a few more surprises for her yet.'

Geena Williams and Patrick Mangan were sitting in the Leeson Lounge. The snug little pub was popular among the legal and business professionals who worked in the offices that occupied the Georgian houses of Mount Street, Baggot Street, Pembroke Place and Fitzwilliam Square. It was a week after the TV3 exposé, as Mangan called it, to anyone who would listen, on Deborah and the Mooneys. The atmosphere in the office had been so heavy with suspicion about Deborah that it would have taken a Black and Decker to cut through it. Mangan was delighted.

In his nonchalant way, he had brought round every conversation with his colleagues – even the cleaners and the maintenance man, to what he was terming 'the Deborah situation' and assured them that 'this could mean the end of the firm': the Criminal Assets Bureau would probably shine the spotlight on Jennings and Associates – not that they had anything to hide, he explained to his colleagues, but with the 'Deborah situation', the CAB would be right to assume that the whole firm was in on whatever was going on between her and the Mooneys. If any wrong-doing was discovered, they could all be in the firing line and then the other solicitors might be struck off by the Law Society. His concern, of course, was not for himself but for Deborah and he hoped, indeed he was sure, that she was beyond reproach and all of this mess would be cleared up.

As the loyal employee that Jennings regarded him to be, Mangan felt it was his duty to confide in his boss and had duly informed him over a few pints the night before that some of the other solicitors were already looking for work elsewhere because of professional embarrassment over the 'Deborah situation'. There wasn't a grain of truth in this, of course, but what the hell? thought Mangan. It made him look good and compounded Jennings's growing antipathy towards Deborah. Perfect.

As he downed a third of his pint of Guinness in one satisfying gulp, Mangan relived the image of Jennings scowling at Deborah as they had passed each other in the stairwell, when he and their boss were leaving for the pub. There was now no chance that Jennings would contemplate inviting Deborah for an after-work drink. As far as Patrick was concerned, it was abundantly clear to all in the office that he did not trust her.

The Leeson Lounge was packed with office workers finishing their week's work with a few drinks, and although many of the pub's customers knew that Mangan had been married, he and Geena had become something of an item there. Nobody cast a second glance when they got close, as they invariably did after his fifth pint of Guinness and her fifth double gin and tonic.

Now he cast a lascivious glance over her full body, her large breasts and sturdy frame, which he privately regarded as 'generously curvaceous'. The curly black hair that cascaded down her back, and the way she held back her shoulders and stuck out her chest gave her a voluptuous air that was hard to ignore. As Mangan had said to one of his friends, 'She's no Deborah Parker, but there's something about her that makes me want to fuck her brains out.'

And that was exactly what he had been doing at eight o'clock on the previous Friday when Deborah, who had been finishing off some work, had walked into the women's toilets in their Mount Street offices. She had pushed open the door to be greeted by Mangan's milky white buttocks flexing over a spreadeagled Geena Williams. Mangan, she decided, was a disgusting excuse for a man. And that had been her opinion before the business over the missing cheque.

As for Williams, Deborah had given her a wide berth since the party in Dobbins. When she observed her with Mangan, Deborah understood the woman's antipathy towards her.

'So you don't think she'll say anything to Jennings about us?' Geena asked.

Mangan dug his hands into his pockets, feigning to scratch the inside of his thigh, but really trying to control the beginnings of a hard-on. 'Listen, darlin', there's no way she'd dare breathe a word of it. She'll look like a stupid cow if she does.'

'What do you mean, she'll look like a stupid cow if she tells him? She already is. Everybody in the firm knows that. I've seen to it!' Geena told him gleefully.

Mangan smiled at her, using the opportunity to pat her inner thigh by pushing back her short black skirt. It was only a matter of time before he and Geena would be in the back of his eight-year-old Toyota Corolla.

'She knows Paul and I are good friends, Geena. There's no

way she's going to risk going to him with this. Sure what would it achieve? We're safe as houses, so we are!'

It was Mangan's closeness to Jennings that had attracted Geena to him. Ordinarily, she would never have touched him with a barge-pole, but she was savvy enough to know that it would be a long time before she made senior without considerable help.

When Geena had first made a play for Mangan, after Deborah's departure from the Shelbourne Hotel at the Christmas party, she had done so with one objective: to fast-track her rise within the ranks of Jennings and Associates. In Geena's world only the ruthless survived, and what better person for her to align herself with than a pathologically political power freak whose humongous sex drive would give her the leg-up she needed?

As he inched closer to her, Mangan mused that Geena was his number-one asset in his bid to destroy Deborah Parker. Geena was a pathological bitch, whose mouth was bigger and dirtier than the river Liffey; if he wanted word spread about something, he did it through Geena, safe in the knowledge that the vicious lies would never be attributed to him. It was a useful symbiotic partnership, which, as far as he was concerned, would end when he had put Deborah Parker out of her job. Then he could become acquainted with any number of the women in the firm . . . And he might use Geena to fulfil his long-held fantasy of a threesome. But those thoughts were for the future. He had plenty to do before he reached that milestone.

Geena interrupted his thoughts. 'You look very pensive there, big boy. What's on your mind?' she said, eyeing his crotch. The two accountants sitting opposite looked away.

Mangan seized the moment to drop his latest bombshell,

which he knew would be all over the practice by Monday's morning coffee-break. 'Listen, you're not to breathe a word of this, but I'm really worried that we're all going to be in the dock over Parker. She's done something that has seriously placed us all in jeopardy. We're in big trouble if it gets out.'

Geena pushed her breasts into his chest and licked his ear.

Mangan elaborated: 'Look, your brother's in the force, isn't he? He's in the CAB, isn't that what you told me? So this information came from him. Right?'

She took the bait. 'Of course it did, whatever it is you're going to tell me.'

'I think I might be able to explain the origins of Parker's fancy car and all the expensive gear she wears, not to mention the apartment. We think she's on the take.'

In those two brief sentences, Mangan was aware that he had managed to convey the impression that he was involved in some covert operation with Jennings to expose Deborah Parker and that he had given Geena permission to treat her with the contempt she so openly displayed towards her these days. Mangan was satisfied that Geena was highly effective in helping him annihilate the woman who was blocking him from his true entitlement: senior partner, Crime Division at Jennings and Associates.

'You cannot be serious! She's too squeaky clean for anything like that. Anyway, how could she be on the take from us? We're hardly a cash business.'

'It turns out that she was given some kind of a big retainer by the Mooneys. Only Paul never got the cheque. He's given her a week to come up with it. It's for something in the region of twenty grand. Don't quote me, though. You'd better attribute this to that brother of yours,' Mangan said.

★   ★   ★

Geena got into the front passenger seat of the car and used the lever to pull it forward as far as it would go, then got out and squeezed into the back until she was kneeling in front of Mangan. She pulled her hair back from her face and began to suck. She hated giving him a blow-job, but she felt she should reward him for the information he had just given her. As she worked away, she took her mind off the task in hand as she contemplated the telephone call she would make as soon as she got home. Her brother Dan might get a promotion, too, if what Mangan had told her was right . . .

16

Stephanie walked into the room, which was suddenly silent. With her long, shapely legs, cased in black fish-net stockings, her short black leather mini-skirt and the pale grey silk bustier that Michael Junior had bought for her in the D&G shop in Puerto Banus, she was the embodiment of what many men would call 'sex on legs'. And that was what she was tonight.

It was Friday night, Exclusive Escorts' busiest of the week, and she was working.

Her brown hair was expertly cut – courtesy again of Michael Junior's wallet – in sleek layers around her lovely face. Her huge brown eyes were made up to maximum effect, with subtle shades of gold highlighter emphasising the soft brown on her lower lid and creating an altogether sultry look. Stephanie had looks for which other women would kill, but she had an easy, unaffected manner too, which put everyone at ease. It was one of the reasons why she was popular with both staff and customers.

The other girls working tonight, Jan, Carla, Sharon and Tiff, might have been envious, knowing that she was the first preference for most of the customers, but there was an acquiescent aspect to her personality that made them feel sorry for her. They knew from past experience that before long the boss would have worn her out.

Tiff, the most senior of the girls, had been working for the

Mooneys for the past five years and was now the designated receptionist at their newest base, a fabulous penthouse in the Irish Financial Services Centre. She was responsible for ensuring that the punters paid up and were satisfied with the service. She had taken a shine to Stef, recognising in her the vulnerable girl she also had once been and hoping that Stef would soon realise she was a beautiful young woman who could go it alone in life without help from the likes of the Mooneys.

Tiff had had that chance fifteen years earlier when she had gone on the game to get away from her violent, drunken husband. Now, at thirty-six and with four kids in tow, she knew that she hadn't a hope in hell of finding a decent way of life. 'Tell me, Stef, what's a lovely girl like you doin' in this business? Have you looked in the mirror lately? You could have any fella you wanted,' she asked Stephanie, who was sipping a glass of champagne to warm herself up for her night's work.

Carla jumped in: 'So does that mean we all look like the back of a bus, then, Tiff?'

'Ah, you know what I mean, girls,' Tiff said. 'This one didn't grow up on the scene in Dublin the way we did. There's somethin' different about her. Sure haven't you all said it yourselves? I mean, we all polish up well, all right, but we know where we come from. This one,' she said, 'looks like she's just come back from finishing school in Switzerland or wherever it is they go to learn how to walk proper. You do, Stef. What in hell are you doin' in this game?'

Stephanie ran her fingers through her smooth hair, causing it to fall in tousled strands around her face. It was a gesture she used when she didn't want to be drawn into a particular conversation. She lowered her head, as if examining her patent leather knee-length boots. She knew that the girls wouldn't rest until she gave them something to work with: she'd been through this inquisition with them before and it had become clear to her that Tiff had designated herself as her mentor and wanted to help her. 'I suppose I got into it because it was the easy route. It's good money. The work might be tiresome, but the hours are short and I get to walk away at the end of the day. There's nobody I owe loyalty to. That's what I like about it, Tiff. It's business. Then you get to walk away at the end of the day and you don't get hurt.'

Tiff's heart went out to her. She had rarely heard such sadness. Tiff knew that she would die for her fifteen-year-old daughter, but this girl, with all the natural assets God had given her, had no one. And she had clearly been badly hurt before she came to live in Dublin.

'What about your family, Stef? Do they know what you do?' she prodded, hoping to catch a glimpse behind the barrier Stephanie had erected around her personal life.

Stephanie wasn't rising to the bait, though. She stood up and announced, 'I don't have any family and that's why this business suits me down to the ground. I don't need anyone. I've always been on my own and, working in this business, it's sure to stay that way – just the way I like it.'

She walked over to the window, which afforded panoramic views of the Dublin city skyline. To the right over the river Liffey and up towards the quays, she could see that the streets were thronging with revellers, young people of her own age, out on the town for a good time. Most would return home to their families at the end of the night. Something Stephanie had never known.

Then she was snapped out of her trance: the buzzer had announced the arrival of their first customer. It was Michael's special friend, although Stephanie did not know what made him so special. All she knew was that she gave him whatever he wanted and did not receive a penny for her efforts. As Michael Junior had told her when she quizzed him about it, 'He is an esteemed professional man who did me a big favour.'

17

Hanley and his team were gathered around the big conference table in their offices at Harcourt Square. It had been five months since he had had his private meeting with Tom Daly. In that time he and his team had worked around the clock in an effort to dig up any dirt they could on the Mooneys. Nothing would give Hanley more pleasure than to take away the big house on Killiney Hill from Michael Senior, but as yet, they had nothing that might bring the man's world crashing down around him.

Daly had told Hanley that he would receive 'all further relevant information that may arise from the tappings', and Hanley had thought it strange that Daly, or whoever had ordered the interception of the Mooneys' calls, was not providing them with the full transcripts. It was common practice for an investigating team to be given all information, no matter how insignificant it might appear to those who were gathering it. It was left to the investigating officers to judge its relevance. He found it dubious that this was not happening where his investigation was concerned.

At the conclusion of that meeting at Garda Headquarters, he had been tempted to ask Daly why, according to the numbered pages on the transcripts, he was only being given access to certain conversations, but had thought better of it. He knew that had Daly wanted to explain it to him he would have done so. Still, it had disturbed him in the months since. He felt that he hadn't been given a full deck to play with and that something more sinister was going on than the Mooneys' making millions from crime.

None the less, his team had gathered a large amount of information from their inquiries and the telephone taps had been of some assistance. What nobody had bothered to check during the original investigation was Michael Junior's involvement in any businesses outside prostitution. Hanley had been furious to discover that the man had not been investigated for failing to pay taxes or living off the proceeds of crime. However, had they then held the information they possessed now, they would have had to pass it on to the Criminal Assets Bureau: it was unrelated to the assault case and could not have been brought up in court.

It was Mooney's mother who had played a key role in unravelling the latest information, which would ultimately, Hanley hoped, put the nails in the family's respective coffins. It was thanks to Hanley's trusted right-hand woman, Detective Maria Lynch, that they had been able to focus on Lelia.

Maria had long been friendly with TV3's Alex King, and before his programme was aired, he had tipped her off about his footage of the Mooneys, knowing it would make her look good if she could tell her bosses about the programme before it was screened. For this little favour, he had known that Lynch would repay him with some juicy information, or addresses he might need in the future. It was the way the media and the police co-existed in a world in which journalists were increasingly involved in exposing crime. But what King hadn't screened, which had amazed Maria, was the footage containing incriminating remarks made by Lelia Mooney. She had scoffed at how pathetic the Irish police were, and then said,

'Jesus, if they had half a brain between the whole lot of them, they would have looked under my maiden name. Sure that's where the real money is. I may be blonde, but I'm certainly not dumb!'

Maria Lynch had taken the unused footage home and studied it time and again in an effort to ascertain what the crocodile-skinned Lelia could have meant. She had checked with the Companies Registration Office at Dublin Castle three times by phone and had even gone up there to check the files. But there had been no mention of Lelia Mooney owning anything. Then she had completed a reverse check, asking staff at the CRO to give her a list of any companies registered to an address at Mount Argento, Killiney Hill, Dublin, and still came up empty-handed.

It was only when she was sitting at home two nights ago, watching *The Green Mile* on television that it dawned on her. She had immediately telephoned Hanley, who had then telephoned his priest brother in the diocese of Finglas, and discovered that Lelia Mooney was née Black. It was so obvious they were furious that they had never checked it before. Countless inquiries into bent politicians and criminals' assets had shown that the new trend among those wanting to hide their money was to put it in their wives' maiden names.

The following day, Maria had taken herself straight back to the CRO offices and had returned with a stack of B10 forms – used to set up a company in Ireland.

The team sat in Hanley's office and waited for her to speak. 'Well,' she said, 'before I go into this, I think we need somebody from the Criminal Assets Bureau in here. We need to get orders permitting us to examine the bank accounts of these companies. We are also going to need the Revenue to tell us if any tax returns have been filed for them. I suspect not. We need the expertise of the CAB's boys to carry out those searches for us.'

They were impressed with what she had given them so far. She went through her folder until she found the pages containing the synopsis of Lelia Black's assets – all ten million pounds' worth.

'It seems that the lovely Lelia has been cashing in on the property boom in Ireland for the past thirteen years or so. From what they have listed as holdings, the Mooneys would appear to have been purchasing run-down buildings and renovating them. They are now letting them and will presumably hang onto them until they reach their true potential. For example, I have already checked this one here,' she said, handing each of her colleagues an A4 sheet on which she had catalogued her findings. 'They bought this house in Waterloo Road, one of the most expensive addresses in Dublin 4, for seventy thousand pounds in 1989. It seems to have been the first of their purchases and they must have known what they were doing because at the time that was a lot of money, even for them.

'Anyway, I talked to the neighbours on the way in here today and they say it was totally run-down when the Mooneys bought it. In 2000, they sold it for a whopping eight hundred grand, leaving them with a spare fifty thousand after they bought their villa in Marbella. The killer, though, is that the house was registered as a business and they were able to write off every penny of the renovation work against tax. To top it all, they seem to have at least seventeen such properties.'

Hanley had turned a deep red. 'This really takes the biscuit, doesn't it? What kind of pension will we have when we retire? And we're forced to follow every bloody rule in the book to chase the likes of the Mooneys, with their foreign villas that we couldn't even afford to rent for a week. It rubs salt into the wound that they can make millions as if they were legitimate businesspeople, leaving young women half-dead on the side of the road, and get away with it. I'll tell you one thing, though, they're not the thick gobshites we thought. It's time we re-evaluated our approach to dealing with them.' Hanley slammed his fists on his desk.

Sergeant Brian Williamson was, like Maria Lynch, in his late twenties and hard-working. He was recently married and his wife, Brenda, a nurse, was expecting their first child. Also like Maria, he knew that Hanley's forte was his ability to inter-rogate suspects and trap them with their own words. Hanley was held in the highest regard the length and breadth of the force, but it never ceased to amaze his young protégés that, after all this time, the Attorney General could be so easily incensed by criminals.

Williamson decided that this might be the time to throw him the gem of information he had picked up over a few pints in the Bleeding Horse on Harcourt Street the previous night. 'But you know what the thing is now, boss. It seems that more and more, these guys are getting help from the establishment in the pursuit of their activities. I was having a few pints with Dan Williams from the CAB last night and he let slip some-thing that could take us down a new route altogether. If what he told me is true, we could be looking at bringing the Mooneys down in style,' Williamson said.

Hanley nodded at his young sergeant to continue.

'According to Dan, and it's only his word because his sister works for Jennings and Associates, they suspect that one Deborah Parker is in business with the Mooneys. Apparently her firm's threatening to get rid of her so they can keep it quiet.

There's something about a cheque for twenty grand plus gone missing that the Mooneys allegedly gave her as an annual on-call retainer. It makes sense, boss, especially with her holidaying with the Mooneys. She's kept very quiet about that too.'

Hanley was thrilled: with the properties registered in Lelia's name and this latest piece of information, he had enough to order an investigation of Deborah Parker's bank accounts under the Criminal Justice Act and into the Mooneys' assets under the Confiscation of the Proceeds of Crime legislation.

He telephoned his opposite number in the CAB and told him he would need some assistance on the Mooney case. This time, he would get the proof before he acted. The problem for an impatient old-school officer like Hanley was the old saying that 'Proof confuses instinct'. This time, he swore he would throw instinct out of the window and play the whole thing the establishment's way – by the book.

18

Knocktopher Village, May 1979

Sheila sat, trembling, in the hall of the big house. It had been seven years since she had last crossed its threshold, and she had not expected to see it again. Yet here she was, placing her fate once more in the doctor's hands and awaiting his pronouncement on her future. Or, more precisely, on the future of her second daughter.

Her mother had made the appointment for her to see him outside surgery hours – away from the eyes and ears of busybody villagers. Sure wasn't it coincidental, they whispered, that the doctor's son had been packed off to college at Trinity around the same time that Sheila had been up the pole?

Now the doctor was standing at the drawing-room door. 'Sheila,' the grandfather of her first child said, 'would you like to come in?'

She despised this man with all her heart. He had never even held his granddaughter. And now he didn't even bother to ask how the child was.

As the doctor sat before Sheila, he had a lump in his throat as he took in the beauty of her third child. His granddaughter's half-sister. He had seen Sheila often with the little girl and on many occasions he had almost stopped his car and called to her, but he had been afraid of what such an encounter with the child might do to his marriage. His wife, Penelope, had been insistent that her younger son was not tarnished by association with an illegitimate child. It would have been the end of him, especially since that child had been born to a Catholic.

The doctor was sure that their granddaughter would have won their love and affection, had she been allowed into their lives. But Penelope had warned him whenever he had raised the subject that it would ruin their family. Nor did she miss an opportunity to point out that her family had supplied them with the wealth to live in such splendour.

Sheila wondered if the doctor's son had turned out to be a similarly cold and calculating man. She understood that he would have been ruined socially had he married her, but he had never even visited his child. The callousness of this family made her feel ill.

She could not know that her former lover had wanted desperately to see his baby, but when he told his mother, she had warned him about the codicil in her will. And when she had informed him that Sheila had married, he had vowed never to return to Knocktopher.

'So, Sheila, your mother has explained to me what happened,' the doctor began. 'I can understand your distress and I think that unless you are prepared to keep the child living in the house, the only option is to put her up for adoption.'

Sheila's heart sank.

The doctor continued, 'You do realise that you will never see her again? You must relinquish all rights to her if you take this route. You have to be clear about that. I must emphasise to you that until a family is found for the child, she will be placed in a children's home. There's no telling how long it could be before they find her new parents – most couples want babies, not four-year-olds.' He paused. 'Sheila, I am so sorry for all of your troubles. If there was *anything more I could do to help, I would . . . Do you mind if I ask, has the same thing happened to the older girl?'*

'No, Doctor. He hates your granddaughter. It's only this one that he would ever lay a finger on. You see, as he has told me so many times, she is his own flesh and blood and he feels he can do as he pleases with what he owns.' She bit her tongue to prevent herself adding, 'Including me.' But she didn't need to: the doctor knew; everyone knew. No one helped. Neither did she add that her husband took perverse pleasure in insisting that her elder daughter witness his degradation and humiliation of her mother. In any case, one didn't speak of the atrocities that took place behind closed doors.

'Will the social workers want to know why I am giving her up?' she asked.

'I don't think so. I have not experienced a case like this before – at least, not where the mother has taken the child out of the situation. I think you're very brave to do what you're doing. I will set the wheels in motion for next Friday, if that's all right with you. Try not to worry too much, my dear. What you are doing is for the best.'

With that, Sheila left the house, having refused his offer of a lift back to Gardener's Lane. It was a beautiful summer day and she wanted to enjoy it with her little daughter before she was forced to give her away.

A week later, they drove back from Kilkenny in silence. The doctor was powerless to offer Sheila any consolation. More than once, he had contemplated stopping his green Aston Martin, taking her in his arms and hugging her. But he knew that this would not help, just underline his family's hypocrisy.

Sheila's hands had been shaking violently when the social worker handed her the pen to sign the consent form. She had broken down, knowing that the child would never be able to trace her and that she herself was forbidden any contact with her.

As they travelled back, she clutched the little girl's teddy bear and prayed that some day she would meet her precious child again and be able to explain to her why she had given her away. She tried to console herself by reasoning that when she was older, the girl might understand. It was then that she burst into sobs, knowing that she never would. What could she say if she ever did meet her? She could never let her know what had happened.

Her left eye was dripping rivulets of blood. Her right arm was badly sprained, if not broken. Clumps of her hair lay on the floor. Even now, as he pinned her into the corner of the room, she was thinking of what she had seen him do to their little girl.

'You did what?' he yelled. The perspiration dripped from his forehead on to her chest, which he had exposed when he ripped down the top of her dress. At twenty-five, Sheila was beyond caring. Indeed, were it not for her children, she would rather have been dead. There were times when she prayed he would just kill her and put her out of her misery. And then she thought of the children.

'The doctor knows now. Someone knows, Eamon. You touch any more of my children and it will be all over the village. See how you like that.' She spat the words at him, knowing he would be too afraid to touch them now.

'That little bitch!' he said, pointing in the direction of her first-born's bedroom. 'I wouldn't touch her if she was the last female on earth. As for little Frank, you'll not say I ever touched him! Are you calling me a queer now, is that it?'

Sheila almost laughed at him. He was complaining of being thought queer yet justifying his abuse of their daughter, who was now gone from her for ever. He was insane.

'What's mine is mine, and I'll do whatever I want with it. Do you understand, harlot?' he roared.

She could feel him getting hard and knew what was to come. He was always at his worst when he was angry. It was clear to her that the beatings excited him, and there was little she could do to escape them. Who would listen to her? Not her mother. The doctor? She wouldn't go to him for help again, if she could avoid it. The priest? He would only tell her that she was obliged to meet her husband's needs.

He took a pair of scissors off the table and cut off her briefs, then pressed them into her face. 'Never let me see you wearing a pair again. I will make you pay for this. You might have been able to take away the little one but you will always be available and ready for me. Do you understand?'

He stormed into their bedroom, lifted her underwear drawer out of the chest and threw every item into the fire. 'In future, I'll get to you even quicker,' he said, then stuck himself inside her.

The evening finished as it always did, with Eamon saying a decade of the rosary, then Sheila kneeling before him and begging his forgiveness. As she said the words, though, it was not his forgiveness she was seeking: it was that of the daughter she would never see again.

19

Deborah didn't know what to do. She had walked to the top of Killiney Hill and was standing beside the obelisk, taking in the sweeping view across Dublin Bay. Only a few weeks ago she had been sunning herself on her annual girls' trip to Marbella, with not a care in the world.

She thought back to the day beside the pool of the beautiful hotel they had stayed in. The five-star Don Pepe was one of the most luxurious in the area but, thanks to Aine and her job at a travel agency, they stayed there every year for next to nothing. They had been drinking beer in the afternoon sun, and Deborah had been the first to let go. She had told her friends that Mangan was trying to destroy her.

Julie and Aine had been shocked. Deborah Parker was regarded by all who knew her as cool and capable. The idea of her becoming so concerned about office politics unnerved them. They had wondered, later that night, if something else was going on in her life . . .

Deborah hadn't been very clear when she had told them about Mangan. Sure, he had hit on her a few times and she had turned him down. But didn't that happen in every office without leading to World War Three? So what if he had become close to her boss? Why should she care? they had asked. Wasn't the main issue that she was doing her job well? Nothing they said could make her see the futility of worrying about it. Sure didn't she deal with criminals every day of the week? they had asked. If she was able for the likes of the Mooneys, she was more than able for Mangan – even if he was up to something.

No matter what she said to them, she hadn't been able to convey the impact on her of Mangan's behaviour. It was so insidious, so subtle, that she didn't blame them for not grasping why it was having such an effect on her.

Deborah thought back to their strolls along the stretch of beach between Marbella and the marina in Puerto Banus, to their evenings in the famous Restaurante Tony Dahli, where the eponymous owner, a once-famous opera singer, regaled diners with Dean Martin songs.

In the end, her friends had just advised her to get on with things and she had resolved to confront Mangan about his behaviour. The time for games was over.

Now, on Killiney Hill, she was under suspicion of fraud and consorting with criminals, although she hadn't been accused of it outright. Tears came to her eyes: the halcyon days were well and truly over. Her world was crumbling. Everything she had worked for was falling apart.

As it turned out, she had not had the chance to confront Mangan: events, thanks to Alex King, had taken a turn for the worse. She had just come from an hour-long meeting with Michael Senior and was gazing across the bay at his house, contemplating the devastating news he had just delivered to her.

Earlier that day she had telephoned him and inquired casually if he could trace the cheque he had written for her on the day she had visited him to discuss his son's court case. She had said that the accounts department had mislaid their record of it. She would be obliged if he could ascertain whether it had been cashed. Later, when she sat facing him in his mahogany-panelled study, he had told her that the cheque had indeed been cashed, less than a week after he had given it to her the previous June.

She sat down on the damp grass, regardless of her cream linen suit, and let her face fall into her hands. She just wanted to block out everything that was happening to her. Tomorrow, she would have to tell Jennings that the cheque had been paid and, no, she could not say it was lodged in the firm's account because it had been made out to cash.

The energy drained from her at the thought of what this encounter might mean for her career. And she sensed that her impending downfall would signal only good things for Mangan. If it was the last thing she did, she would have it out with him. And her ace card was to threaten him with what she had witnessed between him and Geena in the office toilets.

It was time to start playing dirty.

20

'I'm getting worried about Hanley's team. They're perilously close to something that's going to force them to take a much closer look at the family. If they come up with anything else, they'll have to put the whole operation under the spotlight. And you don't need me to tell you that if the media gets a whiff of this, they're going to be all over it. The repercussions will stretch far and wide if it ever gets out.'

The man sitting across the desk digested the implication of what had been said. There were too many reputations at stake here. No new case should be opened against the Mooneys: that had been the purpose of the plan they had worked out to put Hanley and his team back on the case. They had known that Hanley, a thorough investigator, had covered all his bases the first time and that had there been anything to find against the Mooneys, they would have learned of it during last year's investigation. By putting Hanley back on to the family, they had been covering their bases, ensuring that nothing was leaking into the public domain about their man.

But now Hanley was uncovering valuable intelligence and they would look stupid, even guilty, if they attempted to whitewash his findings.

The man who had spoken first was waiting for his associate's thoughts on these new developments. He was feeling threatened. If what they were up to got into the public arena, heads would roll at the highest level. But, hey, he mused, I have a get-out clause. I was merely the conveyor of orders. If it came to an inquiry, my role would be perceived as benign. He folded his arms and sat silent.

'How are the tapings going?' the man behind the desk asked.

'There is still the same level of contact between them. Twice-weekly calls, at least.'

'And are the visits as frequent as before?' the official asked, leaning back in his swivel chair.

'More frequent. The man cannot get enough of it. The operation is without boundaries. Even for this kind of business, I'm shocked by what goes on behind their closed doors. It really is a case of *carte blanche* as far as our man is concerned, if what I'm reading into the telephone conversations is correct,' the first speaker replied.

'Who has had access to the transcripts?'

'Just myself, my man and Hector.'

'Hector?' the official asked, angry at the idea of another individual knowing about their set-up. 'Who the bloody hell is Hector, and why does he know about this? Jesus Christ. My instructions were that this was to be bloody watertight, aside from the gullible Hanley. You're compromising us all,' he bellowed.

The other man let him rant. In fact, he enjoyed watching the officious coward suffer. For the life of him he could not understand why this bureaucrat had risen to such a high level in his organisation. Except that he was a yes-man through and through. He looked at the man who was effectively giving him his orders, yet who clearly knew nothing of the business he was meddling in. For that was what it was. Meddling. Unnecessary interference in the workings of an institution of whose operational procedures he was ignorant.

'Oh, forgive me. You have nothing to fear from Hector. He is totally safe and on our side.' He knew that he was making the official sweat and enjoyed every second of it.

The man's nostrils flared. He looked deranged and out of control. 'What the hell do you mean that we have nothing to fear from *Hector*? My instructions to you were unambiguous. Only the people I referred to in the beginning were to know about this. Even the subject of this operation does not know that he is being monitored. The boss will be concerned at this latest development. Now, for the last time, I want to know who Hector is and why he is involved in our business.'

Now the other man could barely contain his glee. 'Hector,' he said, 'is not a person, my friend. Hector is the computer the Irish police force uses to transmit data from monitored telephone conversations. If I confused you you have my sincerest apologies. It is just that I assumed you knew that, given the high level of your personal involvement in this operation.'

The official was seething. Not only had he been made a fool of, the other man had threatened him with his knowledge of the official's involvement in the affair. Forgetting about Hector, he shot back, 'We are all involved in this operation – it's not just my head on the block. You would do well to remember that when you deal with me.'

The other man sat back and casually crossed his legs. Body language was everything – he had learned that in the early days of his career and had used it to telling effect in undermining past targets. 'But that is where you are wrong. No guillotine awaits *me*. I am merely carrying out orders. There is no record of my role in this nasty little business. I have nothing to run from at all.'

The official knew that his cards had been marked. He had lost this battle but had no intention of losing sight of what the

133

war was really about. It was about power and staying in his position. It was about protecting the man who had placed him there. 'OK, so those in the loop include you, me, your man, your boss, my boss and, of course, Hector,' the official said, in a slow drawl of contempt. 'Our subject hasn't a clue and the Mooneys are oblivious. There are two questions: can we put a stop to Hanley's investigations, and can we be certain that he has no idea as to the real motive in monitoring the Mooneys?'

'Hanley is too far advanced in his inquiries for us to tell him to stop. The man is the best in the business and he can smell a rat a mile away. From what I can gather, he already has sufficient evidence to work on and any interference would stick out like the proverbial sore thumb. People like Hanley don't anticipate interference from the likes of us, and were he to receive it, it would only make him more determined to let the cat out of the bag. One way or the other, if we try to stop him now, he will use his media contacts to ensure that it gets out. Before we know it, we'd have opposition politicians screaming about a cover-up and the police protecting organised criminals. And as we are both aware, protecting the Mooneys is the last thing this operation is about. No one would guess that it is someone else who needs protecting.'

'So what is this allegedly sufficient evidence Hanley has obtained? Correct me if I'm wrong, but that's what everyone thought last time and it transpired that his team were economical with the truth about how they had run their inquiry. Who is to say that the whole thing won't fall apart on them again?' the official queried.

'We're not just talking assault here, remember, so the investigation is being run on a different level. The last time, when you and I knew nothing of the information we have in our possession now, they were merely conducting an inquiry into assault and rape. Now Hanley has been given a new remit to look at all aspects of the Mooneys' activities. We did this so that we would know what was going on and to keep track of our man. Hanley is coming up with the goods all right. In fact, the whole thing is getting so big that he has even invited the Criminal Assets Bureau to join the party. As you and I both know, cops don't like to share the glory with other investigating teams, but whatever he has so far, it's big enough for him to think he can hammer the Mooneys. If he was warned off now, he would want a reason. And Hanley is the man to find it.'

'OK,' said the official, in a sombre tone. 'It looks like we may have shot ourselves in the foot by trying to keep tabs on our subject, but how likely is it that, if Hanley nails the Mooneys for whatever offences he comes up with, our subject's involvement will come out?'

The other man was incredulous. Didn't this moron have the slightest inkling about the type of people he was dealing with? Obviously not. 'It's very simple,' he enunciated. 'Your man needs to protect someone, because otherwise his own position comes under public scrutiny. Actually, his position will be untenable if this gets out. There is one reason, and one reason only, that the Mooneys provide our subject with their facilities for nothing. He is their meal-ticket in the event of an investigation like Hanley's being successful. And now, thanks to Junior's acquittal on the assault and rape charges last year, our man is in it up to his eyeballs and, consequently, so is your boss.'

He paused to allow the weight of what he was saying to sink in, then concluded, 'Thanks to the actions of the man we now have to protect, the Mooneys, my dear friend, feel they have secured themselves a first-class ticket to crime evasion for the rest of their lives. If anything happens to bring them down, the whole system will come tumbling with them . . .' With that, he left the office, leaving the official to contemplate the potential ramifications of Hanley's investigation.

He was worried. He cursed himself for having devised the idea of keeping tabs on their subject via Hanley. He had thought he was being so clever in using the investigation as a cover. Hadn't he been sure that it couldn't possibly bear results. Hadn't he seen to it that phone taps were placed on their subject and the Mooneys to cover all his bases? So clever indeed that the shit was piling up, and if Hanley couldn't be stopped, an avalanche of bad publicity would follow. Something had to be done about the situation and, he reflected, it might have to be done privately – so that when the shit hit the proverbial fan, no one would point the finger at him.

21

Alex King drove his five-series BMW coupé slowly up Killiney Hill. As one of Ireland's top investigative journalists, he normally spent his time whizzing from one source to the next, or being chased from the homes of big-time white-collar fraudsters who invariably were taken aback by his audacity. 'Just who do you think you are, coming to my home uninvited? You're trespassing and if you don't leave immediately, I'll call the police.' This was the normal type of response he received from the professionals he approached.

At thirty-three, he had twice won the coveted Investigative Journalist of the year award, and was part of an increasingly powerful band of high-calibre journalists who were slowly but steadily exposing some of the élite of Irish society. His prime targets were people who had acquired vast amounts of wealth by unknown means, yet whose contact with certain members of the establishment shielded them from public scrutiny.

The Celtic Tiger of the nineties had turned Ireland into one of the fastest-growing economies in Europe. Alex had no qualms about his comfortable status. He had worked hard for everything he had achieved. Now he was doing his bit to expose those who had gained their wealth illegally. Irish property prices were among the highest in Europe. Stylish hotels were popping up on the Dublin skyline to cope with the demands the booming economy was placing on business accommodation in the city, and despite high inflation, life was good for the professional and middle classes.

Also, in the late nineties, it had become apparent that a number of big-time criminal gangs was flooding the streets with hard drugs and making phenomenal amounts of money. They were killing each other almost every week, but few paid much attention: the unspoken feeling at the time was 'Let them – that way, there'll be fewer to worry about.' The ethos of apathy prevailed until the same criminals began to target journalists, murdering one and threatening others. The shutters came down and a raft of wide-ranging legislation was introduced to quell the growth of organised crime.

Who would have thought, Alex mused, as he drove slowly up the steep hill, that the laws designed to target criminals would lead to the exposure of some of the best-known figures in the country's political and business circles? Hardly a month passed without the media learning of yet another high-profile individual being under investigation for money-laundering or living off the proceeds of crime. He considered the irony: those who stood on platforms preaching about standards, ethics and respect for society and had demanded invasive powers for the police had shot friends and colleagues in the foot. Now, for every 'scumbag' of an ordinary criminal the police caught, you could be sure that another 'respectable' criminal was round the corner.

As far as Alex was concerned, there were two underbelly classes in Irish society: the real criminals, who shot each other, imported drugs, ran prostitution agencies and smuggled Kalashnikovs into the country, and those who made their fortune through money-laundering or tax evasion. They did this while the majority of law-abiding citizens saw their pay packets diminish by almost fifty per cent. Ordinary people were sick of it, and as a result Alex had become something of a celebrity. People liked his exposés.

It was when the two groups' worlds collided that he became excited – as had happened with the Mooneys and Jennings and Associates. Who would have believed that one of the leading criminal-law firms in Dublin would allow its senior associates to consort publicly with one of the most notorious crime gangs in the country?

Sure, Deborah Parker and her pals had tried to disguise the association by staying in a hotel – one of the best in Spain but undoubtedly paid for by the Mooneys, although he couldn't prove that yet – but it supported Alex's theory that the professional classes were more than willing to avail themselves of the fruits of their clients' ill-gotten gains. Not once, in his nine-year career, had it occurred to Alex King that the solicitor–client relationship rested on the fact that a solicitor did his job to the best of his ability and worked with the tools available to him, which, in the case of a solicitor, were the facts supplied by the client. Instead, he had so bought into the idea of the merging of the two worlds that he couldn't see past his own prejudice. So Deborah Parker had suffered – or, in Alex King's eyes, had been rightly exposed. He had the video evidence to prove it. And she had not bothered to seek a retraction of his story. Furthermore, the latest piece of information that had come into his possession about her would further enhance his theory.

As he turned the sharp bend, his entire body tensed. It was always the same when he was cold-calling at the home of a potential interviewee or source. Inside, he was hyper and hopeful, but outwardly he was calm, almost reticent, not wanting to put off his target by appearing too eager. If he did, they sensed how much he needed them and invariably refused to co-operate.

As he pulled off the hill and brought his gleaming black car to a halt outside an imposing pair of black wrought-iron gates, he was filled with the hope he always experienced when approaching the home of an ordinary, as opposed to 'respectable', criminal. The latter would tell him to piss off and threaten police and injunctions, while the ordinary criminals were frequently so admiring of a journalist who had the nerve to approach them, or so curious as to what that journalist might know, that five times out of ten he got to meet them.

Lelia Mooney couldn't believe what she was seeing on the CCTV screen that was perched on her marble kitchen island. The location of the set had been a source of argument between herself and Michael, but she had won in the end. It was left in pride of place in the kitchen where, as Lelia had pointed out, it would not go unnoticed: visitors who had missed the cameras on the way in would realise how well off they were because they needed such heavy-duty surveillance.

'Jaaays-us,' she said to her friend Geraldine Gilford, at the other end of the phone line. 'Jaaays-us Christ! All me fuckin' wet dreams have come together at once, love. There's a bleedin' ride – and I mean ri-ide – at me fuckin' front door. He's got silky black hair and a gorgeous arse. He's wearin' lovely jeans and one of them gorgeous Ralph Whatsisname shirts.' She continued breathlessly, 'God, Ger, he's lookin' straight at me now in the camera an' he's got divine – that's what all the women around here say – blue eyes. I don't care who he is, I'm lettin' him in and that's that. Fuck, I hope he hasn't got the wrong address. I'm goin', Ger, before I wet meself. I'll ring yez later and let you know who he is.'

Lelia ran straight to the bathroom and applied a heavy coat of crimson lipstick. Luckily for her, she had just returned from a visit to Toni and Guy in Dublin and her hair was perfect. She applied a thick coat of shimmering blue eye-shadow to her lower lids.

By the time she came out, the man had been pressing the intercom for about three minutes. It was only when she saw him turn to leave that she answered – Lelia Mooney had a policy of leaving people waiting: otherwise they would think she had nothing else to do. 'Mount Argento. Who are you calling to see, please?' she said, in the strained South Dublin accent she had striven to acquire since moving from Finglas.

Alex had thought that the newspaper photographs had prepared him for Lelia – but that accent! He was praying that his facial expression didn't convey his disbelief and amusement. He ignored her question about whom he was calling to see: if he announced himself immediately, she probably wouldn't let him in. Instead he began, 'Mrs Mooney, I have some interesting and disturbing news about your solicitor, Deborah Parker. I wonder if you might spare me some time? I might be able to shed some light on her dealings with you. You might benefit from what I've learned.' He waited, thinking she had gone off to fetch her husband before answering.

The minutes ticked by. He glanced at his watch. This had happened so many times before. They just left him standing and wouldn't confirm whether or not they intended to see him. It was the cruellest thing an interviewee or source could do to a journalist. Suddenly the big gates swung open. He jumped back into his car and almost swerved into the driveway for fear that she might change her mind.

★   ★   ★

An hour later, he left the house. He had been berated by the lovely Lelia when she had realised who he was, but he had homed in on her dislike of Deborah Parker when he had told her about the other woman's secret dealings. OK, he hadn't got what he'd come looking for – an interview with Michael Senior about his 'business' activities and the precise nature of his relationship with Parker – but he had employed a faithful journalist's trick in taking the next-of-kin into his confidence. It worked almost every time.

All he had to do now was hope that Lelia Mooney could exert sufficient pressure on her husband to persuade him to call him. Having met Lelia, Alex felt that any man would be well advised to do what she wanted, rather than listen to her whining about Deborah Parker who, in Lelia's words, was a 'conniving bitch not to be trusted'. She had told Alex that she had already informed her husband of her own suspicions about Parker.

'You did what? You let *him* into *my* home? Is that what you're saying? Well, Jesus fucking Christ, you really are as thick as you bleedin' well look. Do you know that? You silly fuckin' cow, Lelia. How many times have I told you that if reporters call here you're to send them away. You've given him a fucking *in* now, Lelia. For Christ's sake, woman, did he have a bag or a briefcase with him? Or was he just wearing his camera strapped around his neck? You *stupid* bitch. I've heard it all now. You think he's really nice . . . For fuck's sake.'

Lelia wasn't fazed. She had been expecting an outburst. She knew that the best way to handle her husband was to let him blow off steam, then have a proper chat with him about it. Before he'd got home, Lelia had decided that the best way to handle the situation was to conceal her dislike of Parker and to feign concern for him. She knew that if he found out she didn't like the girl he would accuse her of waging a vendetta and she would never win him round to seeing King. Of all things, Michael Mooney Senior was a fair man and he had never stuck the knife into anyone unless they upset him. She knew that the same principle applied to Parker, so her concerns about the woman's deviousness would not wash with him. He would want proof. He was decent like that. Well, Lelia thought, he'll get his proof. 'Look, Michael, I really think you should talk to him. He had some interesting stuff to say about her. I don't think you can trust her any more,' she said evenly.

'Lelia, if you're telling me this, you must have an agenda I don't know about, love. In case it has slipped your tiny mind, me dear, that young woman has got our son off some very serious charges. We owe her a debt of gratitude so we do.'

Lelia persisted, 'But, Michael, that's just the thing. It seems that *she*'s the one who owes *us*, love. According to King, she's not as pure as the driven snow, and he has the evidence to prove it.'

Mugsy was becoming irate. Sure, he knew that Lelia had a weakness for attractive men, but there was something more to her need for him to meet King and he couldn't put his finger on it.

He knew that she didn't like Deborah Parker, although she hadn't told him so and surmised that this was where her 'concern' was coming from. 'How do you know he has the evidence to prove she's bent, or whatever it is he's alleging?' he quizzed.

'Michael, love, I know that twenty grand is nothing to us, but she's only gone and done a runner with the money you gave her. Your man King told me so. He says he has the evidence to prove it.'

Mugsy sank into the big pine carver chair, which looked incongruous alongside the sleek lines of the designer kitchen units, which had been in the house when they bought it. He considered what she had just told him. If there was one thing Michael Mooney abhorred, it was being taken for a ride and as he digested his wife's bombshell, he conceded that King might be talking the truth. He replayed the conversation he had had with Deborah the previous week and recalled how she had told him that her accounts department had mislaid their record of the cheque. He was also worried that King might have been filming inside the house. If so, they would be the laughing stock of Killiney, although all of the other criminals' wives would probably think it was gorgeous.

Mugsy knew that, in terms of the media or the cops pinning something on him, he was not invulnerable. Now that King had been in the house, he might prove intractable. He would have to meet him now, although he might be difficult to handle. At least he would shed some light on the disappearance of his twenty grand – and Michael Mooney was going to get to the bottom of this with Parker.

22

In the year after her mother's death, Deborah had been given to an overwhelming amount of introspection. She still missed the one person in the world she had always been able to rely on and trust implicitly, but she had decided that her best way forward in a world that, for her, was devoid of family, was to put her head down and get on with things. She was determined to make a success of her life for her mother's sake: she was sure she looked down on her from above. Her mother had been present when she graduated from University College, Dublin, with a first-class law degree. The years of slogging had been worthwhile just to see the pride on her mother's face when the dean of her faculty had announced that Deborah was one of the top three students in her year.

Now, she held a coveted position in one of the most respected criminal-law firms in Dublin. It was a cut-throat business but she could honestly say she had earned her success through sheer hard work, dedication and her ability to gain the admiration of the criminals she sought to make her clients. Not once had she stabbed a colleague in the back or undermined them in furthering her career. Not once had she had to sleep her way to an easy life. Until now. 'There is only one way that this campaign will stop and that is if I sleep with him. That's what he wants from me. Patrick Mangan is a fucking control freak,' she told Aine and Julie, as the three sat on her terrace, taking in the view of the Irish sea.

'Debs, you cannot be serious. There is no way that sleeping with him will solve anything. And, anyway, he hasn't exactly asked you to,' Aine said, perplexed.

'Don't look at me like that,' Deborah said hotly. 'I have no intention of sleeping with him. If he was the last man on earth and I was desperate I wouldn't let him near me. But that's what he wants, and that's what all of this is about.'

'Look, Debs,' Julie said, 'this is just jealousy on his part and you're lending it a considerably greater degree of significance than it deserves. For God's sake, you've been written about in half the newspapers and magazines in the land. His nose is bound to be out of joint. Don't let this thing get out of proportion.'

Deborah stood up and slammed her fists on the table, sending a wineglass crashing to the ground. 'Are you both forgetting that this guy sent me an e-mail telling me that he wants to fuck my brains out? How much clearer do I have to make it?' She glowered at them both, her brown eyes filled with fury. 'Don't you two get it? We're both at the same level in the company so he has nothing to be envious of. This is about his pent-up sexuality and the fact that he didn't like it when I turned him down. The bastard can't take no for an answer. Don't you understand? This is about sexual harassment and my life is falling apart.'

'OK,' Julie ventured. 'You're a lawyer, Debs. If this is about sexual harassment, then come up with the proof and nail him. It should be no problem – that's what you do.'

'You know as well as I do how insidious sexual harassment can be,' Deborah stormed. 'The beauty of it is in its subtlety.'

'Subtlety?' Julie repeated. 'What is subtle about an e-mail

saying he wants to fuck you? You'd get him on that alone – if that *is* what this is all about. You do still have the email, don't you?'

'Yes – and I intend keeping it for the rest of my life, believe me. If I don't manage to stop Mangan now, I will in the future. If I really wanted to play him at his own game, I would send it to his ex-wife. Let's see what happens when she reads the data on the top of the page showing him to be the sender and me to be the recipient. Only I wouldn't do that to the poor woman – she's another of his victims. She was married to a serial sex pest. And I don't intend getting him for sexual harassment. That would end my career. You and I both know it.' Deborah drew a deep breath. 'And it's too late now to take it to Jennings. Mangan's inveigled his way so far into his confidence that the man despises me – he can barely look at me without contempt. Maybe he doesn't know he's doing it, but he is. As far as I can see, he has totally bought into Mangan's perverted way of thinking. They don't even dis-cuss their caseloads with me any more at the Monday-morning meetings. I leave Paul's office and then they have their own little chat. It's like a private club.'

Deborah collapsed on to her chair, exhausted. She looked beseechingly at her friends. 'I don't blame you for not taking me seriously. I know it all sounds ridiculous and that you think I'm just offended that they've become such close friends. But I swear to both of you that is not what this is about. Jennings has been taken in by him, and Mangan has gained so much power that he has the respect of the rest of the people in the office and I'm out in the cold. With the way things are going, I think I'm about to die of frostbite because I don't have the appetite for Mangan's brand of political skulduggery.'

Aine intervened: 'Deborah, *we* know what you're saying

about the e-mail and his ex-wife – *we* know you'd never want to upset her and his kids like that. But Mangan doesn't. As far as he's concerned, you're a thundering cow who's destroying his career. Now it's time to call his bluff. Nobody is saying you have to *tell* anyone what you saw, but you could threaten him with the e-mail.'

By the end of the evening, Deborah had decided her friends were right. She would have to confront this thing, because if she didn't get a grip on herself soon, she would fall apart. Just as Mangan had been hoping . . .

Her working weeks had taken on a steady pattern now: in at eight forty-five and out at six. The atmosphere was horren-dous. In theory, Geena Williams was supposed to provide her with back-up support when she needed it. It was how juniors learned the ropes, but when Deborah had asked for assistance recently, Williams had either told her she would get her the files she required 'when I'm ready' or had deliberately botched-up the documentation she needed. Her actions fru-strated Deborah's efforts to work efficiently. It was an affront to professionalism, Deborah thought. 'Geena,' she had said to her after she hadn't bothered to complete a file, 'part of your job is to learn from the more experienced people in this firm and to assist us when we require it. The next time I ask you to do a job for me, I would appreciate it if you'd just do it.'

Geena had sat there in her swivel chair and looked at Deborah wide-eyed. Then she said, 'I agree with you. I'm here to assist the senior solicitors.' She crossed her legs slowly, her short skirt riding up her meaty thighs. 'And that is what I do most of the time here – assist the senior people. I spend most of my days doing work for Paul and, of course, for Patrick. I'm very busy, you know.'

Deborah had had enough. 'Yes, Geena,' she said silkily. 'I have seen with my own eyes exactly how you assist some of the senior people in this firm. I suggest that you remember that the next time I ask you to do something.' And with that, Deborah began to walk out of the office. Then she turned back. 'By the way, that motion I asked you to prepare for filing yesterday, I need it on my desk in thirty minutes.'

And then there had been the blazing row she had had with Paul Jennings. She was now under suspicion of fraud. He had given her until the end of the month to find Mooney's twenty-thousand-pound cheque. Deborah was certain that the entire office had heard him shout, 'Find that money – money that was given to you for this firm – or I'll call in the police. You don't need me to tell you that that will mean the end of your position here if we find out it's been cashed, and that I'll report you to the Law Society. After that you will be investigated and undoubtedly struck off.'

When she insisted that she had given the cheque to Mangan, he had warned her about the laws of defamation and added that Mangan was 'the only bloody senior person I can trust in this office at the moment'. He had also said that there was no question that if Mangan had received the cheque he would have handed it over.

Deborah hadn't yet summoned the courage to tell him that Mooney had confirmed it had been cashed. Nor had she told Aine and Julie. It was just too much of a nightmare and she needed time to work out a plan of action before she came clean with him.

One way or another, she had to extricate herself from the mess she was in and, in desperation, she was considering contacting the person central to her position now. She had refused to return his calls in the past, but now he might be the only person who could help her – if he was even prepared to listen to her.

She took out her mobile and dialled the number she had stored in her company phone but had never used. Alex King was an investigator, after all. If anyone could find out what had happened to that cheque, it was him. If the police didn't get there first.

23

Knocktopher Village, May 1988

'Oh, dear God, we have to help that woman. We have a responsibility to her. This situation cannot continue.'

The doctor's wife had been sitting with her hands folded in her lap while he told her of the emergency visit he had paid to Sheila at Gardener's Lane earlier that day. She looked up at him, her hair held off her face by an Alice band. Her piercing green eyes staring through him, she spoke clearly and did not waver. 'My darling, you really shouldn't get so caught up in your work. She's only a patient, for goodness' sake. You should be more detached.'

The doctor couldn't believe his wife's coldness. Certainly, a woman like Penelope might find it difficult to understand his patient's predicament – but didn't she have a compassionate bone in her body?

'Don't you understand? She has been admitted to the city hospital for a hysterectomy. He has ripped her insides out. The bruising alone will take months to heal. He has left her so that she may never bear another child. It's the worst I have ever seen,' he said.

'That's just as well, given what I have heard of the man she chose to marry,' Penelope sneered.

The doctor had had enough. He rose from his chair and shouted at her for the first time in their thirty-five-year marriage. 'You are

151

a cold, bitter woman. Have you no decency? We have a respon-sibility. She never chose to marry him, we forced her. She loved our son. And he – as you well know – loved her.'

But Penelope was not to be swayed. She remained implacable. 'We will have nothing to do with those children,' she hissed.

'But we must consider the girl. She has had a cruel life and we are to blame for it. She is only fifteen – and you would fall in love with her if you met her. She looks so like—'

Penelope held up her hand and rose from her chair. 'Enough. I will listen to no more. We do not do charity cases, darling. Whatever would our friends think?'

'But she is the daughter of your son, woman. She is your granddaughter, for crying out loud.'

'She is nothing of the sort. She is a fifteen-year-old bastard, thanks to her harlot of a mother. That's all she ever was and all she ever will be.' Then she walked from the room.

The doctor sank back behind the desk in his surgery. Please, God, do not let the child have inherited her paternal grandmother's genes, he prayed. He vowed that if it was the last thing he did, he would make amends to that girl. Some day.

24

Michael Junior was cock-a-hoop. His decision to take the lease on the penthouse in the Irish Financial Services Centre development had proven a good one: the location, which was frequented by the professional classes, gave his sixth brothel the perfect cover. The fact that none of his customers came from the centre, which was home to some of the world's leading financial firms, was even better. It meant that none of those who used the nearby restaurants or lived in the locality were suspicious of what he was up to. And if the police caught up with his latest venture, he would pay the meagre fine imposed by the court and open up shop elsewhere.

The laws on prostitution were designed to protect the working women rather than to punish those who lived off the profits. Among liberal-minded individuals, there was a consensus that those who provided the service should be free to do so. Sure wasn't Ireland a democracy and an open-market society? Few thought of it as a trade in human flesh, which was what it was, or knew that the women became virtual prisoners to their pimps, who introduced them to depravity, domination and drugs. Nor did they take into account the fact that the likes of the Mooneys used their millions to fund drugs-distribution networks and imported weapons to conduct their turf wars. It went unnoticed that most prostitutes worked for criminals, who thrived on power and the fear their reputation instilled in others.

After Judge Deering had quashed the charges against him Michael Junior had taken legal advice on the implications of his activities – but not from Deborah Parker: he knew that if he admitted them to her, she was obliged by her professional oath to report any crimes she had knowledge of. Instead, he had approached one of his own clients.

'It's very straightforward, really,' the man had told him. 'Under the Criminal Law (Sexual Offences) Act of 1993, a person such as yourself could fall into one, or indeed all, of three categories. You might be arrested for organising prostitution, for living off the earnings of prostitution or for brothel-keeping. The most you would suffer for organisation would be a fine not exceeding ten thousand pounds or if you were unlucky a five-year prison term . . .' He had continued, 'In the instance of living off the earnings of prostitution, the penalties are smaller, a fine up to a thousand pounds, six months in jail, or perhaps both. For brothel-keeping the penalties are the same as for organisation. But the overcrowding in the prison system militates against brothel-keepers being sent down.'

Michael Junior had been glad of the free advice. Mind you, there was little free about it since his benefactor was availing himself of Michael's services more and more frequently. But given the excellent advice he had offered for Michael's last court appearance, and the loophole he had outlined in the State's case against him, he had earned it.

Reclining on the huge cream sofa in the penthouse, Michael waited for the legal man to ring the intercom. He had noticed that the man was becoming fond of Stephanie. And Michael was beginning to resent this: she was his most popular girl –

and his own girlfriend – but the man monopolised her on two or three nights a week. The more he thought about it, the more he felt that the legal man was a sexual deviant with a grudge against women. He had heard strange stories from Tiff, who was worried about Stef and what the man might do to her, that he had taken the precaution of filming them in the act. Something about the man's desire to be dominated by Stef disturbed him. He replayed the scene in his mind: the man tied up by Stef, whom he had instructed to perform oral sex, then him tying her up and taking her from behind.

It was almost as if he was playing out a role in which he was denied his freedom by the woman, then inflicted pain on her as a payback. Every time Michael watched the video he was sure, from the agonised expression on the legal man's face, that there was a psychological cause for his behaviour.

The intercom buzzed, but Michael let the client sweat for a few minutes before buzzing him into the penthouse. The man was becoming a bit too demanding. Michael considered showing him the videotape he had made because, at the end of the day, the only person who could lose was the customer. Michael knew that, under Irish law, he could not be charged twice with the same crime, so he was in the clear.

As for Stef, there was no doubt that she would deliver the man's requirements. And when she had finished, Michael would make a few requests of his own, no matter how bruised she might be. That, as he had told her during her 'interview', was one of the perks of his job.

25

It was the strangest of nights to date in her new career. The legal man was usually demanding and she had been furious when Michael had told her she had to work on a Sunday – she needed a day of rest. But Michael hadn't seen it that way.

She had dressed in the gear she knew the client liked, suspenders, white stockings and a gel-filled bra. The hand-cuffs were at the ready and the silk scarves beside the bed. She had been unnerved when he entered the room and just sat in the armchair to stare into space. God, she had thought, what in hell is he dreaming up for me now?

He removed a cigar from his breast pocket and began to smoke it. Was he going to do a Bill Clinton?

It came as a surprise when he told her, 'I just came to see you. I don't want to have sex tonight, just talk.'

And talk was all they did. He asked her about herself. She lied, of course, but the conversation lasted for over two hours and, by the end, Stephanie had accepted that the man had no other intentions that evening.

As he left the room, he handed her an envelope. In it were two fifty-pound notes. 'Take care of yourself,' he said, as he left.

As far as Stephanie was concerned, it was he who needed to take care. He had just asked her if she had ever had the love of a mother. She had a feeling that he had not.

26

They sat in the conference room at Harcourt Square, keenly focused on the top-secret intelligence documents on the table before them. Brendan Hanley, Maria Lynch, Brian Williamson, Ronnie Weldon and Dan Williams, who had been seconded to the team from the Criminal Assets Bureau, had just made a significant breakthrough in their case and they were discussing where they should go with what they had.

Dan Williams's superintendent had secured a court order for a search of Deborah Parker's bank accounts.

By coincidence, the judge who had issued the warrant was none other than Thomas Deering. He had been intrigued when the application was made, because Deborah Parker's reputation was impeccable. Still, there was nothing the judiciary hated more than the legal system's image being tarnished.

Since then Williams had been in touch with a number of financial institutions. All were obliged to co-operate with the police, since a law had been introduced to prevent criminals laundering their dirty money. Soon he had come up trumps.

The official at Ulster Bank had been amazed when he discovered that Deborah Parker's account had wavered from its normally impeccable state. The amounts being paid into it were unusual. A review of her account for the past six years had shown that, in addition to her salary, which had increased substantially after she moved to Jennings and Associates, she had received monthly transfers from another account of five hundred pounds. That had never been called into question as the figure, in banking terms, represented a small sum. What had shocked the bank official was the discovery of a twenty-thousand-pound deposit in Deborah's account last summer. His calculator told him that since last summer the combined value of the monthly deposits, including the twenty thousand pounds, was sixty thousand and five hundred pounds.

Williams relayed this to his colleagues as they examined the pages in front of them. It seemed to Hanley that they had conclusive evidence linking the Mooneys to some form of illegal activity involving their solicitor. He had been so wrong about her. Most of his colleagues, who knew her from the courts, had said she was a likeable, hard-working individual, who played things strictly by the book. Now he had more than sufficient evidence for another warrant to search her offices. He was certain that if she had so casually paid twenty thousand pounds into her account for all to see, there would be more elsewhere. Hanley reckoned that there was no safer hiding-place for it than a solicitor's office. He was glad he wasn't in her shoes: by the time he was finished with her, she wouldn't have any left.

'Good man, Dan. You get going on the paperwork for a warrant to search Jennings and Associates and I'll have a word with your super about signing off on it,' Hanley said, rubbing his hands. 'The next thing we want to get to on our agenda is the properties. Again, Dan, we need you to liaise with the Revenue officials in your own offices. We must ascertain precisely how much was spent on property by the Mooneys in the past twelve or thirteen years. I need a full tally of how many were sold and when, what profits were made on each of them. I want this information by the end of the week.' He made a mental note to get Maria Lynch to tip off her reporter friend Alex King about their operation: he would attribute any success to Hanley's team and the National Bureau of Criminal Investigations, rather than CAB, because it was from his own offices, Hanley knew, that King's bread was usually buttered – by Lynch. She was a great girl. Hanley found it hard to conceal his soft spot for her.

There was no doubt that Lynch would fast rise up the ranks of the force. She was a good officer with a talent for lateral thinking, which often took an investigation down paths that otherwise would have been unexplored.

Lynch looked at Hanley, signalling to him that he should not pursue the avenue he had discussed with her when it had been just the two of them yesterday morning. But he was so engrossed in the progress they were making, and so excited about the prospect of a raid on Jennings and Associates, that he did not notice. 'Now, Lynch, about those phone numbers? Can you do us the pleasure of telling us who they belong to?' he asked.

Lynch sat up straight and eyeballed him, but there was only so far she could go with the others in the room. She felt bad about keeping secrets from the rest of the team – if they got to learn about it she would be branded a professional networker and she didn't want that. They all knew that the key to a successful investigation was teamwork but on this occasion Hanley had asked her to keep an element of the investigation to herself. She accepted that he was her boss and she had to abide by his wishes, but she didn't want to lose the respect of her colleagues by letting them know about it.

'Stop kidding with them, boss,' she said. 'You and I both

know that you're only teasing them. I'm afraid that today I have nothing new to offer you.'

Hanley could have kicked himself and responded, saying that it didn't do the rest of them any harm to keep them out of the loop and rose from his chair laughing, praying he hadn't given rise to any suspicions. They already thought he was sleeping with Lynch.

As he left the conference room having adjourned the meeting until the following Friday, he thought about that rumour. The idea would have been attractive, were he not nursing a twenty-two-year-old daughter through her grief at the death of her mother two years earlier.

As soon as he reached his office, he called Lynch on her mobile. 'So it must be good,' he said, when she answered.

'Oh, yes, boss, but I can't get to the bottom of it using the usual clearance procedures.'

Hanley's antennae shot up. 'Are you telling me, Lynch, that this is a restricted number?'

'Yes – and I'd have a better chance of getting into Fort Knox than I do of getting the identity of the account-holder. Somebody's being protected here.'

'How right you are,' Hanley said.

He put down the phone. Even at his level of the police force, the private numbers of certain individuals were protected by a blocking system. He always laughed when people assumed he could access any information about them because he was a police officer. Sometimes the police had to jump through several hoops before they could get hold of certain information. Just like everyone else. Now he needed permission from the top of his organisation before the identity of the individual in whose name the number was registered could be revealed to him. It was just as he had thought when he met Tom Daly in January. Something sinister was afoot and Hanley was going to make sure he wasn't part of it . . .

As he drove to his home in Blackrock on Dublin's south side, he considered how to proceed in the case. For sure, he would take a look at the legislation tonight and see what grades of public servants were afforded the extra security privileges that prevented even the National Bureau of Criminal Investigation accessing their private phone numbers. He was certain that this went high. And there was no doubt that this was about to get dangerous.

As he wove along the coast road in the rush-hour traffic, he thought of Mairead – she would have advised him to back off. 'Brendan, dear, you have only a few years left in the job. Move on to something else, love. We have Elaine to think about. You know how worried she'll be if this blows up into a big affair.'

After the heart attack, five years earlier, Mairead and Elaine had urged him to request a desk job and stop chasing hardened criminals. Certainly, he had considered it, but as serious crime spiralled out of control, he had wanted to do his bit for society.

Elaine was almost twenty-three and had just finished her commerce degree at University College, Dublin. He had vowed, after Mairead died of cancer, that he would supply all the support and love her mother had given her – and more. He had promised himself that she wouldn't have to worry about him and another heart attack.

He thought about what the lads in the office would say if they knew he was contemplating backing off. Brendan Hanley, the so-called Attorney General, who struck fear into the hearts of hardened criminals? The man whose outwardly soft manner belied a cunning and intimidating presence that sent shivers down the spines of interviewees and, indeed, those in the force who met him for the first time? They wouldn't believe it.

But no matter how guilty Hanley felt about upsetting his daughter, he knew that he had a service to provide. His job was to protect the security of the State and protect it he would, even if that meant rooting out wrong-doing at the highest level in the land . . .

27

It was what the media would have termed 'a dawn swoop', although it occurred at half past nine, just as Patrick Mangan, Paul Jennings and Deborah Parker were emerging from their office building to get into a taxi to take them to the Four Courts. In fact, Mangan had no court business today, but he had insisted on accompanying Jennings because he said he wanted to sit in on a trial where Jennings was instructing a top criminal-law barrister. Deborah had thought it strange that Mangan was so insistent upon accompanying him. She had even remarked to herself that he was looking unusually smart today, in a well-cut suit and pristine shirt.

Maria Lynch had the most unlikely appearance for a detective. In her tailored trouser suit, with her sleek blonde hair and flawless makeup, she looked more like a solicitor. She addressed a startled Paul Jennings first: 'Mr Jennings, I am Detective Garda Maria Lynch of the National Bureau of Criminal Investigations. I am accompanied by my colleague Dan Williams of the Criminal Assets Bureau. Mr Williams has in his possession a warrant, issued at nine o'clock last night, to search your premises. It was approved by a judge of the District Court under section fourteen of the Criminal Assets Bureau Act of 1996.'

The newspaper photographers' cameras flashed in his face

but Jennings was pugnacious. He asked her to explain the purpose of the search.

'We are investigating possible collusion between a named employee of this company, one Deborah Parker, and or individuals of this company and a family of well-known criminals who are living off the proceeds of crime. We have reason to believe that your premises may contain documentation that may be of assistance to us in our inquiries into organised prostitution and widespread tax evasion in this jurisdiction.'

Lynch waited for his response. When none was forthcoming, she warned, 'Failure to comply with our requirements and permit this search to proceed will result in a breach of subsection seven of the Act and will result in a fine not exceeding fifteen hundred pounds or imprisonment.'

Jennings called Mangan to one side and whispered in his ear, leaving Deborah standing alone. It was the picture that would make the evening news and the front pages of all the national newspapers, broadsheet and tabloid, the following morning.

She could hear the press pack shouting at her, asking all sorts of questions, but none were getting through to her. Her head was spinning. She pushed her hair off her face and tried to retreat into the office. Jennings placed his arm across the doorway, providing the photographers with another sensational picture.

Deborah knew this was a set-up and that it involved Mangan, but it was pointless to try to intervene in front of the national media.

Mangan was telling Jennings, 'The girl is a liability, Paul. Damage limitation is what is required now. We have one opportunity to show the world that we're not involved in whatever seedy business she's up to and this is it. You've got to let her go and my advice to you is to do it in front of the hacks.'

Deborah was astonished. She could not believe that Jennings had asked Mangan for advice. Christ, she thought. This guy is so dangerous. He has the man who headhunted me eating out of the palm of his hand. How did he do it?

Jennings had taken the opportunity to disassociate himself from Deborah in front of the cameras. He took her arm and moved closer to where Alex King's cameraman was posted and raised his voice to ensure that the mike picked up his every word.

'Deborah, I am afraid that you have left me with little option but to suspend you. You have failed to explain clearly why you were pictured dining with a family of suspected criminals in Marbella, and you have misplaced twenty thousand pounds, which was given to you, in trust, by a client. Your actions have placed the reputation of this firm in jeopardy and we do not wish your name to be associated with it until these concerns are cleared up. You should also know that I intend to report you to the Law Society for professional misconduct and apparent misappropriation of funds. You will hear from us in due course.' He held open the door and gestured for the officers to come in.

Deborah walked fast down to Baggot Street. There was a clap of thunder and the heavens opened. The one-way traffic leading from Baggot Street on to Pembroke Street was bumper to bumper and she ran across the road, hoping to catch a cab that would take her out to Dalkey: she was in no condition to drive. She stood there, soaked to the skin, and shivered as the media posse, which had followed, attempted to get answers on the nature of her dealings with the Mooneys. She wanted to shout, 'Set-up', and explain the situation, but she knew she couldn't. One word about being framed or sexual harassment would lead to an instant writ from Mangan. And where was the proof? A one-paragraph request for sexual favours was hardly going to explain her so-called involvement with the Mooneys. But she knew that by saying nothing, the journalists were concluding that she was guilty. 'Set-up' was what most of her clients said had happened to them. The only difference between her and them now was that she had no one to turn to. When the TV3 jeep pulled up, she had no option but to clamber inside beside Alex.

They were huddled in their usual corner in the Leeson Lounge, both fast on the way to being drunk.

'You see, Patrick? I told you it was only a matter of time before she cracked,' Geena said.

Mangan couldn't believe how valuable she had been in his campaign to oust Deborah, and had no intention of dispensing with her services just yet. He had to be sure that Hanley's case against Parker was watertight before he gave Geena the heave-ho. And even then, he thought, as she gazed into his eyes, he might not get rid of her altogether. She was one of the few women who could give a good blow-job and her breasts were huge.

'What are you thinking, Patrick?' she asked him.

Mangan's mind was on what was to come in the back of his car. Fuck it, he thought. I might just throw caution to the wind tonight and book us into a cheap hotel. I can always say I was too pissed to drive. A few minutes passed as he contemplated that prospect. Then, 'I'm thinking how glad I am that your brother's in the CAB. I mean, if you hadn't let him know about her stealing that twenty grand, it would have taken them an age to discover what she was up to. I'm assuming that when they trawled through her bank account, they came up with other stuff as well. Why else would they have come into our place today?'

Geena had no intention of feeding him the latest information from her brother. She needed Mangan to ensure that she climbed another rung of the ladder and wanted a promise that her future with Jennings and Associates was secure. 'This is fabulous,' she said. 'You're going to emerge from this the golden boy, Patrick. Paul will do practically anything you say now, won't he?'

'Well, the first thing I'm going to say to him is that we need someone to take on most of her cases. You're not quite ready for the bigger ones, Geena, but you could handle most of her stuff. The firm owes it to you. If only Paul knew how invaluable you have been in exposing her – but he must never find that out,' he told her.

Her green eyes sparkled mischievously and her curly hair tumbled seductively over her shoulders. When she raised her eyebrows in a gesture that implied there was indeed more dirt to be had on Parker, Mangan felt himself harden. He pulled her close to him and stuck his tongue into her mouth.

He took her to a cheap hotel in Gardiner Street, in the middle of the north inner city. He was unlikely to encounter anyone in the legal profession around here. He was so excited that he made her come three times.

When they had finished, he fell asleep thinking about Deborah Parker, as he always did . . .

28

Alex King took in the classical lines of the furniture and the modern artwork on the cream walls. The rain had stopped and a gentle breeze was causing the floor-length muslin drapes to flow into the room. The Philippe Stark television and Bang & Olufsen stereo completed the modern look of the room. This kind of furniture comes at a price, he thought, and at a price much greater than a solicitor can afford. Most solicitors, with less than ten years' experience, earned under thirty thousand pounds and those in Deborah's position about forty thousand. With Ireland ranking as one of the most expensive places to live in Europe, with a fairly punishing tax regime, someone like her would scarcely be able to afford this type of lifestyle.

He thought back to when she had telephoned him and asked to meet him. He had been so excited about scooping the exclusive interview that every investigative journalist was hoping for. They had arranged to meet in a little bar in Greystones, where he lived. Although it was just a forty-minute drive from Dublin city centre, the County Wicklow town was a world away from the hustle and bustle of the city. Like Deborah, he loved the sea, and his Victorian harbour-front home, which afforded stunning views of the coastline, was his pride and joy. He had purchased it in a run-down condition seven years ago, when he was twenty-six and trying to get by as a freelancer. He'd had to live hand to mouth to meet the mortgage repayments, but it had been worth it.

He had slowly restored the house to its former glory, sanding floorboards, repairing magnificent fireplaces and the beautiful cornice that had been ravaged by years of damp. It was now worth almost eight times what he had paid for it, and even with the cost of the renovations, he would come out with well over half a million pounds' profit were he to sell tomorrow. The basement apartment that he now let downstairs more than covered his mortgage, and with the generous salary increases he had received each time he got an award, he was now earning just under a hundred thousand pounds, with little to spend it on – he never seemed to have time for anything but work.

To the onlooker, Alex King had everything; good looks, a great car, a beautiful house, a flourishing career and a healthy bank account. The only thing he lacked was a woman in his life. He hadn't found anyone who shared his dedication to work and who could allow him the freedom he needed to pursue his career. He often had to leave dates early, not turn up at all, or go out on surveillance in the middle of the night. He chuckled as he recalled the expression on a former girl-friend's face when he told her he would have to leave her at Frère Jacques, a beautiful French restaurant in Dame Street. The food and wine were exquisite, and Elizabeth, with her long red hair and blue eyes, had been enjoying his company, as he regaled her with stories about some of the country's best-known politicians and business figures. Alex had thought he had met his match. As a doctor, she was familiar with unsocial hours and middle-of-the-night call-outs. But that evening he hadn't been prepared for her reaction when he took the telephone call on his mobile. He hadn't told her what his latest investigation was about, and when he did, she had been less than impressed. She hadn't minded that he had had to leave – he had made his situation clear to her – but she spilt red wine on the linen tablecloth when he told her why.

'You're going to buy a what?' she asked.

Embarrassed, Alex had urged her to keep her voice down – the other diners were staring at him now.

'Did you just say that you're going to buy a gun? You have got to be joking. This is the last straw, Alex King. I told you I don't mind what you do, but that's illegal and it is also highly dangerous. If you go, we're finished.'

Alex had tried to explain that he was doing this as part of an investigation into the arms trade on the streets of Dublin to demonstrate how easy it was to acquire a weapon. He had told her that his criminal contact was a man he had used many times in the past and that there was nothing for her to worry about. She could read about it in the paper the following Saturday. But Elizabeth told him that she could not be involved with someone engaged in such dangerous pursuits.

That had been three years ago, and since then he had had no more than a handful of relationships lasting no more than a few weeks.

Now Alex reminded himself of how lucky he was to be sitting in Deborah Parker's apartment: only two weeks ago, she had arranged to meet him, then cancelled at the last minute citing work pressures.

When she walked into the room, her beauty hit him in a way it never had before. Yes, he had thought her good-looking, but now, in sweat pants and a soft grey cashmere sweater that hung loosely from her slender frame, she was stunning. There was no other word for it, he thought, as his eyes lingered on hers. She had a fresh face with lovely big brown eyes, but what got him was the smile: fragile and innocent, it transformed her face. This was the first time he had seen it.

He pulled himself together and handed her a brandy he had taken the liberty of pouring for her. She had been shaking badly when they came into the apartment and he had prayed that she wouldn't pass out from shock.

'Thank you for bringing me home,' she quivered. Her eyes were glassy with tears.

Alex didn't know what to think. Either she was a very good actress or she was torn apart by what was happening to her. He started to speak, but she signalled with her right hand that she wanted to talk first.

'Look,' she said, her voice stronger again, 'I know what you must think of me and I know with that raid this morning that I must look worse to you than I ever did. But I swear to you. I haven't done anything.' She continued, breathless, 'I know you must think I'm into something with the Mooneys after Marbella, and I wouldn't blame you for it, but I swear to you I'm not. I go there every year with my two friends. You can ask them, if you don't believe me. We always stay at the same hotel. Aine is a travel consultant. She gets us a discount from the Don Pepe every year. As for the Mooneys and the meal we had with them, what do you want me to say? I met a client in a restaurant, a very generous one, and he insisted we join his party. That's all there was to it, I swear to you. I'm only sorry that I didn't return your calls and explain it to you. Perhaps then none of this would ever have happened to me.'

Distracted by her beauty, Alex reminded himself that he was there to do a job. 'Let's get one thing clear, Deborah – I can call you Deborah, I take it? What happened to you has nothing to do with me. I was merely reporting the facts as I witnessed them. I have the video footage to prove it. There is more to this than meets the eye and I will damn well discover what it is. You're in a mess, all right, but it is not of my making.'

'I'm sorry. This thing started long before I went to Marbella and I didn't mean to suggest you were to blame for any of it. But something is happening to me and I don't know where it's coming from. I'm under investigation by the police and I've just lost my job. In case you didn't hear Paul Jennings when he was threatening me this morning, I'm under suspicion for the theft of twenty thousand pounds from my firm. It can't get any worse.'

But Alex knew from his own investigations that it would. The question was, did Deborah Parker, or was she really being set up? And how come she hadn't mentioned the other thing he had discovered about her trip to Marbella? 'I already knew about the twenty grand,' he said. 'I've talked to Mugsy Mooney and he filled me in on it. Here is the question I have for you. Why, if you didn't steal it, did you tell him you were looking for a record of it in your accounts department? Why not just tell him the truth that you lost it? You have to admit it looks shady from the outside.'

Deborah was astonished that he had known about the cheque. How had he found out? From his police contacts? Or, even more frightening, had it been Patrick Mangan? It was by no means unheard of for solicitors to have regular contact with journalists. They forged relationships all the time down in the Four Courts. One thing she knew for certain was that he hadn't heard it from Paul Jennings. Her boss, or former boss, as it now seemed, wanted to keep the whole thing quiet to protect his firm.

The idea that Mangan had been behind the police and King

finding out about the missing money sent shivers down her spine. If he was capable of stitching her up with the police and a top investigative journalist, where would he stop? She was panicking now. Should she continue talking to King and try to get him on side, or throw him out so that he couldn't have anything else to feed back to Mangan – if Mangan was his contact?

She walked over to the big picture window that ran the length of her living area and looked out at the sea. Was there anyone she could trust? Please, God, she prayed, take me out of this nightmare.

She decided to trust Alex with some of her story. She had lost everything anyway.

'Patrick Mangan is setting me up,' she said. 'He has wormed his way into Jennings's confidence – in fact into his life – to such an extent that he has Paul eating out of the palm of his hand. The man has wanted me out of the way since the day I joined the firm. The missing twenty thousand is down to him. He is the person I gave it to and he is denying all knowledge of it. He says I stole the cheque and now he is the kingpin in Jennings and Associates and everyone hangs on his every word. No one has trusted me since your exposé on Marbella.'

Alex tried to stop her, but she continued, 'Don't ask me why it is happening or how I let it happen, but I did. And as for my excuse to Mugsy Mooney, I was hoping he'd come back and tell me that the cheque had not been cashed. Then I intended to tell him that we had misplaced it and ask if he would write another one. I don't even know if it *was* cashed.'

Alex nodded, which confirmed to Deborah that it had been cashed.

'Do you know who cashed it?' she asked, hoping he wouldn't say it was her.

'No, and neither does Mugsy,' Alex replied, 'but I can tell you it won't be long before Hanley and his team discover where the money went. I don't need to tell you that the new powers afforded to the police enable them to track most transactions very easily.'

Alex was trying to take it all in. He glanced at his watch and saw that it was half-past one. He had to edit this morning's material for the five-thirty news bulletin. He hadn't done his piece to camera yet, never mind any voiceover on the footage, and he knew that when he turned his mobile on there would be a stack of messages from his police contacts informing him of what they had discovered in the search of offices. 'Listen,' he said, 'you've just told me a lot and I need to know that you're giving me the full truth. You have to level with me. Is that the full picture?'

Deborah sat back and drained brandy from her glass. 'I've told you everything except my suspicions as to why Mangan is doing this to me. Yes, there was some professional jealousy, but I don't think he's motivated by that alone. He has wanted to sleep with me ever since we met and I believe his campaign stems from my refusal.'

Alex was taken aback. Sure, she was a great-looking woman. He had thought so when he saw her in Marbella and even more now. There was something sexy about an attractive woman showing her vulnerable side. But this was a legal firm she worked in and, above all else, a guy like Mangan would be aware that sexual harassment constituted instant dismissal in this age of litigation. It sounded a bit far-fetched.

Before he had time to ask, she volunteered the information he sought: 'Yes. I have the proof in black and white, but there is no way I'm giving it to you yet. I need to know that you're on my side. And I am not asking you to take sides. I know you'll

177

make up your own mind as to who you believe, but right now, I'm asking you for help in trying to get Mangan off my back and in trying to sort out the mess I'm in. I promise you I'm not hiding anything. If you help me, I will give you an interview.'

A few minutes later, Alex pulled his BMW away from her apartment complex at breakneck speed and began the journey to TV3's offices. And as he sat in one of several traffic jams along the way, he couldn't help wanting to believe her. The woman had clearly endured psychological torture, and Mangan was responsible for it – if she was telling the truth. But he was conscious of her attractiveness too. He hoped she wasn't playing him. No. His instincts were usually right, and he felt he could see the glimmer of truth in what she was saying.

Well, tomorrow night, he would find out when he met up with Maria Lynch to find out what they had really been looking for in Parker's office.

It disturbed Alex that he wanted to believe Deborah: this was not something he normally experienced on an investigation. But she had left out one salient point. There had been more to Mooney's role in her affairs in Marbella and she had not told him what it was. Still, for the moment he was prepared to give her the benefit of the doubt.

29

'So, you see, she can't have been telling you the truth. The money was right there in her account. We already knew that from a trawl Dan Williams conducted through his CAB office. That's why we went in there in the first place,' Maria told him. 'We knew she had lodged the twenty grand in her account and we wanted to find out what else she was hiding. Hanley isn't known as the Attorney General for nothing, you know. It was his theory that there are few better hiding-places than a solicitor's office and, boy, was he right! I mean, who would have thought that we would see the day when the CAB and the NBCI raided a solicitor's office? The days of the professional classes being immune from scrutiny are well and truly over, I can tell you.'

Alex was astounded. He had spent the best part of the last twenty-four hours feeling sorry for Deborah Parker and her trauma – and he couldn't accept Lynch's theory, even if she was one of the best officers on the force. If Lynch was right, Parker was probably getting ready to flee the country with Mooney's twenty grand, and it would have to be a brave woman who would take on Mugsy Mooney. He shuddered to think what the man might do to Deborah if Lynch was right.

'Are you absolutely sure?' he asked.

Maria picked up her gin and tonic and eyed him. Alex understood the look: it said, 'Not you too . . . ?' He confirmed her suspicion with a wide grin. She told him he wasn't the only one to fall for Parker's charms. 'Don't worry,' Maria said. 'Hanley fell into the trap too. The lads think the only reason he ordered the search was to find something to clear her. He thinks – thought – she's an angel, but that search has pushed the knife even deeper into her.'

Alex stared forlornly into his pint of Carlsberg. If Lynch was right, he had been fooled by Deborah Parker's crocodile tears. He returned to the conversation and, in particular, to Lynch's last words. 'What do you mean? Christ, Lynch, don't tell me you have even more dirt on her?'

Maria looked at him teasingly, until he insisted that she elaborate or he would tell the force she was gay. The threat was a joke. Her sexuality was not.

'OK.' She laughed. 'Hold your horses, Mr Hotshot Journalist. I was just waiting for you to get over your heartbreak before I let you in on the rest. Before I do, I need your word that you won't use any of this until you have my say-so.'

'Scout's honour,' he said. He knew that Lynch trusted him. She had been dealing with him for the past three years and he had never broken an agreement. And he was one of only a handful of investigative journalists on the crime scene who were not in the pockets of the top brass.

The boys at the top leaked sensitive information about security issues to a few favoured journalists. In return, those journalists rarely criticised the actions of senior officers. The relationship was mutually beneficial, but senior police management were able through it to exert huge control over the media.

However, Alex King was beyond exploitation. He refused to join the coterie around the management so Hanley and Lynch were happy to trust him. Alex had earned the respect of his police contacts by once telling the Commissioner to fuck off. When Alex King had been investigating alleged links between members of the force and a gang specialising in passports for sale, Commissioner John Kelly had turned up at his home. It was said he had asked Alex not to run the explosive story 'for the sake of the force'. He had promised full co-operation on future investigations, but Alex had yelled, 'Fuck off, and stop attempting to pervert the course of justice.' The Commissioner's driver had wasted no time in relating the tale to his colleagues.

The passports story was aired, Alex was named Investigative Journalist of the Year and four members of the force were convicted. Commissioner Kelly had been forced to acknowledge Alex's diligence in exposing corruption within the force. And Alex had become a hero of the disillusioned officers.

Maria told him what they had learned: 'When we conducted the trawl through her bank accounts, we discovered she has been receiving large sums of money into her account since she began practising law. It would appear to us that the Mooneys are not the only ones she is taking from, but in this case it seems she has been put on a retainer by someone. The account is held in trust by a firm of solicitors, so the identity of the sender is unknown to us. It stinks to high heaven, doesn't it?'

Alex thought back to the convertible Golf GTI and the expensive furnishings. His initial suspicions had been right. 'God! I feel such a fool, Lynch, I really do. Give me everything you've got on this woman because, when the time is right, I am going to bury her.'

Later, as Alex walked away alone from the pub, a practice he always observed when meeting police contacts – they didn't like to be seen with journalists, unless it was in the pub after a win in a big court case – he thought of the irony: Lynch was a detective investigating a high-profile case, giving him copious amounts of information, but it had never occurred to her to ask him what he might have uncovered in the course of his own inquiries. He liked Lynch, but the arrogance of some detectives, who believed that only they had access to the juicy information, never ceased to amaze him.

If only she had bothered to ask what he had come up with . . . The devastating link he had uncovered between Mooney and Parker would confirm the theory of collusion between the pair. Now he knew for certain that Deborah Parker wasn't coming clean with him, he would have no qualms about reporting his revelations on air.

But at the back of his mind something still didn't fit . . .

30

Assistant Garda Commissioner Tom Daly walked into the Hole In The Wall just as Brendan Hanley took his pint of Smithwick's from the lounge-boy. The pub was located on Blackhorse Avenue, just a stone's throw from police head-quarters, and it was a favourite with many of those who worked there. The lunches it served ensured that it was always brimming with police, and on winter evenings the blazing fires ensured that customers stayed until closing time, rather than brave the elements outside.

But it was four o'clock in the afternoon and the lunchtime throng were now ensconced at their desks.

'There's a pint of the black stuff on its way for you,' Hanley said, as Daly moved into the seat beside him.

Daly did not bother to tell him that since moving into the higher echelons of management ranks he had taken to drinking G and T. He had been relieved when Hanley contacted him: there must have been serious developments in his investigation. With the powers-that-be in the Park and the Department of Justice keeping a close eye on the case Daly was keen to report any positive news to his superiors.

'Well, Tom, you're looking on top form. Life treating you well, is it, as you wait to take the throne?' Hanley said. He had referred to speculation that Daly would become the next

Commissioner of the Irish police force. Subject to ministerial approval, of course.

Daly reflected on what Hanley had just said to him. To anyone else, the remark about his long-hoped-for promotion would have been harmless, but police officers who specialised in intelligence gathering or, like Daly and Hanley, had spent years running covert operations against the IRA spoke their own language. Points were made through innuendo and if one wasn't *au fait* with the double-speak, one couldn't make head or tail of a conversation like the one being held now. Daly was aware that Hanley knew something was afoot with the phone-tapping and that his promotion might be jeopardised by it. At the same time, this hadn't been a threat: it was more an invitation to him to come clean or risk a cock-up that might lead to exposure.

'Ah,' he shrugged, 'pullin' the divil by the tail, Brendan. You know how it is, taking orders from above and just getting on with things. A man's got to earn a living.' He had now informed Hanley that his hands were tied as far as the operation and the reason for it went. 'You're going great guns on this Mooney business, I gather. You must be looking for something if you've deigned to visit officialdom,' he said. This was a reference to Hanley's disdain for Irish police force politics which had dissuaded him, and many more good officers, from advancing his career. He had little time for the networking and back-stabbing required to get to the top. He believed that policing was just about policing, and didn't want to be bogged down in bureaucracy.

Hanley accepted that Daly's hands were tied, but if he himself was inadvertently becoming embroiled in something bigger, he wanted to know about it. 'Well, Tom, it's like this. The Mugsy business has entered a new phase and, without doubt, we're close to having enough evidence to take to the Director of Public Prosecutions – we'll certainly get the go-ahead to proceed with a case against him and his son. We're tying up some loose ends, and we have a number of avenues of inquiry to pursue following the raid on their solicitors' offices. When you give us clearance on a couple of procedures we need to follow, it should be all systems go. Mind you, it's more that young solicitor, Parker, who's being tainted at the moment than Mugsy and Co. You know, I think Mugsy's probably sound enough, but the son – he's a nasty piece of work. Mugsy's of the old school, turning a few tricks here and there, making a fair few bob out of it, but Michael Junior deserves to go down. We'll get him on organisation of brothels and living off the proceeds of crime. No doubt about it.'

Daly tried to stay calm as he absorbed what Hanley had just said. This would go down a bomb with the official – if he told the official what was happening.

Daly already knew that the procedural go-ahead Hanley sought was clearance to obtain the identity of a private telephone number of an individual on Eircom's flagging system. Certain members of government, the police force, the armed forces and the judiciary had restricted-number privileges so that they were protected from threats and intimidation by the public.

Daly considered his options. If he refused to give the go-ahead, Hanley would make it his business to find out what was in the can of worms and blow the whole thing wide open. So he would provide him with the sanction he required and let him get on with his inquiries. After all, there was nothing in writing to say that Daly was involved with the tappings. The Interception of Postal Packages and Telecommunications Act contained a clause that allowed the Minister for Justice verbally to sanction a tap if the urgency of an investigation required it. That was the procedure that had been followed with the Mooneys and the man the official wanted monitored. Anyway, Hanley might not stumble on what was being hidden even if he knew the identity of the account holder: it was common knowledge that people in senior State positions frequented brothels all the time.

'Consider it done,' he told Hanley. 'Your young protégée – Lynch, isn't it? She'll get a call later with the name of the account holder,' he said, and drained his pint.

Hanley watched him leave, then ordered another pint of Smithwick's. It was clear to him that he had been set-up with this monitoring of the Mooneys and reporting on their activities. He knew now that when he had received his instructions from Daly there had been no expectation that he would come up with anything tangible enough to make a case against them. That had been evident from the shock on Daly's face when he had told him he was getting ready to move on them. It was also clear to Hanley now that someone wanted the Mooneys kept out of the courts and out of the public spotlight. But why? Had that person helped them before?

He ran a hand through his hair as he contemplated the reasons for establishing the operation if there had never been any intention to charge anyone at the end of it. Clearly Daly was receiving his instructions from higher up the ladder, which meant either the Commissioner himself or the Minister for Justice.

He leaned back and stared at the ceiling. Then it hit him. Like a bullet in the head. The Commissioner couldn't be involved in something like this: the man had six months of a seven-year term left to serve and he wasn't going to jeopardise the handsome pension and offers of prestigious posts on the boards of the country's top firms that he would undoubtedly receive when his term ended. This business was between Daly and the minister, because there was no way that Daly could have provided the transcripts of the phone tappings without ministerial authorisation. Who else would the minister pressure if he wanted something like this done except the man whom everyone knew wanted the top job? Hanley also knew, from his covert-operation days, that the Minister for Justice could verbally sanction a telephone tap, and that if anything had been put down in writing, Daly was too shrewd to have become involved.

It was all coming together now. But who were they protecting – and why? And what did Deborah Parker have to do with this web of deceit? Or was she just an innocent victim of this sordid cover-up? Hopefully, the note his team had discovered during the search of the office would lead them to the answers they sought.

31

August 2002

She looked at herself in the mirror, the sunken eyes, pale skin and limp hair. She couldn't take much more of this – not that she hadn't been used to hardship. In some of her foster-homes she had been put to work like a slave. When she was seven, they had finally found her a permanent home. And, wow, had she hit the jackpot! For five years, she had lived with the Mallons in Cork and had cherished every second of her time there.

Rory Mallon was the kindest man she had ever met. He was a doctor in the village of Schull in the west of the county, and he and his wife, Melanie, had been on the waiting list to adopt a child for six years before their dream came true. They had received the gift of a beautiful little girl called Stephanie. That was not the name given to her by the adoption agency, who had informed her mother that they would have to change her name. The Mallons had been told that they could change her name but when they had asked the child if she wanted to keep her name, she said she wanted to be called Stephanie. It was the memory she had of her mother: she had hugged her tightly, with tears in her eyes, and said, 'Goodbye, Stephanie.'

From the outside, their house looked like a tiny cottage, but inside, Stephanie saw that it stretched back for what seemed miles – it had twelve rooms.

It had taken her a long time to forget that she didn't have to call them Mr and Mrs Mallon, as she had been told to address adults in the children's home, but she hadn't felt comfortable addressing them as Mum and Dad. The Mallons had told her to call them whatever she liked. In the end, Melanie had become Minnie, while Rory was Big Daddy because of his rotund stature and cuddly appearance. They had laughed when she announced her names for them and Rory had taken her on his lap to cuddle her – not in the way she had been cuddled before. When Rory Mallon cuddled her, it was with love, warmth, and the devotion of a father.

And then they had died, in a house fire, when she was at Irish College in Donegal five years later.

After another spell in a children's home, Stephanie was farmed out to a new family. At thirteen, she was fighting with an explosive mixture of emotions. She was too sullen, they had said. She was too strong-willed for a girl of her age. Three foster-homes later, the social workers decided that she was too difficult a child. She even had a problem with the chores her foster-parents gave her, they had reported.

Stephanie went back to the sweathouse, as the children referred to the State-run home she was placed in, and the slavery began again: scrubbing floors, polishing windows, washing bed linen by hand, preparing vegetables for the twenty-five other children and their so-called carers. At fourteen, she ran away to Cork city, where she learned to live alone.

Cork hadn't been kind to her either and now she was in Dublin, heading for the big-time, making nearly a thousand pounds a week, after Michael Junior had taken his cut. And a slave yet again. She took out her makeup bag and piled on the foundation. 'Flawless finish'. She giggled into the mirror.

'There's nothing flawless about me any more, that's for sure.'

She sat on the stool of the vanity table and inhaled the white powder Michael always left for her when a hard night lay ahead. Michael Senior would go ballistic, she knew, if he found out that his son was loading the girls with the white stuff. As far as Michael Senior was concerned, the white powder was for the enjoyment of himself and his cronies, not his employees.

As the cocaine took effect, she thought of the irony of the situation: Michael Senior had adopted a benign attitude to his son's criminal activities. It was all right for Michael Junior to be involved in crime, but he, Mugsy, was the one who would decide which crimes were acceptable and which were not. Stephanie suspected that the only reason he was against the girls using drugs was because they might bring the police to his door. If there was one thing the Irish police no longer tolerated it was drug-dealing.

It was only half-past nine and the legal man would be arriving in an hour. Transformed by her makeup, she put on the black stockings he liked, then tied the little black and white apron round her slim waist. Tonight, Michael Junior had informed her, she was to be the legal man's maid. She would wait on him hand and foot and do whatever was requested of her. That was what the man had said he wanted: a woman who would take his wishes into account.

At that point Michael Junior came in and announced that he wanted to carry out a 'routine inspection'.

'Oh, for God's sake, Mick, do you have to do this now? I'm just about to get to work.' The only time she ever felt strong enough to answer back was when she was wired with the drug.

'Didn't I tell you to address me as Mr Mooney when we're

working? Didn't I tell you to treat me with the utmost respect? Shut the fuck up and do what I say,' he shouted.

Stephanie decided that now was as good a time as any to put a stop to his abuse of her body. She couldn't take any more of it. And, she had enough dirt on him to bury him so maybe it was time she threatened him with it. 'Listen, Michael, I will not get down on my knees and I will not continue to service your warped mind,' she spat at him. It felt good to defend herself. 'Just piss off and leave me alone, would you? At least while I'm working.'

The heir to the Mooney throne was outraged. He had never been on the receiving end of disobedience from his girls – aside from last year's little incident, and Rita Brady had paid for that. He went to the bedside table and took out the handcuffs that awaited the legal man's arrival. Roughly, he pushed Stephanie on to the bed. The apron fell off.

She knew he was going to rape her. And it wouldn't take him long to get at her, in a suspender-belt, stockings and a pair of high black shoes.

He grabbed her left arm and attached the handcuff to her wrist. 'No, Michael, please,' she cried, as she heard it click into place. 'For God's sake, don't. I'm your girlfriend.'

He laughed as he knelt over her body and attached the second handcuff to the brass post. 'You should have thought of that thirty seconds ago. You're an expendable piece of ass, that's all, and don't forget it. You'll be all right for another few months and then you'll be wasted, just like the rest of them. Look at Tiff – she's the living proof. Why do you think she's on Reception? Because there isn't a man alive who she could help get it up if she was the last slag on earth. She's been shagged half to death and now it's your turn.'

When he had finished, blood poured down her legs. Even on that day in the Willows, she hadn't experienced such pain.

Roughly, he rubbed his semen into her face. Then he unlocked the handcuffs. 'Now get yourself ready, fast. The legal man will be here any minute.'

They sat in a dingy late-night café just off the quays. When the legal man had seen the state she was in, he had told Michael Junior that he wanted to take her out for dinner. Michael had been surprised, but he had told him to feel free.

Seeing him out of the usual context, Stephanie felt there was something familiar about him that she hadn't picked up on before. She couldn't put her finger on it, but it was as though she knew him, or someone who looked like him, from a long time ago. She didn't tell him so.

Perspiration was gathering on his forehead, despite the bitter cold outside. He was mesmerised. Never before had he looked upon what he was doing as injurious to the girls. As far as he had been concerned, they were willingly plying their trade, and while it was illegal, he knew that the police rarely targeted the girls or their customers. They stuck to the pimps and only then if they were known to be endangering the women who worked for them. This was precisely why he had chosen the Mooneys' operation for the fulfilment of his own sexual needs. They were regarded by professional punters as safe operators. At least, until the attack on Rita Brady.

He had never married – he had only ever loved once and that was some time ago. He wanted sexual gratification, though, and until now he had seen nothing wrong in obtaining it through payment. But he had not been asked to pay since he had provided Michael Mooney Junior with legal advice last year. It had been around the time of Mooney's court case that his needs had become more specific: he could no longer penetrate a woman from the front because he could not look them in the face. It had to be from behind. Subconsciously, he knew this related to his guilt at what had happened to Rita Brady, although he had never acknowledged it. And lurking deeper in his subconscious, he knew that he wanted to punish women – or at least one woman. The woman who had destroyed his life.

They had been there for almost two hours before Stephanie told him what Michael Junior had just done to her. Then he apologised if he had upset her with his own requests. When he looked at her, at the mess she was in, he felt ashamed and embarrassed. Shocked.

Stephanie was at her wit's end. She didn't know if she should trust him. But who else could she turn to? Certainly not Michael Mooney Junior. Certainly not Tiffany – she had been in the game for so long, she would never get out: Tiffany wouldn't dream of helping Stephanie. At least this man had explained his actions, as few others ever had. She had no choice but to trust him, she thought.

Eventually, he took her to his beautiful house on Wellington Road. In Dublin's embassy belt, he had bought it three years ago with the proceeds of his mother's estate, which had been shared with his older brother, from whom he had been estranged for the past twenty years. Apart from his housekeeper, Stephanie was the only woman who had entered it.

After he had settled her, he went downstairs and poured himself a stiff whiskey. He wanted her to report the rape to the police, but first he had to consider the ramifications for his own career. His conscience was clear about the rape and any charges that might be brought against Mooney, because he wasn't jeopardising any police investigation if she chose to take his advice. He had been involved in enough rape cases to know that semen could stay in the human body for up to seventy-two hours, so if she went ahead in the morning, the police would have enough evidence to convict Mooney on conspiracy to pervert the course of justice charges.

As for himself, his career would be over. He would have to report to the authorities what he knew of what had happened to Rita Brady and would lose his job. Of that he had no doubt. Indeed, he was only sorry he hadn't done it a year ago. But tonight he had been provided with an opportunity to make amends, however unfortunate the circumstances. He would own up to his misdemeanours and take whatever steps were necessary to protect the girl. He had missed that chance with another woman but this time he was not going to take the cowardly route.

32

Knocktopher Village, January 1996

'*You told them about the note my Frank left, you two-bit whore. You'll pay for that, by God.*'

Eamon was drunk. He always was now. Ever since Frank had taken his life two years ago.

'*Yes, Eamon. I told the people in the village that "your Frank" took his own life and how I found him in the bath with his wrists slashed. Well, he was my Frank too. And everybody knows now.*'

Sheila no longer cared. She wanted him to hit her. She wanted to fight back. The antidepressants weren't working: they would not block out the pain. Because of him, she had lost everything. Two of her children were gone, one dead, the other living God knew where. The third would never come back to Knocktopher. She wanted to provoke him. Either he would kill her or she would kill him. But she would be free of it. Prison would be better than this life. '*I told them how the water turned pale red. I told them how he blamed you.*'

Eamon had returned early from Harney's bar. Few people there spoke to him any more because he was usually too drunk. But tonight had been different: it had taken six pints of Guinness and six whiskey chasers before he realised that none of the regulars had uttered a word to him. And then Jimmy Hanlon, himself the worse *for wear, had come out with it: 'Ye killed your own son, Eamon. Not content with having the little one sent away and givin' your wife more than any woman deserves in the beating department, you killed your own son. The whole parish knows it now. Not that we didn't know you were a wife-beater before. You're not fit for hell, man.'*

Eamon had stood up and looked around. Twenty sets of cold eyes were on him. The silence was deafening. He was a condemned man. For the first time in his life, Eamon was hurting.

'You bitch,' he said, as he staggered towards her. 'You vindictive fucking bitch.'

He walked slowly towards her, suddenly perplexed at the lack of panic on her face. Usually, she was terrified – that was what he liked about it . . .

He kissed her on the lips. A tender, slow kiss. His tongue danced over her face and he never closed his eyes.

Sheila was waiting for her opportunity. The knife was on the table and she intended to use it tonight. He had her pinned against the wall now, holding her eyes open, pulling the skin tight on her face. 'You won't close them tonight, woman. You'll look at me as you take it from me. Do you hear?'

He punched her in the stomach viciously, again and again and again. As he did so, Sheila stood there, waiting for her opportunity. Tonight she would kill him. Each thump was stronger, but the beating that was designed to elicit fear brought strength instead. And memories. The years flashed through her mind as she stared into his face and saw again her children's terror.

She thought of her first child's third birthday, her little legs dangling above the flames. She thought of her other daughter and of what she had witnessed on that beautiful summer evening. She looked into his mouth and remembered how he had acquired the gaps in his teeth. She thought of her son, of how Eamon had berated him for treating women with too much respect.

And as he pounded his wife, Eamon thought of his son too. The eighteen-year-old son's note flashed before his eyes. 'Leave her alone, Da.'

There was no need for Sheila to use the knife. Just as Eamon was about to hurl his fist yet again into her stomach, he looked at her, wide-eyed with shock. 'Jesus. Help me,' he said. His face was contorted with pain. He reeled back, staggering. 'Jesus, woman, get me some help.' He tensed in a violent spasm and then he was on the floor.

She looked at the gleaming serrated knife in her hand, the knife that had been held to her face and throat so many times, smiled and placed it on the table. She looked at her husband briefly, and then left the cottage and walked slowly to the village pub to use the phone. When she went in, in her dishevelled state, Jimmy Hanlon bought her a brandy. She drank it – to kill the pain, she said.

There was an eerie silence in Harney's bar, as the customers waited for her to admit that she had killed her husband. Sheila savoured the moment. Then she said, 'Did you know, gentlemen, that my husband has a heart, after all?'

There was a collective gasp as the villagers looked at each other in confusion. Then Sheila told them, 'Yes, gentlemen. My husband had a heart and it has just killed him. May I use the phone, please?'

33

Maria Lynch, Brendan Hanley, Brian Williamson, Ronnie Weldon and Dan Williams were in a conference room at Moran's Hotel on the Naas Road, a twenty-minute drive from their offices in the city centre. Hanley had elected that the team have an away-day to clear their heads and take an overall look at their investigation.

When a major investigation was nearing completion, it was common practice for a team to locate itself away from phones, faxes and interruptions for a brainstorming session, such as the one Hanley and his team were having now. But in this instance, Hanley had not told the others the real reason for it.

Today Hanley planned to tell the others who else was involved. But it had been because of his last conversation with Assistant Commissioner Daly that he had decided to get out of the office. Daly had provided him with the man's identity, but there was no doubt in Hanley's mind that if they had their session at Harcourt Square, a listening device would be in place and every word monitored. The big-brother scenario was at play and Hanley knew that when it came to matters of political sensitivity the boys at the top would stop at nothing to protect themselves. He was taking no chances on this one: he knew that if they became aware of what he thought he had discovered, his superiors might mount a public-relations campaign to discredit him. Here there was no chance that Commissioner Kelly, Tom Daly or any of the officials Hanley suspected Daly was colluding with could exert any control over them.

Hanley had resolved that if this was the last case he worked on, he would see it through to the end and that everything came out. The very fact that such a powerful legal man was involved and might have used his position to compromise last year's case against Michael Junior had seen to that.

But the problem for Hanley was that while on one hand the man appeared to be involved with the Mooneys as a customer, it also seemed that he was being blackmailed. He had no intention of exposing him because he frequented brothels. But telephone records showed he had been involved with the Mooneys at the time of Rita Brady's attack. The question that that information posed was central to their inquiries now: did the man know that Michael Junior had been responsible? According to his telephone records, he had made contact with Michael Junior that night, which probably meant that he had been at the brothel.

The blackmail issue intrigued Hanley. It was clear, from the note they had discovered in Parker's secure filing cabinet on the day they raided Jennings and Associates, that the woman was blackmailing him. But why? Was it because she was aware that he was a customer? If so, she was about to take a major fall and Hanley would see to it that she paid for her crimes.

He could not believe how wrong he had been about her. His normally reliable policeman's instinct had well and truly failed him. 'Can you just recap for us, Dan, exactly what you found when you accessed the account from which the money is being paid into Parker's Ulster bank account', he asked Williams.

'Sure thing, boss,' Williams said. 'It's quite bizarre, really. The legal man has been paying her five hundred pounds a month for the past six years. I had to use the legislation to get the identity of the account-holder from the bank, but it's in black and white. It's that well-known legal figure whose appointment was a source of such controversy.'

Maria Lynch could hardly contain herself. If Williams was talking about the same person whose identity she had finally been told, then this put a new complexion on things. Why was Deborah Parker blackmailing him?

Hanley could see her confusion and was enjoying it. He had told her not to inform her colleagues of the man's identity until he was ready for her to do so.

'Refresh us, if you would, with the details of the letter you found in Parker's office, Dan,' Hanley instructed him.

Williams took it out and read it aloud. It was from a rural firm of solicitors.

'Dear Miss Parker,
We are instructed by our client to lodge in your account the
sum of five hundred pounds each month. As outlined in
earlier correspondence, the sum will be lodged in your
account on the first of each month. Our client has requested
that you make no further attempts to establish contact and,
as legal advisers, we are instructed to administer these funds
as requested by our client. Yours sincerely . . .'

Williams continued, 'I contacted the solicitors and tried to flex a bit of muscle, but they were shouting legal privilege and saying they could never reveal the full details of the instructions they had received from the man who is making the payments. It was only when I presented a search order to the bank that I discovered who he is. We will be imposing on the solicitor/client privilege relationship if we try to get any further regarding the reason for the payments and, anyway, I suspect that the only people who can enlighten us there are either Parker or the legal man himself.'

Hanley told Lynch to reveal the identity of the man whose telephone conversations with the Mooneys were being monitored by the powers-that-be.

When she had done so, Hanley summarised the situation. 'So, what we have now is a senior legal figure, who we all know secured his post through nepotism, consorting with criminals and availing himself of the services of prostitutes. He is also being blackmailed by one of the country's most high-profile solicitors, who is under investigation for misappropriation of funds. The question is, what does Parker have on this man? Because whatever it is, the Mooneys most likely are keeping him on board with that knowledge too.'

There was a look of incredulity on each of Hanley's officers' faces. No one could understand why Parker would blackmail this man. But it was apparent to them all that before long they would be arriving at her apartment to escort her to a police station and find out.

They would spend the afternoon going through the already well-established case they had against the Mooneys for living off the proceeds of crime. The millions were in Lelia's name and, no doubt, the family would employ the biggest legal beasts in the jungle to fight their case. They would probably claim that the money did not belong to Michael Senior, but Hanley's team were pretty certain of securing an order to freeze their assets.

Now Hanley wanted to decide how best to tackle the latest unfolding scenario before moving on to the more complex issue of freezing monies. 'So where we take it from here is crucial,' he said. 'I think it's time we paid a visit to the legal man before we question Parker. We already have him for collusion with the Mooneys, so it shouldn't be too hard to get him to spill the beans about whatever he has got up to that has enabled Parker to hold him hostage. But this must be kept watertight. The last thing we want is for his brother to discover what we're up to. You don't need me to tell you that if he's targeted, his brother will pull the curtain on our operation quicker than we could scream, "Cover-up." ' Which is exactly what it is, he thought, and wondered yet again what on earth this investigation was really about.

34

Knocktopher, February 1996

Sheila opened the door and stepped back in astonishment when she saw who had come to visit. In the two weeks since Eamon's heart-attack, she had had a steady stream of visitors calling to com-miserate on the death of her husband. It was well known to everyone that he had forced her to live a dog's life, but in country towns and villages, tradition was still observed.

He was the last man she had expected, but Sheila had no intention of being rude to him. He might have been the father of the man who had deserted her, but that was long ago. Now she would let bygones be bygones. God had taken her husband at last, and now it was just Sheila and her daughter. Although that daughter was almost twenty-three now and no longer lived at home.

The doctor looked at her. At forty-two, Sheila Dunne was a beautiful woman. She had big kind eyes and he had seen her last week emerging from the village hair salon. She had had her straggling black hair cut into a smart bob and the new style framed her face, emphasising the bone structure and strong features. He wondered what his granddaughter looked like now.

Sheila kept her face blank.
A day hadn't gone by since 1979 when she hadn't thought about

her younger daughter and wondered what cards life had dealt her. She often worried that her child wasn't safe, then consoled herself in the knowledge that nowhere could have been as dangerous for her as her home.

'Would you like to come inside?' she asked the doctor.

He walked through to the cosy sitting room and took the new chair. It had replaced the wing-backed one her daughter used to hide behind. He coughed nervously. 'I have come to see you because I wish to help you. My wife knows nothing of this and I would ask that you consider keeping it that way,' he said.

Sheila stood up, indignant. 'If you think that now that man is dead you can come in here—'

He cut her off: 'Please. If you will just hear me out. It's about the child.'

'Which one?' said Sheila sarcastically. 'The one I had to give away because I married that animal or the one who is your granddaughter?'

The doctor bowed his head. 'There is nothing I can do yet to help the older girl. Not while my wife is alive.'

Sheila sat down again. She was surprised by his admission that it was his wife who had prevented any contact with the child. It was well known that the doctor had married money, so obedience to his wife must have been the price he had to pay. She nodded in acknowledgement of what he had said, but wondered why it had taken him all this time to tell her that. But the answer was obvious: he would never have approached her for fear of what Eamon would do had he suspected a liaison – even though the doctor was at least thirty years older than she was.

'I have come about the little girl we took to Kilkenny. I was wondering if, in light of your husband's death, you might want to find her.'

The shock Sheila felt was reflected on her face.

'*If this is bringing back painful memories for you, I apologise, but I know you mourned her and I wondered if I might be able to help you.*'

Sheila broke down in tears. Of course she still mourned her daughter – every day. There was nothing in the world that would give her greater pleasure than to make contact with the child and try to explain. But she would never tell her what had happened to her at her father's hands.

*She wiped her eyes with a handkerchief from her apron pocket, and looked at him. '*But how can you help me? They told me I could never trace her. How can I get her back now? You told me I'd never be able to get in touch with her.*'*

The doctor explained about the new legislation and how, if one side wanted to contact the other, they could do so through Social Services. It was up to the recipient of the letter – in this case, her daughter – to respond. If she wanted to see her mother, the girl could inform Social Services and both sides would receive counselling before any meeting took place. Normally, the process took months, but through his own contacts in Social Services, the doctor could expedite matters.

'*Doctor, I don't know what to say to you.*' *She felt alive with hope.*

'*I must caution you, Sheila, the girl might not want to see you. You must take that on board.*'

Sheila said she accepted this, but in her heart of hearts, something told her that her little girl had not forgotten her and that she wanted to meet her too.

*As he prepared to leave, the doctor asked a final question: '*If I could ask you a favour, please?*'*

'*Anything you like, within reason,*' *she joked, her voice full of joy.*

'*In the future, perhaps you would call me Thomas. I'm only called Doctor by my patients.*'

As she watched him walk towards his car, she wondered how she had managed to be so cordial. Why had she shown him so much understanding? But as Sheila knew, everyone had a cross to carry: no one was immune to pain and suffering. Even the landed gentry.

And the pain on the doctor's face was apparent to her as he turned hesitantly towards her before he got into his car. 'One other thing,' he said, faltering. 'How is Deborah doing in Dublin?'

35

It had been six weeks since Alex had left her at her apartment, believing she was being set up by Mangan and privately hoping to help clear her name. Now he was bitterly disappointed in her. He had thought that Deborah Parker would be exonerated, and that he would be instrumental in this. It had been the first time in his career that he had wanted a suspect to be cleared. But he had been wrong.

Since then, he had learned that Deborah had taken him for a fool. Maria Lynch had made that abundantly clear when she had informed him of the monthly deposits to her account, and that the missing twenty thousand pounds was there too.

Alex contemplated tonight's exposé. Lynch and her team were about to move in on Parker and they wanted to pile on the pressure through the media first. That way, the powers-that-be couldn't prevent them proceeding with their investigations. In normal circumstances, he would have been thrilled to get such a scoop but everything about the Deborah Parker story filled him with despondency. It disturbed him that, despite the mounting evidence against her, he did not want to put the final nail in her coffin. She had certainly got to him.

He stood at the entrance to Deborah's apartment complex. His back was towards the gates and the cameraman zoomed in, capturing the smart, landscaped drive that gave way to the stunning view of the sea. It would provide the perfect backdrop to his story of collusion, blackmail and corruption.

He was doing a piece to camera, which would be used to trail tonight's news. It would make sensational viewing.

Alex cleared his throat, then took a final look at his notes. The cameraman counted down from three, and signalled to Alex to begin.

'As the police investigation into one of the most powerful crime families in the country comes to its conclusion, TV3 will tonight bring you the story of what is going on behind the scenes. I stand here at the home of disgraced solicitor Deborah Parker. She has failed to come clean with TV3 about the precise nature of her dealings with the well-known Mooney family. Behind these gates, Deborah Parker lives in an exclusive apartment worth at least half a million pounds. The twenty-nine-year-old solicitor has been suspended by her prestigious law firm and is under investigation by the Ethics Committee of her governing body, the Incorporated Law Society of Ireland. But that is just the tip of the iceberg in this story of collusion and corruption.' He paused for effect, staring into the camera for three seconds, then delivered the lines that he knew would keep viewers glued to their television sets. 'Tonight, on *TV3 News*, we bring you the real story of this woman's involvement with organised criminals. We reveal details of the ongoing police investigation into her links with them and information not yet known to the police authorities about the extent of them. Join me, Alex King, tonight, for the inside story on a woman who tried to con one of the most powerful crime families in the country.'

The cameraman slashed his hand through the air as Alex finished: the take had been a success.

Usually he felt a rush of adrenaline at the completion of a

successful story, but instead Alex felt empty and dejected. He knew that the story was correct and that, ethically, he was obliged to reveal the facts of the case. But he didn't want to hurt Deborah Parker.

36

Deborah sat with Julie and Aine. They were silent: there was nothing to be said to fill the time as they waited for the report to appear on the news. King could have nothing on her, Deborah had insisted. Julie and Aine had wanted to believe her, but they knew that something explosive was about to make its way on to the television screen and on to the front pages of the national newspapers the following morning.

From her own legal perspective, Julie knew that there was no way an experienced journalist like Alex King would run with a story like this unless he had cast-iron proof. And both she and Aine were becoming fed up with Deborah's lack of honesty. They couldn't accept that Patrick Mangan's hatred was the sole reason for her suspension. There was more to it than she was letting on and they had come to the conclusion that she was, at the very least, being economical with the truth.

Following the broadcast, their suspicions were confirmed.

Deborah just sat there motionless. Her face was as white as a sheet and the sweatpants they had become so used to seeing her in over the past few weeks clung to her legs as perspiration drenched her.

'You can't believe him,' she said. 'You just can't believe him. I didn't do it. He is making a big mistake. There is no way that this is so. You must believe me.' She was staring at them with bewilderment.

Julie had had enough. 'Deborah, the man has said it in plain language. The missing twenty grand was lodged in your account. It's not just a case of missing money any more. It's in your bank account. The Criminal Assets Bureau have the proof.'

Deborah started to protest again, but her friends were having none of it.

Aine intervened: 'Deborah, this is getting worse by the minute. How can you expect us to believe a word you say if you won't come clean with us? The man paid your bill at the Don Pepe. *He paid your bloody hotel bill*, for God's sake. What more is there to be said?'

But there *was* more, according to Alex King's report. Julie was presenting all of the facts to her now and there was no escaping them. 'You are under investigation for blackmail, for God's sake. Blackmail of a well-known legal figure, Deborah. Who is it? What are you involved in? Unless you tell us now, we're out of here. We are not going to be party to this.'

Deborah went to the roll-top yew-wood bureau at the side of the room and took out her unopened Visa card statements of the last five months. 'If you want proof that I'm not involved in anything, I'll give you proof,' she said, and opened the statements until she came to the one covering their trip to Marbella. 'I paid my own hotel bill. Remember? I went downstairs ten minutes before you guys to pay?' she said.

'OK, Deborah, you went downstairs before us, all right but we never saw you paying any bill. If you paid it, show us the proof. That will be a start, I suppose.' Julie snorted disdainfully.

Deborah was flummoxed. There was no record of any payment to the hotel, as Alex King had said. At least she could prove to them that there was no twenty-thousand-pound deposit in her account. She riffled through months of un-opened bank statements. She had been under such pressure for the past year, thanks to Mangan and his campaign to destroy her, that she had abandoned her monthly account checks. She knew she had enough money to pay her bills and hadn't bothered to keep account of her financial affairs, as her mother had advised her to do.

When she found the statement for June 2001, she sank to the floor. It was all there in black and white: twenty thousand pounds had been lodged in her account and, of course, Deborah Parker had no idea why. She had let her affairs go totally out of control.

Her friends waited silently, but Deborah knew there was no point in trying to explain King's allegations of blackmail – she had had no idea what he had been talking about.

Julie and Aine left her kneeling on the floor, surrounded by bank statements and Visa card bills. Tomorrow, she would appear before the Ethics Committee of the Incorporated Law Society to explain her involvement with the Mooneys. And now this. Alex King had clearly timed his exposé for max-imum effect. She was a condemned woman.

She had no defence against the accusations and no doubt that whoever she was meant to be bribing would have cast-iron proof too.

Mugsy Mooney got into his car to pay Deborah Parker a visit. He had bought her line that the cheque had gone missing because, at odds with the fact that he didn't like solicitors, he had a soft spot for Deborah Parker. But now he had incon-trovertible proof that she had stolen his money.

37

At first, Deborah had assumed it was a posse of reporters at the front door, but then she looked at her watch and realised that it was only forty minutes since the report had been broadcast. There was no way they could have made it to Dalkey so quickly. But it was Mugsy's frame she could see on the security screen, so she buzzed him in, knowing that he would not leave until he had an explanation. When she opened her apartment door he brushed past her and she followed him into her sitting room. He stood in the centre of the room, his face red with anger.

He poked a finger into her chest. 'I want to know what ye've done with me money and I want to know now,' he said threateningly, his eyes boring into her.

Her heart was pounding and she ran her sweaty hands through her hair. 'I didn't do anything with your money, Michael. I have no idea how it got into my account. Well, actually, I do, but you wouldn't believe me if I told you.'

'Listen, love, I've heard enough of your crap. You come to my house and you tell me that the cheque is lost or something to that effect and all the while it's sitting in your bleedin' bank account. I would have said that was a pretty devious thing to do to a man like me. I don't need to tell you that I don't like to be crossed.'

Deborah didn't know where she would get the strength to

stand up to him. A man with a fearsome reputation like Mugsy Mooney did not like to be criticised or lied to. And, after all, she had lied to him. But she had nothing to lose by defending herself now and she was damn well going to let him know that he had made her look even more suspect by paying her hotel bill.

'Listen, Michael, I know that there are other issues King has referred to about my banking, but that's personal and that's the way it has to remain. I can assure you that I'm not blackmailing any legal person either. I don't even know what he was referring to there. But I can tell you this. You inflamed the fires of curiosity by your actions,' she said.

Mugsy's stance softened. 'Look, love, I hear what you're saying, and I'll straighten that out with King and anyone else who happens to ask me. I might be a con-man, but I'm an honest one and a man of my word. I would never hurt a woman in any way. I should never have got the hotel to revoke your credit-card payment. It was just a gesture of thanks for all the hard work you'd done for us last year. How in hell was I to know that you were being investigated by the CAB?'

It was three hours before she had told him the full story. He now knew about the monthly cash transfers. He knew about Mangan's vendetta to remove her from her post and he knew, as she had pointed it out to him, that the bank docket referring to the twenty-grand deposit would contain a date and the initials of the person who had lodged it in her account. She looked shattered. Mugsy wanted to believe her, if only to satisfy himself that he had not misjudged her.

The first thing he was going to do was contact Alex King and inform him of his erroneous reporting. She might not have had anything to back her claims that she had not put his cheque in her account, but she could certainly prove that the monthly cash transfers were unrelated to blackmail – even if she was unaware of the identity of her benefactor.

Mooney was intent on getting to the bottom of the matter. He hoped that the trail would not lead back to Deborah Parker: if she was lying, the repercussions for her wouldn't bear thinking about . . .

38

The legal man's hands shook as he picked up the telephone to dial the number of the National Bureau of Criminal Investigation. This afternoon he would resign from his job, and he wanted to make contact with the police authorities for two reasons. The first was to ensure that Stephanie was taken seriously by Hanley's team because he knew that, as a prostitute, she would be regarded with suspicion; and the second was not just to admit his role in the sordid affair but to explain to them that he was not being blackmailed. Alex King clearly did not know the identity of the legal person to whom he had referred in his report – at least, he had surmised that from the way the story was told – but he believed that a prominent legal person was linked to the Mooneys' operations. Now the legal man was certain that the police had surveillance footage of him entering the penthouse. He had decided last night that he was going to come clean about his links to the Mooneys, although he knew the police would think he was doing so as a result of King's exposé.

He had also to call his brother. But he would not do that until he spoken with the police and resigned from his post. Otherwise his brother would attempt to cover up his activities. His brother was so ruthless that he would put a stop to the police investigation altogether. Of that he was certain. After all, his brother was his mother's son.

When the operator at the NBCI heard the name of the man who was seeking to speak to Hanley, he put him straight through.

Hanley could hardly believe that the legal man had contacted him. Earlier that morning, he had been preparing a warrant for his arrest.

Twenty minutes later, he replaced the receiver. He had had only a superficial conversation with the man, but he now knew that Michael Mooney Junior should indeed have been convicted for the vicious assault on Rita Brady, although he could never be now. He would get Mooney for the attack on Stephanie, though. The legal man was on his way to a meeting with her now. And he would get Mooney Junior for brothel-keeping and living off the proceeds of crime.

The legal man had asked Hanley to keep their intended appointment secret and Hanley had agreed to do so, knowing, as the man did, that if the powers-that-be got wind of it, steps would be taken to prevent it. The legal man's brother would see to that. Only one point caused Hanley concern. Why was the man insisting that he was not being blackmailed by Deborah Parker? Hanley had incontrovertible evidence to say that he was, yet the man was denying all involvement with her. Hanley was adamant that he would get to the bottom of it. He just had to make sure that Tom Daly and whichever officials were interfering in police business didn't get in his way . . .

The meeting took place at the Willows Hotel in Ballsbridge, just round the corner from the legal man's Wellington Road home. Stephanie had laughed when she heard where she was to go and he had offered to change to another venue when she explained it was the location of her first encounter with Michael Mooney Junior. She declined. There was a bitter irony about the coincidence and it was nice to know that she was going to stitch up Mooney in the same hotel where he had begun abusing her almost a year ago.

Hanley and Lynch walked through the foyer and into the huge conservatory-style lounge at the rear of the building. It was a beautiful sunny August day and the sun was beating in through the huge windows. They walked to the corner where the man they both recognised from the courts was seated. As they approached, Hanley said, 'God, Lynch, this case is full of stunning-looking women, isn't it? This one has the same look as our Miss Parker.'

'Can't say I can see the resemblance myself, boss,' she replied curtly.

There was no need for introductions between the two men, but Hanley introduced Lynch to the legal man, who introduced Stephanie. The formalities aside and two pots of coffee ordered, the legal man set about outlining Stephanie's request to make a complaint against the Mooneys, Michael Junior in particular. She had been tortured and abused, and her body bore the evidence to prove it. The legal man would also provide a statement to support her. He told them he was prepared to turn State witness and confess all regarding his knowledge of Mooney's whereabouts on the night Rita Brady had been attacked last year. He admitted that he had been one of the customers of the Sandymount brothel that night, and that Rita had been hired out for him until she got the jitters, when Michael Mooney Junior had pulled her out of the penthouse and into his car.

Hanley sat back and listened. This man could offer all the co-operation he wanted, but he need not think he would escape prosecution. He had withheld information pertinent to the commission of a crime and he would suffer for it. Hanley had no intention of doing any deals with a man protected by a brother who held one of the most influential posts in the land.

But before Hanley could tell him that he was not engaging in any trade-off deals, the legal man said, 'I have already informed the president of the District Court that I am resigning. I am seeking no refuge from you in any of this. I gave advice to Michael Mooney Junior on the flaws in the State's case, then presided over the case and made a ruling in it of inadmissibility. I realise now that aside from procuring the services of prostitutes and perverting the course of justice by not revealing my knowledge about the circumstances of the attack on Miss Brady, my position is untenable. I will accept whatever is coming to me.'

Hanley and Lynch sat open-mouthed. They knew they had had a lucky break in securing the man's co-operation, but now he was placing his entire reputation and future on the line to make amends. His brother would go ballistic.

The former District Court judge continued, 'I know you have questions as to how and why I became involved with the Mooneys and I can assure you that there are deeper personal reasons for my behaviour that I am quite willing to discuss with you, Detective Hanley, but only in private.'

Lynch sat up straighter in her rattan chair, her shoulders back, looking furious. Hanley shot her a stern look. If the judge wanted to discuss something man to man, he would allow him his dignity. He was going to endure so much humiliation when this got to trial that Hanley would protect his modesty now.

'But about the girl,' the judge continued, 'Stephanie has been through quite enough, as she will tell you herself when she provides her statement. Surely there is some way of protecting her? She is guilty of nothing but trying to fend for herself in what has been a harrowing life, I can assure you.'

Hanley had no intention of bringing any charges against her. She was going to help him get Michael Mooney Junior and that was enough for him.

If her allegation regarding the rape was substantiated by the police doctor and she was found not to have been involved in controlling their prostitution agencies, she would have nothing to fear. Even when the case came to court, Hanley told her, her identity would be protected.

When Stephanie left with Lynch, to give her statement, Hanley got down to business. 'Can you tell me about your associations with Deborah Parker, please?' he asked.

The response was quick, Hanley noted. His interviewee didn't even stop to think before answering. 'Detective, I do not have any associations with Miss Parker. The only contact I have ever had with the woman is in my courtroom and even that was limited. As you know, the barristers are the people who do the talking in cases.'

Hanley had to hand it to him, the man was a good deceiver. All that practice, he thought.

'I have to tell you again, Judge, we have evidence to show an incontrovertible link between you and Miss Parker. We can do this the easy way, whereby you co-operate with me, or we can do it the hard way, whereby the evidence will be presented to you in court,' Hanley told him. 'Either way, Judge, we will find the explanation.'

The judge sat forward and asked, 'Exactly what kind of evidence are you talking about here?'

Hanley sniggered. 'Judge, do I have to tell you that I am one of the longest-serving detectives in the force? It insults me that you presume I'm going to give away my case. Please. Just answer the question.'

This time the judge responded impatiently: 'Detective, I would ask *you* not to insult *me*. I'm not taking you for a fool. I merely ask because if I knew what this so-called link is between myself and Miss Parker, I might be able to clear it up for you. The claims will be made in your Book of Evidence against me, so I'm going to learn what you're talking about before it gets to court anyway.'

The man's logic was impeccable. Really, Hanley thought, he didn't have much to lose by telling him. 'Judge, as you are aware, we have been investigating Miss Parker's finances. And the upshot of what I'm alleging is that we have traced regular transactions from your bank account to hers. I cannot fathom how you can deny this when we have traced it to your address, albeit at your original family home,' he told him.

And then it dawned on the judge. 'Detective,' he said, looking relieved, if confused. 'I do believe that you're referring to my father's bank account. But for the life of me, I cannot for one minute imagine why he would be paying huge sums of money to Deborah Parker.'

Hanley found himself in a true quandary now. This meeting had been designed to answer questions. Instead, it had left him even more confused. As they parted company, each man left the meeting certain that the other was in the dark.

39

Private Investigator Dermot Fortune had never been engaged by a criminal before – at least, not to the best of his knowledge. He had assumed that they did their own dirty work. But Mugsy Mooney was asking him to become involved in a case so high-profile that he found it hard to resist. Anyway, the money on offer was attractive and, with his contacts, he could find out what Mooney wanted to know without much effort. Although he didn't tell Mooney that.

When his contact at the bank had informed him that the deposit slip was signed by a D. Parker, he had offered an extra thousand pounds and obtained a photocopy of it. Fortune then took himself to London and the offices of a handwriting expert he had used in several marital-breakdown cases. Mooney had provided him with a copy of Parker's signature and Fortune presented it to the handwriting analyst. The man was a permanent employee of Scotland Yard's Fraud Division, but he was known to provide his services to a wider clientele – at the right price, of course.

Two days later, Fortune returned. The signatures were not written by the same hand, he assured Mooney, then extracted another five thousand pounds from him to implement the next part of his plan.

Two weeks earlier, armed with the information Deborah had given Mugsy about Geena and Mangan's relationship and her theory that she was being set-up, he had sat outside the offices of Jennings and Associates. A big-bosomed woman with curly black hair came strutting out of the office, flaunting herself. She was just as she had been described. There was no mistaking that she was his target. He followed her to the Shelbourne Hotel on St Stephen's Green, knocked her drink off her table and bought fresh ones for her and her three friends. He took up Geena's offer to join their group.

On their second date they were sleeping together in his apartment in Dun Laoghaire and by the fourth, she had given him the whole Deborah Parker story. He had told Geena that he was involved in recruitment, on the look-out for good legal talent for one of his biggest clients. Geena had wasted no time in telling him how one of her colleagues, Patrick Mangan, expected her to sleep with him so that she could get to the top, and of how Mangan had effectively driven Parker from the firm. She assured him that she might be able to assist in his recruitment drive because she had no intention of sleeping with anyone to get to the top. When Fortune told her that he was looking for a long-term relationship, she told him that she suspected Mangan had framed Parker for the theft of the twenty thousand pounds.

It had been as easy as that for Dermot Fortune. Returning to his contact in the bank, he asked how long they kept their security videos. He had been cast down when the official told him they were wiped after six months. But coincidentally there had been a mugging in the bank on the day the twenty grand had been paid in and the video had been kept for the court case. The only reason the official knew this was because the mugging had taken place on his birthday and he remembered from the television reports on Deborah Parker that the money had been lodged on the same day.

Fortune had relayed the information to Mugsy and the five thousand pounds was promptly supplied to secure the bank official's co-operation. It was only a copy of the original video, of course, but it was enough for Mugsy Mooney.

40

Mugsy Mooney had thought long and hard before calling Alex. He hated journalists. They were a shower of nosy bastards, and if they weren't so interfering, always running stories about the high life enjoyed by criminals like himself, the cops wouldn't be on his back half as much. But he owed Deborah Parker a favour and he was a man of his word. The girl was in the doghouse, partly because of him, and Mooney was intent on convincing Alex that he had been wrong about her. He enjoyed the idea of proving a journalist wrong. They were always so self-righteous.

Alex found it difficult to accept what Mooney was suggesting: that he call his editor immediately and tell him he was going to Marbella with Mugsy Mooney.

'Look, I'm just telling you, son, that I can prove to ye that I paid the bill for the girl,' Mugsy said persuasively. 'She knew nothing of it, but we have to go there to prove it. You see, they know me at that hotel. It's where I used to stay before I got me villa.'

Alex could not understand why Mooney wanted to help Parker. 'Listen,' he said, offering advice to a criminal for the first time in his life, 'she got to me and she is obviously getting to you too. Why would you possibly want to help clear her name? What's in it for you?' he asked.

'There's no great mystery to it, son,' Mugsy said. 'It's really very simple. You see, I did the girl a bad turn and now I intend to make up for it. I promised her I would.'

Alex was mystified. 'But why go out of your way for her? Your money still ended up in her account. She's obviously bent. The woman is under suspicion for blackmailing a judge now.'

'The reason I'm going to help her, son, is to prove to you that you were wrong in that side of your story. You see, she promised me she would do her level best to get me son off and, in fairness to the girl, she did. Now it's my turn.' He continued: 'And another thing too. I believe the girl in what she's saying about the missing cash. I've had a private detective on it to get to the bottom of it.'

So Alex had called his editor, who had reluctantly sanctioned the trip to Marbella. These days, it wasn't good practice to allow your journalists to run around the Continent with known mobsters, but it was too good an opportunity to turn down.

Alex had been fascinated to watch Mooney in action. He wasn't a fearsome-looking man, but when he meant business, his eyes held a frosty look that did not invite challenge. At first hand, Alex saw how the combination of charm and hostility had ensured Mooney's progress up the criminal ladder. He was likeable, for sure. But you didn't mess with Mugsy Mooney.

Mooney had booked them into the penthouse suite of the Don Pepe, and at half-past eight on the night of their arrival, a night porter knocked gingerly on the door. 'Now, Miguel, I want you to show me friend here the Visa slip I told ye about with Miss Parker's name on it,' Mugsy had told him.

Miguel looked at Mooney imploringly. 'Please, Señor

Mooney, *por favor*, I have to beg you that this is against hotel policy. I will be fired from my job if I am found out to be involved in this business . . .'

Mugsy let him know that he would not tolerate non-compliance. 'Yeah? Well, Miguel, you should have thought of that when you were putting me in touch with that coke-supplier friend of yours when I used to stay here before I got me own villa. Now, for the last time, have you got the girl's billing details?'

Miguel had produced several photocopies. The first was of the original Visa slip, signed by Deborah, the second contained the chit cancelling her payment and the third was the bill, paid by Mooney, hours after Deborah had checked out in the early hours to board her flight in Málaga.

Alex felt an overwhelming sense of relief, for Deborah's sake and for his own. She had been truthful, after all. And his journalistic instinct had not failed him. He was also at ease now with the other feelings he had for Deborah. He was sure that she was attracted to him too. Or at least that there was some kind of chemistry between them.

He also felt a fool. When his own contact in Marbella had promised to find out who had paid Deborah's hotel bill, he had not been very thorough. The TV3 libel lawyers would hit the roof when he told them of this development.

When they had returned from Marbella, Alex knew that he had no option but to telephone Deborah. It had been three weeks since his exposé and now, thanks to Mugsy Mooney, he was having to eat humble pie.

Mugsy had made him promise not to reveal to her the full extent of his findings regarding the twenty thousand pounds lodged in her account. 'My PI came up trumps for me. Ye see, money can buy you anything, son, and it's bought me the truth. My man says to me that the money was lodged by a fella named Mangan. Now, how about that? Can you believe it? Jaysus, I nearly fell off me seat when he told me he was sure. But I want to be the one to deal with Mangan directly. Say nothin' to her about it, do ye hear me, son?' Alex could certainly deliver the news about the hotel bill to her.

'You want to meet me?' Deborah shrieked. 'I can't believe you, Alex King. You reporters really are the lowest form of the low. Do you know that? You promised to help me. Then you destroyed my career, printing your libellous nonsense about blackmail and theft and collusion with criminals. And now you have the nerve to ask me to meet you. You *have* to be joking, right? Next thing I know you'll be trotting out some syco-phantic crap about believing me and wanting to make it all up to me. Am I right?'

Alex decided he loved the sound of her voice when she was angry and, yes, she had hit the nail on the head. He had intended admitting to her that he had been wrong and that he now believed most of her story. It was another trick he employed to get his targets on board. When everyone else was against someone, he would use that knowledge and pretend to believe in their innocence. It worked most of the time.

But Deborah Parker wasn't most people.

'Deborah,' he said, 'I accept that you didn't know Mooney paid the hotel bill. I have the evidence to prove it. I cannot apologise enough for what I did to you and I know that you will probably sue me for it. But, contrary to what most people think of reporters, I have a heart and a conscience and I want to try to make amends.'

'And what about the blackmail?' she spat. 'Have you decided I'm guilty of that? And the twenty grand that ended up in my account – you can't forget I put that there, can you?'

Alex badly wanted to tell her about Mugsy's private detective and how the unsuspecting Geena Williams had revealed Mangan's involvement with the missing funds. But Mugsy had made him promise, and he wasn't about to cross him.

'I don't know what to say to you about the alleged blackmail, Deborah,' he said. 'I have nothing to prove it didn't occur. The police still say it did, by the way. But I can tell you that I will do whatever it takes to clear your name. I know it's too late, but it's the least I can do. Please accept my offer and, if not, please accept my apologies. And, as I said, I have the proof you need to show that, as far as you were concerned, you paid your own hotel bill in Marbella.'

There was no more to be said.

They arranged to meet at the Club, one of Dalkey's inviting pubs, whose claim to fame was that a considerable number of police officers frequented it.

They sat in the cosy bar, which seemed to be populated by the same people every time Deborah went in. While the lounge was filled with the pub's younger clientele, the small bar was occupied by those who seemed to prefer an intimate atmosphere. It was why Deborah had chosen it.

Alex had found her sitting in the little window-seat, away from the rest of the customers. As he approached, he could see that she was attracting knowing glances. None were approving. Her appearance shocked him. She had lost weight and taken on an ethereal quality. But her fragility only enhanced her beauty in his eyes. He sat down beside her. Gone were the sharply tailored suit and the high heels and in their place a pair of faded Levi's, worn loafers and a white cotton T-shirt. Her hair was tied back in a ponytail and her skin was golden.

237

Probably from all of the walking she had done since she lost her job.

In loose chinos and open-necked shirt Alex resembled a model in a Ralph Lauren advert. As Deborah observed him, she wished she didn't find him so attractive. She despised him for what he had done to her life and her career, and also because she was so aroused by him. Part of her wanted to slap that handsome face, but another part wanted to do things with him that she hated him for making her think about . . .

They were the last to leave the pub and it had been a fruitful evening. Alex had promised Deborah he would take his new evidence to Maria Lynch the following morning. The original hotel bill signed by Deborah would do little to remove the suspicion of blackmail, but it was a start, and Mugsy Mooney's information would force Patrick Mangan to show his hand over the twenty grand. As Alex had listened to Deborah defending herself against that charge, he had felt like a prize bastard, knowing now how the money had ended up in her account.

When Deborah invited him back for coffee, he jumped at the chance.

The coffee did not materialise, but instead she brought out a bottle of Château Musar, the delicious Lebanese wine she had been saving for a special occasion. She really didn't know why this was a special occasion, but she wanted to savour the wine – and Alex King's company.

When she offered him a glass, he walked back from the window to stand before her. 'A toast,' he said, quietly. 'To our new relationship.' He had raised his eyebrows as he uttered the words.

But the *double-entendre* was not lost on Deborah. She held his gaze and felt the colour rising in her face. She was feeling panicked, confused – and something else too: physical stirrings, over which she had little control.

Alex sipped his wine, without taking his eyes off Deborah. Then he leaned over the couch and kissed her, the wine passing from his mouth to hers in a sensual gesture that left her weak with desire. She swallowed and felt his tongue flutter along her lips. He took her glass from her and placed it on the floor. Then he held her hands and pulled her up to him. They stood, searching each other's eyes. Then Deborah brought his head down to hers and kissed him.

41

Cork City, March 1996

Sheila got out of the car, having checked her makeup in the rear-view mirror. She wore a beige woollen coat over camel trousers, and in her hand, she carried a photograph album.

The doctor had come back to her sooner than she had expected. He had informed Social Services that his patient wished to make contact with her daughter. Four days later, the senior social worker had telephoned him with the news that Stephanie wanted to see her mother.

Once she had turned eighteen, Stephanie had made contact with Social Services and advised them of her address in Cork city. Since the age of fourteen she had been living rough, and it was a credit to her survival skills that she was never apprehended by the authorities. But the Parkers were made of strong stuff. She had few good memories in her life, but the one she cherished was of the pretty woman hugging her and saying, 'Goodbye, Stephanie.' She had often wondered if it had been a dream she had conjured up to give herself the will to keep going. But deep down she knew that it was real and that the pretty woman was crying because she didn't want to let her go. It was this memory that had led her to inform Social Services of her address in the dingy little flat in Cork. If her mother were to make contact, she wanted to know.

That had been two years earlier and now, aged twenty, Stephanie had received the telephone call. She had attended a counselling session with the social workers and a psychologist. They had wanted to prepare her for the meeting and caution her that her expectations might not be fulfilled. 'Your mother has another life,' the social worker told her. 'You must remember that it may not work out for you. You may be so resentful of the new life she has built that you might not get along with her. You must go into your meeting with these things in mind, Stephanie.'

Stephanie had been furious, but she knew inside that the woman had loved her very much. Nothing they said to destroy her hopes would have any impact on her belief.

It was half past eleven in the morning when Stephanie walked into the hotel foyer. She was weak with apprehension and had not slept a wink. She had imagined standing in the lobby, searching faces for one she recognised. How many forty-two-year-old women were likely to be in the hotel at that hour of the morning? Probably at least a dozen.

But there was no need for guesswork. Stephanie had been about to walk further into the lobby when she turned suddenly, as if distracted by a shadow. Instantly she knew she was looking at her mother. She stood still, unable to focus on anything but the woman. Her heart was filled with joy, fear, anticipation.

Sheila left her bag on the coffee-table and walked over to her. Tears were falling slowly from her eyes as she placed her hands on Stephanie's shoulders. Then she touched Stephanie's face. 'I'm so sorry, Stephanie. I'm sorry I ever said goodbye.'

Stephanie threw her arms around her mother and held her tightly. She knew instinctively that her mother would never have left her if she had had any choice.

She had a vague memory of another little girl, older than her. There were so many questions. A little boy too?

They talked for hours. Sheila did not tell Stephanie exactly what her father had done to her, but Stephanie was streetwise enough to know, although she did not tell her mother that. Sheila explained how her life had been in danger and how the doctor had helped her to find her a home. She told her of her older sister, Deborah, but not that they had different fathers. Even Deborah didn't know that. She told Stephanie of her brother and how he had drowned. She did not tell her how he had tried to protect his mother against the beatings or how the water in the bath had turned red, but Stephanie was sure his death had been caused by her father.

Stephanie was excited at the prospect of meeting her sister. She had always imagined what it might be like to have a real family. People who cared for and protected each other. 'But wasn't my sister curious about me? She was six when I was sent away. Didn't she remember me? Didn't she ever ask about me or try to find me?'

Sheila told her the truth. 'What could I say to a six-year-old? She didn't understand why you were there one day and gone the next. She cried for you when I told her you'd gone to heaven. And she suffered so much trauma in her own life that I didn't want to tell her until I was sure I could find you. She still has a china doll I bought for her on her third birthday. You loved to play with it, and when you went away, she renamed it Stephanie.' She told Stephanie about Deborah's course at University College, Dublin, and how she planned to be a lawyer. She had just graduated and would begin work at the end of the summer.

Stephanie's heart sank. 'A lawyer? Will she even want to meet me? We've led very different lives,' she said.

Sheila's heart went out to her daughter. She knew from Stephanie's refusal to elaborate that her childhood had been hard. The doctor had told her that Social Services had lost contact with her for six years. But Deborah would want to meet her. Of that, her mother had no doubt.

Sheila showed her photographs of the family – Eamon was

243

absent from them all. There were pictures of Deborah and Stephanie was shocked by the physical resemblance between her and her sister. They had the same dark colouring and big brown eyes. But their smile drew them together. It was shy, almost furtive, uncertain. There was also a photo of an older man, possibly in his sixties, but Sheila didn't say who he was.

The next morning, they embraced for a long time. Sheila understood that Stephanie couldn't just pack up and leave now. The girl had her pride. She arranged to telephone her at the end of the week, by which time Deborah would know everything and Stephanie could meet her.

As Sheila got into her car to drive back to Knocktopher, Stephanie wished her a safe journey.

The doctor called to Gardener's Lane, as arranged with Sheila, when he had bade her farewell the morning before. When there was no answer, he returned home, assuming that things had gone even better than expected. He was so pleased that things were turning out well for Sheila Parker.

Later that night, the police came to his door, asking if he could identify a patient, Sheila Parker. She had been involved in a fatal traffic accident on the outskirts of the city.

42

Assistant Commissioner Tom Daly was back in the official's office. This time, there was none of the double-speak of their earlier conversations. There was no time for it. The plan to protect the official's boss had backfired.

'The judge has offered his resignation, citing personal reasons. I don't need to tell you that the Four Courts is already awash with rumours that he's the man Alex King says is being blackmailed. Everyone in the Law Library is asking why and it's only a matter of time before it comes out,' Daly told him.

'Well, you'll just have to pull Hanley off the investigation and put a stop to it before my man has the finger pointed at him. We can't let this go any further. It must be stopped now,' the official said.

'Too late,' Daly replied.

'What do you mean? You take your orders from this department and that's the way it's going to stay. Pull Hanley off now. I don't care how you have to do it.'

'It's too late because your man's brother has already contacted Hanley. He has made a full confession and Hanley's team is going to use it to secure a conviction against Michael Mooney Junior. They also have a second victim, who has come forward with a complaint of rape, assault and battery. They are throwing in drugs-distribution allegations too. It's too late to stop them,' Daly said.

The official had much to lose. He wasn't going to be party to defeatism. It would destroy all of their careers. 'There is always a way to stop them. Mount a campaign against Hanley. Do whatever you have to do, but stop this going any further. If my man is exposed, the Commissioner's job goes down the drain as far as you're concerned. I don't need to tell you that.'

Daly reminded the official that he would lose his job too. As for himself, he pointed out, 'I was merely taking orders from an official of the department that as you lot so frequently remind us, controls my organisation. You're in the frame, Mr Tynan. It was you and your boss who came up with the brilliant idea of mounting this so-called investigation and authorising taps to protect your man's brother.'

The official knew that Daly was right. If this went to trial, the police would have to use the evidence of the telephone taps to link the judge to the Mooneys. Questions would be asked about why the taps were authorised in the first place and a court would be told that there had never been a legal reason for initiating them. They had been put there to protect the boss's brother. The irony would be that the judge had never known anything about it.

'What about the Parker woman?' the official queried. 'Can't you turn this round and put the focus on her? She's an obvious target. You can trump up the charges against her and that would take us out of the picture, would it not?'

It had been done before. Investigations had been manipulated to protect certain parties. But Daly knew that Brendan Hanley had far too much to go on – thanks to having been given the tapping transcripts in the first place. Hanley was an honest cop. He would never allow the finger to be pointed at the Parker woman.

'I would suggest,' Daly said, rising from his chair, 'that you appraise your man of these latest developments in the situation. I don't think I need to tell you that I probably won't be seeing you again.'

As he walked away from the building, Daly dug his hands into his pockets and exhaled. How had he ever allowed himself to become party to this scenario? Had he stooped to such depths just to achieve the top job? In staying close to the Minister for Justice he had guaranteed himself a promotion to the post of Commissioner, but laws had been broken and lives had been ruined – although he still didn't know how Deborah Parker had become embroiled in the mess – as a result of their illegal interference in the course of justice.

There was only one thing for it. He would come clean with Hanley. Then he would leave the force and spend time with the wife and family he had neglected in his struggle for power. It was true that power corrupts, and Tom Daly no longer wanted it.

43

Patrick Mangan was on top of the world. He had received a promotion and a pay-rise. To top it all, he had received a telephone call from Mugsy Mooney.

'Yes!' he exclaimed, thumping his hand against the steering-wheel as he drove up Killiney Hill in his new Mazda convertible – there was no way that Geena Williams would be doing anything in the back of this new car. Anyway, he didn't need her anymore. He had Deborah's job. He had her credibility. And within a few hours he would have the first of her big clients. When he had telephoned Mugsy after Deborah's suspension the man had been less than willing to commit to staying with the firm. And who could blame him? Hadn't one of its solicitors stolen twenty thousand pounds from him? Mangan had assured him that no such behaviour would occur under his watch.

In the drawing room he sat on Lelia's big white couch. He thought the furnishings were perfect, just what his ex-wife used to like, except hers were on a smaller scale. It was strange, he thought, that there were so many men in the room – Mugsy, his notorious son, Michael Junior, a mean-looking chap called Johnny Collins, and someone by the name of Whacker. He shuddered as he thought of reasons why someone might be called Whacker.

Despite the company of the hard men, Mangan was

satisfied with himself. Where, he wondered, had Deborah Parker found the balls to survive surrounded by these guys? Jesus, she was one tough woman.

When Mugsy offered him a drink, Mangan accepted. He was in with the big boys now.

When Mugsy said, 'I think you'll need it, son,' Mangan didn't have the faintest idea what he was talking about. In fact, he had become so supercilious over the past few months that he didn't give the remark a second thought.

Mugsy handed him a double Paddy on the rocks. 'Now, son, I think you and me need to have a little chat,' he said.

Johnny Collins sat up and glared at Mangan. Whacker Browne sniggered. Michael Junior rubbed his hands against his tight Levis.

'Ye see that video there in the machine, Mr Mangan? I want you to go play it. I want you to press the play button and watch what's on it,' Mugsy instructed him.

Mangan thought this was a strange turn of events. Suddenly, the atmosphere had become tense.

He took the remote control from Mugsy, but his hands were shaking now and he dropped it. When he moved to pick it up Johnny Collins, who was sitting to his right, dug the heel of his black biker's boot into his hand. When he lifted it the bolt of pain that hit Mangan as he tried to flex it caused him to drop his whiskey glass on Lelia's shaggy leopard-print rug. 'Me wife will be upset about her new carpet, son,' Mugsy said. 'Whacker, get him a cloth and a bucket of water so he can clean it up.'

Mangan couldn't believe what he was hearing. He began to sit up but Mugsy gripped him by the back of the head and forced him to kneel, his face close to the floor. 'You'll have to clean it up, son. By the way that's what we're here for tonight. To clean up a few messes you've created.'

Mangan began to tremble. There was no way they could have fingered him. Then he looked at the video. 'Oh, Jesus,' he said. 'What are you going to do to me?'

'Exactly what you have done to Deborah Parker, Mr Mangan. We're going to screw you, and then you're going to confess to what you did. Johnny here is going to take you to see Detective Hanley when he's finished with ye. He's my right-hand man, ye see. But he's ambidextrous as well, if ye catch my drift, and there's nothing he likes better than to screw someone who has screwed me over,' Mugsy said, a cold look in his calm eyes. 'Would you like to see the video of yourself in the bank? You come out well on the camera, so you do.'

Mangan was shaking uncontrollably now, but he didn't miss the video camera that was placed on a tripod in the corner of the big room.

Johnny Collins knelt on the floor. The other men sniggered as he undid his belt, then his zipper, simultaneously whispering into Mangan's ear. He took a pair of scissors, which Michael Junior passed to him, and cut down the back panel of Mangan's trousers. He pulled up Mangan's head by the wiry hair until Mangan's face was staring right at the camera. 'Take it from the back angle now,' Collins said to Whacker, who was operating the machine.

When Whacker moved to film from behind, Mangan shouted, 'OK, I did it. I framed the stupid cow. I put the money in her account.'

'Tell us how and why you did it,' Mugsy demanded.

'She gave me the cheque for safe-keeping because you made it out to cash. She was going to court and didn't want to leave it lying around. Paul Jennings wasn't about and I was the obvious person for her to throw it to because she was in a hurry and her office was next door to mine.'

'But why do something like that to a lovely young girl like her?' Mugsy inquired.

Mangan almost forgot his terror. 'I did it because she thought she was so fucking clever. She needed to be put in her place. Of course, you didn't see that side of her. All you saw was her pandering to you with her big brown eyes.'

Johnny Collins got up and kicked Mangan in the back, causing him to slump on to his stomach. Mugsy stood over him and advised him that he was *en route* now to Deborah Parker's apartment to show her the video. Then it would be passed to Alex King from TV3, with all of the faces blocked-out except Mangan's.

Johnny Collins drove Mangan into Dublin. He only left when he saw Detective Brendan Hanley come to the gates of Harcourt Terrace police station to greet the man who had insisted on an audience with him.

44

'So the only thing left to clear up is why she is receiving payments from the man down in the country,' Hanley said, as they ended their two-hour-long meeting.

'That's right, boss,' Lynch said. 'The warrants are being issued as we speak against Michael Mooney Junior. The Criminal Assets Bureau will have them ready in the morning and there will be a court application tomorrow to freeze the Mooneys' assets.'

'So the tally to date is Michael Junior on rape and battery, running a brothel and living off the proceeds of crime. Then we have the father. We could technically have him for false imprisonment of Mangan, but since he did us a favour I think we'll overlook it. We're going after him under Proceeds of Crime legislation, which will result in their nineteen million pounds' worth of assets being frozen. That should keep him tied up in the courts for a few years. We have Mangan pleading to the theft of the twenty grand. Ironic, considering he didn't take it to spend on himself. Parker's in the clear over the twenty grand, of course, so we just need to look into the monthly payments. You're going to handle that, aren't you, boss?'

Hanley was indeed going to handle the two outstanding holes in this case. Since Daly had informed him that the minister had wanted to protect his brother because it would have compromised his own position, Hanley had been curious as to why the man was so protective of his brother. But Daly had told him of some family rift. The minister felt he owed his brother a debt.

The fact that the Minister for Justice had quietly resigned this morning meant that Hanley could approach the man who was making the payments to Deborah Parker. It had been easier with the minister's brother, because Judge Thomas Deering had saved Hanley from having to approach him first. But getting to this relative would be tricky. The man was seventy-two and could legitimately claim that he was too fragile to discuss his personal business with the police. If he wanted to, he could delay the investigation for years. It had been done before.

'Just remind me again, Lynch,' Hanley said, 'what did Parker say when you asked her where the money was coming from?'

'She told me that, as far as she is concerned, the money was left to her by her mother. The reason we found that cryptic note in her office was because she was trying to ascertain that her mother was, in fact, the benefactor. She was never able to find out, though, so just assumed that she was.'

'Why is she so adamant that the money is from the mother if she doesn't have proof? Maybe she *is* telling the truth?' Hanley asked.

'I don't know, boss. I am still not convinced she's being up-front with us. And here's the thing. The mother didn't have a penny to her name yet Parker lives in this fancy apartment. That was left to her too, she claims. It came with the money.'

'Well, don't lose any sleep over it, Lynch. We'll find out where this money's coming from soon enough.'

Hanley left the office and set out on the drive to Knock-topher. He had a lot to think about. This case, he reflected, was by far the most serious he had handled in terms of its implications for so many high-ranking and well-known people.

Tom Daly was about to resign. The minister was gone and his private secretary was rumoured to be on the way out too. Patrick Mangan had lost his job and, in the not-too-distant future, he would lose his freedom. Judge Thomas Deering had resigned and would be dealt with leniently. After all, Hanley couldn't implicate the judge in any perversion-of-the-course-of-justice charges relating to the Brady attack because the case had already been thrown out of court. The Director of Public Prosecutions had advised him that it wasn't possible to reopen it.

Paul Jennings had lost his trusted lieutenant and was disillusioned with his sense of judgement after a visit from Mugsy Mooney relating to Geena's role in the Deborah scandal.

Stephanie Parker – what a coincidence that the two major victims in this case had the same surname – was being cared for by the judge. Their new relationship was platonic and Stephanie had been uncertain at first about accepting his offer of assistance. But the man was deeply remorseful about what had happened, and although she had only begun to get to know him over the past few weeks, there was something trustworthy about him. Hadn't he given up his post because of her? He had offered her the opportunity to live in the main house with him, but she had turned him down. Instead, she had accepted the self-contained flat in the basement of his residence.

The only mystery left to solve was Deborah Parker's

involvement with the old man. And, as he queued in the traffic jams to get on the main road out of Dublin, Hanley prayed that he would soon have a suitable answer to his question.

45

Alex had known her for only four weeks, but he felt as if he had known her all her life. Deborah Parker was an amazing woman. She had beauty, brains and guts – of that there was no question. As she lay in his arms, he recalled the look on Mugsy Mooney's face when Mugsy had regaled him with the story of how Deborah had accused him of being largely to blame for everything that had happened to her.

'I'll tell you something, King. I don't know if you've got something going there, but you'd be mad not to,' Mugsy had advised him. 'She's the only woman who has ever stood up to me. And she wasn't taking any prisoners either. She was right, of course. If it hadn't been for me paying that hotel bill, you would never have had enough information to run with your story and she might not have looked so crooked. Anyway, she gave it to me right between the eyes and I respect her for that.'

He ran his hands through Deborah's hair. Mugsy was the first criminal, Alex thought, whom he had been allowed to get close to and he had gained a real insight into the man, what he was really like as distinct from his fearsome reputation. Despite Mooney's infamy, Alex had become fond of him. He was guilty of massive tax evasion, but so was a significant proportion of the country's business and political circles and they weren't branded by the media.

In their numerous meetings since the first time Alex had

called to Mugsy's home, Alex had come to regard him as a decent guy, albeit a criminal. He had freaked when Alex had tipped him off about Michael Junior's abuse of the girls – thanks to information provided by Lynch after she interviewed Stephanie. And when he had learned of the widespread use of drugs on his premises he had flown into a blinding rage. 'Never,' he had said, 'would I have condoned any of that. That's why I always tried to have Johnny Collins there keeping an eye on him. But ever since he got off those charges last year, he became almost untouchable. I haven't been able to control him because I've always given in to his mother and he walked all over Lelia. As far as I was concerned, he was running the agencies for me and that was it. I suppose I shouldn't have turned such a blind eye to him. Anyway, I'm going to lose it all now. Or most of it, anyway.' He had winked. Alex had no doubt that Mugsy had a couple of million stashed away from the prying eyes of the Irish authorities. Then he wondered if he would have been lying beside this beautiful creature had Mugsy not come into her life. Probably not. And if Mugsy hadn't entered Deborah's life, none of this would have happened to her. In which case, he was glad it had turned out this way. For Deborah Parker was lying in his arms and he had no intention of letting her go.

'I grew up in Knocktopher in County Kilkenny. I had a sister and a brother. My sister died when she was four. She had meningitis, they thought, and my brother died at eighteen in a drowning accident. Our father was Eamon and I never really knew him. He didn't have much time for me. He died in 1996 of a heart-attack. Our mother was Sheila and she died a month after my father in a traffic accident.' Since that night, when she had invited him back for coffee, they had become virtually inseparable. But there were some things about her life that she could not share with him.

'My mother was the most amazing person in the world. I loved her so much that it still hurts.' Alex cradled her head against his chest. They were lying on his bed and the windows were open, allowing the sound of the sea to pour into the room.

'I wonder if I have some family out there somewhere,' Deborah mused. 'I mean, I've already told Lynch and Hanley that my mother is the only person who could have left me any money, but they've looked at my family and they don't seem to accept that. Not that I didn't find it surprising myself, of course. We had little in the way of material things when we were growing up. My father drank every penny he got and my mother never worked outside the home. The only reason I got into college was because of my grades. But my mother *must* have left me the money. If I had any long-lost aunts or uncles who bequeathed it to me, surely my mother would have told me about them?'

Alex touched her face with his lips, then her eyebrows, her nose and finally her mouth. She gave herself to him, never taking her eyes off his face. His hands stroked the contours of her body. He was never rough – even in their wildest moments of passion.

An hour later, when they were drenched and breathless, she asked him what the latest was in the Mooney case. Alex told her they had secured a witness who was going to say that Michael Mooney Junior had raped her. She would also be responsible for securing a conviction against him for drugs distribution and running a prostitution agency. When he told her the witness's name, Deborah laughed incredulously. 'What's the matter?' Alex asked, sitting up. 'What's so funny?'

'Stephanie Parker. That's what you said, isn't it?'

Alex looked confused. 'Yes. Why?'

'Oh, it's just that you can't seem to get away from Parker women, these days, that was my sister's name. What an amazing coincidence.'

'Sure it is, sweetheart.'

She jumped off the bed and went to the bathroom. 'I'm going to take a shower. Do you want to join me?'

Alex did not join her. He knew he was pushing at the boundaries of reason here, but there had been many coincidences in this case. And Deborah had said her sister was dead. Still, some phone calls had to be made.

46

Hanley got out of his car and stretched to his full height. After the three-and-a-half-hour drive from Dublin his back was aching. 'Bloody traffic,' he muttered as he stretched his arms towards the sky. He was parked on the side of a lane that led into Knocktopher village, and wondering what it must be like to live in such a picturesque, peaceful place, so different from the traffic jams, cramped housing develop-ments, drug-dealers and criminals of the city. But Hanley was all too aware that even in idyllic places crimes were committed, which the public and the police never knew about. That was the reason for his visit today – to find out if a crime had been committed here.

The woman in the petrol station a few hundred yards down the road had known immediately where to send him when he asked for directions. 'Certainly, sir, you're on the right road,' she had said, her eyes filled with curiosity. She was used to seeing the same faces every day and would make it her business to find out why a stranger was on the scene, Hanley thought. 'You're just a few minutes away from the big house,' she told him. 'It's the doctor you're looking for, is it? Well, you'll find him there, so you will. He's the only one living there now. The two boys are in Dublin, so they are. It's a rare

261

occasion you see them down here now, what with them both having such important jobs and everything.'

From his vantage-point on the road, Hanley could see the imposing residence. It was tall and cut of old stone. And while it was grand, it had a cold look about it. The October sun was shining on it now, but Hanley could picture it with grey clouds looming overhead.

He hopped back into the car, ready now to find out why Deborah Parker was receiving huge sums of money from the man.

The loud chime of the bell startled him, and he expected an imperious butler to open the door, although the woman at the petrol station had said the doctor lived alone.

When Dr Thomas Deering arrived at the door his manner was anything but cold or imperious. In fact, when Hanley introduced himself, the elderly man gave an almost relieved sigh. 'Ah. I've been expecting someone to call,' he said, with a chuckle. 'I was wondering how long it would be before your lot put two and two together and came to find me.'

Hanley was perplexed, although he didn't let it show on his face.

The doctor invited him into the modest-sized kitchen where a blazing fire created an atmosphere of warmth and welcome. 'When my wife, Penelope, was alive, she never allowed us to use this room. It was for the staff only, she insisted. But I like it here. It feels like home.'

'So I take it you know why I'm here,' Hanley said, as he accepted a mug of steaming coffee.

'But of course,' Thomas said.

Hanley wondered if the man wasn't senile. Why, if he had been blackmailed for all these years, was he welcoming such intrusion into his private affairs?

'It's about the girl, I take it? You want to know about the cash payments. I figured, what with all of this new legislation you have at your disposal these days, that it was only a matter of time before you found out about me,' he said.

Hanley was mystified. In all his years of policing, he had never been greeted so warmly by someone who obviously had such a big secret to hide that they were willing to suffer blackmail rather than have it exposed.

'I suppose I should have come to you earlier, when I read all of those things in the paper about her,' the doctor went on. 'But the truth of the matter is, I made a promise to the girl's mother and it was a promise I could not break – even after her mother died. You see, she made me swear that her children would only find out from her.'

Hanley had intended returning to Dublin that night. He had hardly seen his daughter, Elaine, for the past three weeks and he had hoped he could wrap everything up within a few hours and return home to plan a trip away with her. But the story had been so compelling that they had talked for hours. By the end, he was so exhausted, and sad, that he had eagerly accepted the doctor's invitation to stay the night. Tomorrow the man would take him up to Gardener's Lane and show him where Deborah Parker's life had begun to go wrong . . .

47

Former District Court judge Thomas Deering sat in stunned silence in his living room. He had been surprised to receive an unexpected visit from Hanley and had assumed that he was here to see Stephanie.

Hanley had been dreading making the visit and had not phoned first because he did not want to impart the news to the former judge by telephone. It was just too shocking.

'I have to say when you pointed me in the direction of your father I assumed that there was some other explanation for all of this,' Hanley said, knowing that what he was about to tell the man would have dreadful consequences for him. And especially for Stephanie. Deborah, too. 'Look, Judge, what your father has told me explains a lot, but I think you're going to be very shocked by it,' Hanley said, attempting to soften the blow.

The legal man had a vacuous look on his face. He was in the dark.

Hanley began quietly, 'There is no other way for me to tell you this, but Deborah Parker was receiving cash payments from your father because he is her grandfather.'

He paused. The man looked totally shocked.

'When Deborah Parker's mother died, your father began paying her the money, but he had to keep it anonymous because of your mother, Penelope. She had expressly forbidden him to help Deborah in any way. Deborah assumed that the money was coming from a trust set up by her mother.'

He was certain now that the judge knew where he was going with this. 'Your father has told me about the rift that developed when Sheila Dunne discovered she was pregnant with your baby all those years ago.' He hesitated. 'Deborah Parker is your daughter. I'm sorry.'

Thomas Deering looked as if the life was draining from his body, but Hanley continued: 'And I have to tell you that the young lady staying with you at present, Stephanie, is Miss Parker's half-sister.'

'Oh, dear God . . .' He looked tormented, as if the implications of this were just too appalling to contemplate. Then he said, 'Detective, what you are telling me means that I've been sleeping with my own daughter's half-sister. What I have done is unforgivable.'

Hanley felt sorry for him. It was surely one of the most bizarre coincidences.

He already knew the whole story but he listened as the former judge explained his part of the story. 'I was only eighteen, you see, and my mother was a class-conscious woman. She insisted that the girl didn't want to know me and that her parents were marrying her off to someone else. There was a huge rift. My elder brother, John, was of the same opinion as my mother. They said it would bring disgrace and shame to the family name. Of course, as you know, he had political aspirations. I think he had me appointed a judge to assuage his guilt. Anyway, I left that Christmas to go to Trinity to study law and I have never set foot in that house since. I never even knew the name of the man Sheila married. I just wanted to stay as far away from Knocktopher as possible. I hated Sheila Dunne for deserting me and I hated my mother for refusing to allow me to remain in contact with her for the sake of the child.'

Thomas Deering took a deep breath. 'I know what you must be thinking – that I'm a coward. I've been so weak.'

Hanley said nothing.

Thomas continued, 'It was different back then. We were almost regarded as landed gentry, and even in the 1970s, having a child out of wedlock with a Catholic was still regarded by many as unacceptable. I never forgave my mother. I went to her funeral four years ago, for my father's sake, but no one mentioned Sheila Dunne or her daughter. Why did my father not tell me? And what about Stephanie?'

Hanley answered him with the explanation the doctor had given him: 'Sheila gave up Stephanie for adoption after she discovered her husband abusing the child. Years later your father offered to help put them in touch again. The night before Sheila went to meet Stephanie in Cork, she told your father that she wanted to break the news to Deborah. She made him promise that he would not become involved. Your father felt he had to keep that promise because he had never stood up to your mother, and Sheila, Deborah and Stephanie suffered because of that.'

'But after Sheila had died why did he not contact Stephanie and tell her the whole story? It just doesn't make sense.'

'Your father did not know if Stephanie knew you were Deborah's father. By then he felt that enough people had been hurt – including you – and he decided to let bygones be bygones. He felt he had a responsibility to Deborah so he instructed his solicitor to set up a trust fund for her.'

Thomas Deering stood up. 'How did my father know that Stephanie was Deborah's sister?'

'That came about by accident,' Hanley responded. 'Your

father knew Stephanie's name, of course, but he never tried to track her down because of Sheila's instructions to him. He had been following the stories about Deborah in the news and, consequently, he was familiar with Alex King. King was aware, from his other police sources, that I was on the way to talk to your father regarding the money that we thought was being paid by you because you have the same name. By sheer coincidence, King telephoned Dr Thomas Deering in Knocktopher just twenty minutes before I arrived apparently. Even when he took the call, your father was unaware of Stephanie's involvement in any of this because, as a rape victim, her name could not be used by the media. But King, for reasons unknown to me, believed that Deborah Parker had a sister called Stephanie and he telephoned your father to ask if he knew anything about it. At first, King seemed to be under the impression that the girl was dead, but your father assured him that she was very much alive.'

Thomas Deering removed his half-moon glasses and wiped the tears from his eyes. 'I know you probably won't understand it, Detective, and I wouldn't blame you if you didn't, but the reason I went to those agencies . . . it was because I could never allow myself to become close to a woman. I loathed myself for my weakness in acquiescing to my mother's demands, and in a way I was taking my hatred of her out on those women. That is all I have to say in my defence. I never thought I could become close to a woman again.'

'But you have now?' Hanley ventured.

'Yes,' the former judge said. 'I have become close to Stephanie, but only in the paternal sense. When I saw her that night in such a dreadful condition, the ramifications of the abuse to which I was party hit me in the face. That is a cross I will have to bear for the rest of my life.'

Hanley was suffused with pity for the man.

'Does my . . . does my daughter know yet?' Deering asked.

'Alex King will tell her tomorrow,' Hanley said. 'It's up to you to inform Stephanie because King is certain that Deborah will want to meet her sister. Whether or not she will want to meet her father, I don't know. I guess you'll just have to wait and see . . .'

48

Deborah felt as if she was in a vivid dream and that she would wake up at any minute and everything would become clear. But she was sitting on a chintz-covered sofa in a cosy hotel in County Wicklow and Alex King had just unravelled the mystery of the monthly payments to her, along with the rest of the story.

They were in the small lounge, the only two people there. It was why Alex had taken her to the little gem of a hotel. In summertime, it was always packed with tourists and day-trippers stopping off for the Hunters' famous afternoon teas in the rose-filled gardens. But in winter, it was a haven of peace and tranquillity, just the type of environment Deborah needed now. 'So you talked to her last night and you're sure it's her?' she asked, for the tenth time. 'What does she sound like? What does she work at? Oh, no, I know the answer to that, of course. What does she look like? Did she already know about me by the time you contacted her?' She now knew why Stephanie had been sent away, about the Mallons in Cork, about Stephanie's meeting with her mother and about the doctor's guilt, which had led him to ensure she was financially secure. She knew who her real father was and how he had believed that her mother had been happy to marry Eamon Parker.

'How do you feel about the prospect of meeting them? Do you think you want to?' he asked.

Deborah's expression was as loaded with hope as anxiety. 'I definitely want to meet my sister. I still have her favourite doll, you know. The one that you always tell me looks so odd with my furnishings. I named it Stephanie after she died. Only she didn't die. But, Alex, why, after she had met my mother in Cork, did she not try to contact me?'

Alex had asked Stephanie the same question. 'Deborah, sweetheart, she understood that your mother would let her know when she had told you the whole story. Then she was killed in the car crash, and Stephanie did not know that. As far as she was concerned, she had been rejected yet again. She did not contact you because she didn't want to set herself up for another rejection.'

Deborah broke down then and sobbed quietly for a long time. When she calmed herself, she had decided she wanted to meet her father. 'I don't know how I'll feel about him. I have so much trouble accepting that he just did what his mother said and went on to live his new life. But I suppose I should meet him and see how it goes. I can't promise any more than that, I'm afraid.'

Deep down, Deborah had never believed she was part of Eamon Parker. Now she knew why – even if she had been the last to know.

They spent the night wrapped in each other's arms. There was no lovemaking and no conversation. He just held her and told her that everything would be all right.

In his telephone call to Stephanie last night, they had decided that Deborah should not be told of Stephanie's sexual relationship with Deborah's father. There had been enough hurt and it was time to repair the damage. It was enough that Deborah thought her father had used a prostitution agency because of his loneliness.

EPILOGUE

May 2003

Brendan Hanley, Maria Lynch and the rest of the team arrived at the Four Courts in an unmarked squad car. This was their day of glory. The media were there in full force, and their expressions remained implacable as the camera lenses zoomed in on their faces.

Michael Mooney Junior sat beside his State-appointed legal-aid solicitor – the only defence available to him now his vast assets had been frozen by the Criminal Assets Bureau. When the clerk called his case, silence descended on court number four. The journalists were ready, pens poised.

The State's barrister stood up and addressed the judge. 'Your Honour, I believe we may not be proceeding with trial in this case,' he said.

There was a gasp. The journalists and the jury, who had been sworn in, looked at each other, confounded. The barrister let his dramatic words sink in then delivered the bombshell. 'I believe, Your Honour, that the defence is entering a guilty plea.'

Hanley and his team walked round to Hughes's pub at the back of the courts. It was located at the edge of the old Smithfield market and its dark interior had been home to many celebratory drinks parties for clients of the Four Courts. But unlike many other high-profile cases, when the media pack always joined the police after a good verdict, their party was a closed shop.

The events involving the former Judge Deering, Deborah Parker and her sister Stephanie would never get into the public arena. Alex King was the only journalist who would ever know what really happened.

Michael Mooney Senior stood in a travel agent's office in Dun Laoghaire. He purchased a one-way ticket to Málaga. His assets had been frozen and the house in Killiney had been seized by the Criminal Assets Bureau. Still, there was always Marbella and it was to the sun he was heading – alone, except for the stash in a Jersey bank.

Lelia Mooney struggled with her heavy Louis Vuitton suit-cases. 'Jaysus,' she screamed, as the taxi-driver dumped them on the wet pavement. 'Would ye mind me bags, for fuck's sake.'

He gave a derisory snort when she instructed him to carry them into the three-bedroom council house of her friend Geraldine Gilford, who had informed her that she could stay with her for a month. 'Well,' Geraldine had sniggered to her husband after getting the call for help from Lelia, 'if I wasn't good enough to stay with her in Killiney, then she isn't good enough for Finglas.'

Stephanie and Thomas were sitting in the kitchen of his beautiful home. They were browsing through brochures for degree courses. Stephanie closed the last and announced that she wanted to study medicine. Her adopted grandfather would be thrilled to hear that, Thomas said, when he arrived for his regular weekend visit on Friday.

Deborah and Alex were strolling hand in hand through Central Park. The summer was just arriving in New York, but there was none of the unbearable humidity that gave the city a claustrophobic feel in the height of summer. A gentle breeze was blowing Deborah's hair on to her face. They stood on the bridge and looked into the lake, which had been frozen over just two months earlier on their first trip.

Alex pulled her hair off her face with his left hand. He put the other into his pocket and brought out a Tiffany box, with its delicate blue wrapping. He undid the ribbon with his teeth and flicked open the box with his thumb. 'Your father says he will not let you away . . . again . . . but if it's what you want, he is happy for you to become my wife,' he said.

Later that day Deborah stood at the counter in Tiffany's and handed the ring back to the assistant. If she was going to become Alex King's wife, she had better ensure that they sized it correctly.

That night, she telephoned Dublin. Her father would give her away, and Stephanie, Julie and Aine would be brides-maids. If he was well enough, her grandfather would come too.

It was going to be a busy time for them. Alex's work in exposing criminals and corruption had earned him a job with the top TV network, CBC, and Deborah was cramming for the New York State Bar exams. She sighed with relief. 'At least in a city the size of New York, our professional worlds are unlikely to collide as they did before,' she told Alex.

Given the calibre of criminals he was investigating now, Alex prayed she was right.

AUTHOR'S NOTE

This book is a work of fiction. It contains graphic scenes that some people may find explicit. While these scenes are indeed fictional, they are based on research I conducted during several years as an investigative journalist. During the course of two particular undercover investigations, I was offered the potential to earn the sums of money referred to in the book for prostitution work. In both instances, pimps offered to conduct 'interviews' with me. While I never followed through on the offers, the scenes in the book regarding the 'interviews', as I have described them, with working girls, are based on information provided by prostitutes working at the higher end of the market. While the Willows hotel does not exist in Dublin, I was offered work as a prostitute during a meeting at an upmarket hotel in Dublin in 2001. The ensuing exposé, which I wrote following my meeting, led to a court case and the conviction of several individuals for their involvement in prostitution.

In relation to the lifestyles enjoyed by the criminals featured in this book, many of the details are based on my experience of gangland criminals over an eight-year period of crime reporting. I have been to their homes and have also been invited to stay at their foreign holiday homes. Of course I declined, but I

279

say this because some readers may find the Mooney family slightly exaggerated in their approach to the law and their legal advisers and in the lives they lead. They *are* exaggerated – and this is how I witnessed several well-known gangland figures lead their lives.

Regarding the sections of the law I have used in this book, I would like to point out that they do not always correlate precisely with the crimes I have matched them to: this is deliberate, as I do not want this book to become a manual for potential offenders. I have altered the time-frame necessary to return the results of DNA from a crime scene for the same reason.

Finally, the scenes regarding the payment of retainers to solicitors are fictional: I have never encountered any criminal-law practitioners who would allow themselves to be manipulated by their wealthy criminal clients.

ACKNOWLEDGEMENTS

There are so many people who assisted me with my research for this book that it is hard to know where to begin. But here goes . . . and if I have left anybody out, I apologise sincerely for the omission. It is not intentional.

First and foremost, thank you to the two people who were of greatest assistance in providing me with technical details regarding the handling of investigations, both on the legal and forensic side: the solicitor who kindly analysed my legal scenarios and told me where I was going wrong – in some instances, I have ignored his advice, so that I do not provide would-be criminals with his encyclopaedic knowledge of the courts; Dr Maureen Smyth, forensic scientist, for her painstaking and patient explanation of the procedures used to extract DNA. Again, I ignored her advice and altered the time-frame necessary to test samples so as not to give potential criminals any assistance in the commission of crimes. Many thanks to Superintendent John Farrelly, of the Garda press office, for pointing me in the right direction to find out facts, figures and correct titles; and to the other man in the Phoenix Park who helped me but who didn't want it mentioned: you're a star, you always have been. To my family, and in particular my sisters, Phil and Chris, for their constant encouragement during the writing of this book: thanks for the child-minding. And to my friends, Fiona, Denise Elma, Aideen and Gordon, for their interest in this labour of love. It was great that there were a few people who didn't ask, 'So, what are you going to work at when you've finished writing your book?'

To the men I have christened 'My Three Wise Men'. They are my very own Mugsy, Big Daddy and Attorney General – you all know who you are, and without you, this project would not have been possible. Thank you for giving me confidence. Please be assured that the characters for whom I borrowed your nicknames bear no resemblance to any of you!

Sincere thanks to Jim Binchy and Dave O'Neill.

To all of the police officers, solicitors, barristers and members of the public who assisted me during my time as crime correspondent, you gave me a rich pool of material to draw from. A special thank you to the 'working women' who helped with my research into prostitution.

A very special thanks to Wayne Brookes, my editor at Hodder, and to Darley Anderson, my agent. How can I possibly describe what both of you have done for me? Collectively, you have made a long-held dream come true. Thanks, Wayne, for your never-ending encouragement and support and your fantastic mind, which never misses a beat! And, Darley, you are a lateral thinker if ever I met one and I love listening to your precise and always-reasoned thoughts. You have both made this novel so much better. Thanks to Heidi and Breda Purdue at Hodder, Ireland, and to Sue Fletcher and the team in the UK, for agreeing to publish this. To all Darley's staff, particularly the ever-efficient Julia. To all of the staff at Hodder who have worked on this book behind the scenes, but who I have never met, thank you. Likewise to Hazel Orme for her diligent copy-editing.

Finally, to my husband Andrew, whom I mention last but who always comes first. Thanks for everything sweetheart but, best of all, for little Elise.